Unlicensed Delivery

Inter-Planetary Alliance

Will Soulsby-McCreath

ISBN: 978-1-7399525-4-9 (eBook),
978-1-7399525-5-6 (paperback)

First Edition

WillSoulsbyMcCreath.com

For everyone working the job that keeps their dreams
alive.

Content Warning:

References to people trafficking, scenes of consensual intimacy.

A quick note about language and pronouns:

If you are unfamiliar with neo-pronouns, they do appear in this novel. In particular you're likely to come across the singular they, as well as others like ey, eir, em and xe, xyr, xem.

This book is written from the perspectives of characters whose primary language of communication is a fictionalized future language. You'll find pieces of various European languages dotted through the primarily English base. This is not to say that I think some future semi-unified language would take English as its base, it's just that… well English is my first language and it's what I write in so…

I wanted to make it accessible but still futuristic, so most of the words I've chosen to include are similar enough to their English counterparts that it shouldn't take too much working out. That is, apart from aufenthaltsraum, which is a German compound word created for me by a lovely writer I met online.

Aufenthaltsraum

– Ow-Fen-Thal-ts-Room – A "Spending Time Room" –

A room whose designated purpose is for use as relaxation in all its forms. Can include sections for botany, cooking, crafting, eating, lounging, gaming, vids, etc.

ALSO BY WILL SOULSBY-MCCREATH

The Guardian Cadet Series
Merry Arlan: Breaking The Curse
Merry Arlan: Finding The Heir
Kitty Hughes: An Unexpected Meeting (short story)

Welcome To Humanity

Inter-Planetary Alliance Novels
Unlicensed Delivery

Not That Kind Of Dandy
Not The Fighting Kind
Not The Fainting Kind

Unlicensed Delivery

Inter-Planetary Alliance Novels
1

Will Soulsby-McCreath

15 Standard Days To Liftoff

Matter

Matter sat in the uncomfortable chair. Supposedly chairs like this were designed to suit the maximum number of members of the Inter-Planetary Alliance; but they always wrought havoc with Matter's damaged joints. Then again, maximum tolerance didn't mean maximum comfort, and maximum tolerance was to be expected in an IPA standardised medi-centre, regardless of location or comfort levels.

The harrushetti sat across from Matter blinked his slit-pupiled eyes, an icy shade of grey that perfectly matched his home planet's icy surface. A cream coloured, hand knitted jumper obscured most of his torso except for his hands, striped with the same grey and white tiger-like pattern as the hair on his head. Matter didn't like to question how it was that harrushetti had also developed head hair or at least thicker hair on their heads than the rest of their body. Most bipedal bimanual lifeforms seemed to have, but Matter's curiosity about it was too easily overridden by their discomfort at thinking of themself having a physical form.

Or maybe it was just that they had been planet-side too long.

They shuffled in their seat.

The harrushetti blinked again.

"Are you gonna ask me a question, or what?" Matter blurted.

The harrushetti smiled. Something about it made Matter's hair stand on end. There was no hint of the harrushetti's sharp canines, but Matter's instincts didn't need to see them to know they were there. "I am Dr Brruuh TeaYaBin." The way his throat trilled around the 'rr' noise made Matter's brain superimpose an earth house-cat over his features. Could Matter even make a noise like that? They moved their mouth to mimic the sound silently. "I have been asked to run your cognitivilogical assessment for Deep—" he paused "—Travel."

"Did you miss a word?"

"Excuse me?"

"You paused instead of saying Space. Deep *Space* Travel."

Dr Brruuh TeaYaBin rolled his shoulders like he was calibrating a pounce.

Matter had studied harrushetti behaviour – they had a harrushetti brother-in-law after all – and a calibrating pounce movement screamed of irritation. Matter held their hands up before it went any further. "Sorry, I was just asking."

Harrushetti were known throughout the IPA for their animosity and previous warlike nature – not that any member of the Inter-Planetary Alliance was allowed to be at war, but the reputation persisted, especially thanks to the number of smaller planets within the harrushetti galactic zone who refused to join or trade with the IPA due to their lingering resentment or even outright hostility towards Harrush itself. In all likelihood, if any of those smaller planets, galaxies, moons, or various peoples had joined the IPA first, Harrush would probably still be independent.

"I would rather you refrained." The rr's rumbled through his secondary vocal cords like a purr or possibly a growl.

"What's the difference between a purr and a growl?" Matter asked.

Dr Brruuh TeaYaBin blinked again, a little more rapidly this time.

"Like, I know a growl is a sign of aggression and a purr is pleased but acoustically, what's the difference?"

"Is where it is created. Purrs are in the chest." He touched a black clawed hand to his chest. "Growls are in the upper throat." He touched a hand to the edge of his jaw, disturbing the soft edges of his fur.

Matter's face lit up, sparkling eyes reflecting the grey undertones of the harrushetti they faced.

Dr Brruuh TeaYaBin tilted his head. "You're ouaeahhn?" the pronunciation was exactly as Matter would expect. More of an oo-ah-eh-ah-nn than the proper ooh-Way-AAn. He looked down at his datapad, scrolling through the information. "I cannot find that in your file."

Matter shrugged, shoulders making an unpleasant pop. They really needed to get out of this chair. "Should be in there somewhere. I'm only half – it's pretty rare for people to even notice." Unless Matter got excited, or ran across another ouaeahhn. Even then, most people didn't know enough about ouaeahhn to figure it out unless they were one themself. "It's pretty well guarded info. People can get weird about it..."

"Do you want to talk about that?"

"Not particularly."

"I asked badly. No translators. Let's talk about that. It cannot be easy, hiding half of who you are."

"No translators? Really? Did you just learn a lot of languages? Or do you only work with people who already speak your languages?"

"The translators are good but they cannot cope with idioms and things akin to that. People use those a lot in cognitivism fields." Cognitivism, also known as psychology. "And it is important to understand non-verbal communication, which is not programmed into translators."

Matter knew that all too well. It was a big part of the reason they'd gone on that six week course on harrushetti culture and communications. "That's fascinating, tell me more."

"I think it is important to have immersed yourself in a culture to understand it well enough to be able to assess—" He stopped, his eyes narrowing to slits, nose scrunching up. "I know what you are doing."

"Hmm?"

"You are trying to deflect my attention away from the

task at hand."

A smile tugged at Matter's lips but they tried to contain it. "And what would that be?"

Again his nose scrunched.

Matter laughed. "Sorry, sorry. I'm just razzing you. Anoushaah."

"That is not a word I know. An-ooh-sha?"

"An-ou-SHAAAAH," Matter corrected. "It's an ouaeahhn word – for the record, ooh-way-an or wee-un are better than the nonsense you said earlier. But anoushaah is – it's hard to translate from ouaeahhn, but it's like a professional apology for semi-unprofessional behaviour that was attempted in the name of fun but proved not fun for all parties involved."

"Complex."

"That's ouaeahhn. Each syllable has a meaning. It takes forever for people to learn."

Dr Brruuh TeaYaBin blinked slowly twice.

"Is the blinking a 'thing'?"

"What?"

"It wasn't in the 'Understand a Harrushetti' data pack or the six week Culture and Communications course I took; but you keep blinking and, now that I think about it, Dimae does too."

"It fosters relationships. But we are not here to talk about harrushetti relationship building."

Matter sighed. "We're here to assess my aptitude for Deep Space Travel lasting at least two years and whether I am fully aware of the dangers contained within."

"Are you going to take this professionally?"

"If you mean seriously, then absolutely not. I don't take anything seriously."

Once again Dr Brruuh TeaYaBin's nose scrunched. "I have to admit, that is not a promising position for a Deep Travel Assessment."

"No?"

"No. Deep travel is a—" he paused. "Sp-ps-pserious business." He stumbled over the s in the same way people did when they tried to coax a cat out of hiding. "Name one risk of Deep Travel and how you plan to deal with the emotional repercussions of that."

"Well..." Matter tapped a finger against their lips in an exaggerated manner. "We could all be eaten by Space Whales!"

The cognitivist opened his mouth and paused, as if trying to mentally communicate a word before saying, "Whales do not exist."

"Whales are an Earth Ocean Mammal."

"There is no existence of ps— galactic whales."

"Of course there are! I've had a run in with the beasts before, they suck all the marrow out of your bones and this is why my medi-file – which is what you keep glancing at on that datapad – labels me as having an unspecified chronic condition."

Dr Brruuh TeaYaBin's voice came out flat. "You have chronic pain because a galactic whale ate your bone marrow?"

Matter put on a shocked face. "You don't believe me?"

"About any part of that tale? No. I do not believe you."

Matter grinned and shrugged. "Your problem. Look, I've done long-term and dangerous assignments before. The big risk is death – at which point, I'll be too dead to worry about it. The lesser risk is an accident that leaves me with constant pain – which I already have and am dealing with just fine. Statistically the risk is low either way and as a half-ouaeahhn, half-earthling I am both physically and biologically designed to cope well, especially if I have good, solid relationships with the crew – which I am guaranteed with at least one on this particular ship. You and I both know this assessment is meaningless for an experienced voyager."

Dr Brruuh TeaYaBin wrinkled his pink nose as if he wanted to growl. He scribbled something on the datapad, hands so tense his claws extended.

Maybe Matter had pushed him too far. Harrushetti didn't take well to sudden changes of emotion; they were a steadfast people and Matter's particular brand of humour tended to set them on edge. Then again, if Dr Brruuh TeaYaBin was a quality cognitivist, he would have read Matter's file, which said they had been cleared for Deep Space Travel before. Which meant this whole assessment was entirely for the bureaucratic stamp of it having taken place. The actual content didn't matter.

14 Standard Days To Liftoff

Sebastian

The green-ish, bobbly, frog-like exterior of the ship loomed over Sebastian, the bulbous eye of the pilot's console the only clean part beyond the stark silver scratch where the name had once been.

Standing at the base of boarding plank, extending from the ship's belly, the darkness of the cargo bay seemed ready to swallow Sebastian whole. "Into the belly of the beast," he muttered to Dimae as his foot landed on the boarding plank.

"You have weird idioms," Dimae replied, following him up.

"All idioms are weird."

The cargo bay was huge. Even the catwalk around the edges, sitting about halfway up the space, stretched way over Dimae's ears. It was definitely taller than an average human blue slat household ceiling on Earth Colony 623. It might even have been taller than a YaPar ceremonial hall on Harrush, and that was only halfway up the cargo bay.

Metal grates covered the floor, clearly visible hinge bolts on them. They must be removable, either to create better stability for cargo or to increase the size of the cargo bed – why anyone would need more space was beyond Sebastian's reckoning.

He placed his box of supplies on the ground and headed over to one of the two doors on the lowest level. The one facing the front of the ship. A bland, plain medical bay lay out in front of him. He called for Dimae to come back and pulled a datapad from his backpack. Handing the datapad to Dimae he said, "Make a list of the things you need to get this fully functional."

"By priority, I know." Dimae pressed his chin to the top of Sebastian's head: a harrushetti kiss.

Basti let his husband explore his own domain, leaving the door ajar as he wandered back into the cargo bay. He examined the floors and walls, opening hinge bolts to see if they moved easily or were stiff from lack of use. His examination took him to the door opposite medical bay. He let himself through to find a two-storey engineering bay.

One of the engines hummed and clicked as the lights inside the room flickered on, illuminating the space like midday sun. Sebastian shifted to the edge of the room and started taking out lightbulbs. This would not do for someone like Sauraxen. And while Sauraxen had yet to confirm that she would work his ship, Basti was holding out hope. He could always put the lightbulbs back.

He jogged back out into the cargo bay and pulled the roll of ugly, disgusting, mustard and brown and avocado green carpet from the box of supplies. It had been cheap and that was what Sebastian needed. And anyway, it wasn't like Sauraxen would be able to see the colour even if she turned the light on.

Cable-tying the carpet down to the grated stairs was easy enough. It was something Sebastian had done before, not for a Wrexi, but another lizardoid with serious toe-claws that tended to get trapped in grating. He laid out strips of carpet over the grating of the top floor of engineering, and all the way out onto the catwalk of the cargo bay, taking lightbulbs with him as he went.

Perhaps he would be better off getting a nicer pattern of carpet for the catwalk.

He hadn't planned to pay for dimmable bulbs on the rest of the ship, hoping they would come as standard. But he couldn't find any dimmer switches so perhaps not. Shit. That was another thing to add to the list of expenses. He pulled a second datapad from his backpack and started noting down things he would need. 'Changeable lightbulbs – Pricing? Carpet that doesn't make me want to claw my eyes out – not a priority.'

The ladder to the top floor seemed stable enough, but Sebastian was drawn by the front-most door on the catwalk first. He opened it to find another bland room, a surprisingly large captain's quarters. A desk sat against what was presumably the back of the lower pilot's console, directly opposite the doorway Sebastian stood in – no chair to be found. A huge bed lay tucked into a corner, big enough to fit at least five human-sized adults.

Dimae was going to hate this place. Boring plain metal

everything, no comfort to be found. Basti closed the door. It wasn't a big deal. It would be fine. It could be decorated.

As much as Basti might have liked to air out the space, he knew Dimae had particular customs about privacy. He'd prefer it stayed closed, even if it was dusty and smelled like disuse.

Sebastian took the ladder up to the top floor and was happy to note the flooring up here was not grated. And was, instead, solid metal plates. Boring again for sure, but at least it didn't need any more ugly carpet.

How Matter was going to get up that ladder on a bad day was a problem for another time. For now, everyone would just have to deal with it.

At the rear of the ship sat an aufenthaltsraum: a multi-purpose space designed for spending time, recreation, bonding, eating, cooking, and gardening. The sliding door stood most of the way open, peeking out from its casing just enough to let Sebastian know it existed.

Inside he found a plain kitchen with an extendable hob, a standardised heater— kind of like a microwave and an oven with some other concoctions all rolled into one. A kettle and coffee machine glittered silver over a cooling box with variable temperature drawers. Basti hated drawers but that would be fixable at a later date, after they had been paid for some cargo deliveries.

A huge table with at least fifteen chairs sat to the left of the kitchen area, and beyond it a series of sofas and armchairs that could do with replacing, but would handle some patching up for now. Basti pulled the fabric he'd already acquired out of his bag and started stitching, then changed his mind and left it half done to carry on searching the ship.

Empty botany racks in a labyrinthine pattern lined the back of the aufenthaltsraum. Space for plants. Good. Humans got weird without plants. Actually, most people got weird without plants. And with all of these separate botany racks, it would be easy enough to grow food and health plants for all of the species he intended to have on board. Good. He made a quick note to himself to buy some plants and to come back and finish fixing the sofas before the crew came aboard, and then headed out to check the bathrooms – one on each side of the hallway – and crew quarters that lined the hallway toward the pilot's console.

One bathroom had been completely gutted, leaving an empty storage space. The other was in perfect working order, everything turned on and off and warm and cool as it should.

Eight matching doors led off the corridor, four on each side. Basti opened every single one to see that each matched its predecessor perfectly – or at least they had when the ship had first been built. Now, one room had no lights, well, not no lights, the bulbs were there and brief examination of the circuitry said everything should work, but no lights came on. Basti stuck a note on the door that read, "Lights don't work. Sauraxen's room?"

Another room had no mattress on the bed and the fold-down desk had been unbolted and removed. Basti stuck a note on the door that read, "Convert this space?"

The rest of the crew quarters were, by and large, identical.

Finally, Basti headed into the pilot's console. Clear glass-like substance reached all the way around his head and under his feet, giving him a little bit of vertigo. The control panels lined the back wall by the door and a free-standing console stood beside a chair clearly designed for an average human to sit in. Well, maybe not a human, but someone shaped like a human. That wouldn't work. Basti was glad he'd already arranged for the chair to be replaced because there was no way he would ever get Ymmattrahni to sit in a human-shaped pilot's chair.

When one managed to get an ouaeahhn pilot – a challenging feat to begin with, what with their high demand and Basti's less than stellar budget – one did everything one could to keep, maintain, and please their ouaeahhn pilot.

It would be fine. The chair was getting delivered tomorrow and installed for free – or, well, for cost of chair. Which meant Basti didn't have to try and get Sauraxen to install the chair, especially since she hadn't actually agreed to join yet.

Basti leaned over the ladder hole and called down for his husband. Dimae appeared from medi-bay, looking all the way up from the ground floor of the cargo bay. Wow. Vertigo.

"So?" Basti called. "What do you think?"

Dimae's purr carried through the ship, bouncing off metal walls and creating a homely echo.

Ja. It had been a good choice.

"We got the cognitivist report back while you were up there," Dimae said.

"And?"

Dimae turned his datapad to face Basti.
Captain Sebastian LeaYaPar-Jones: Pass
Chief Medical Officer Dimae LeaYaPar-Jones: Pass
Pilot Ymmattrahni: PFC

PFC: potential for concern.

Basti huffed as he pulled up the communications node

on his wristband. The calling pattern swirled in front of it as he waited for the holo-image to shift into a face. As soon as Matter's face appeared in pixelated form he erupted, "Matter, I swear to the stars!"

"What?" Matter whined.

"Did you mess with your evaluator?"

"My what?"

"Your evaluator, Matter! Your psychological evaluator. The person standing between you and your position on my ship." Sebastian didn't need to wait for an answer with the way Matter flinched. He threw up his hands, heedless of the way it distorted the image. "Come on, Matter! You've got a warning on your eval."

"What's a warning?"

"It means your evaluator thought you were in a bad mental state to join a Deep Space Crew. It means whoever does our first on-ship evaluations will be keeping an extra close eye on you. What did you do?"

"I was just honest."

Sebastian rubbed his face. "You and honest is like recycled ship water."

"Weirdly soapy?"

"Full of hidden shit."

"Oh, go fuck your husband," Matter snarled before disconnecting.

Sebastian rubbed at his temples. Two warnings on his chosen crew already. It wouldn't be a big deal on a larger vessel but with such a small crew, it could be the barrier between him and a Deep Space Travel License at all.

Dimae ran a hand across Sebastian's shoulders – he must have climbed the ladder while Basti was distracted with his conversation.

"You know Matter is perfectly adept at DeST," Dimae said, using the Harrushetti shortening of Deep Space Travel to avoid the tricky starting S. "The early assessment will prove that."

"I know, Sweetie," Basti replied, leaning into the hand.

"Which means you will apologise for telling Matter that their honesty is recycled vessel water."

"I'm just stressed. It's such a big deal."

"I know. But I know because you told me. Matter does not have this information."

"It's not good for a crew to know their captain is stressed."

Dimae nuzzled Sebastian's hair; loosing some strands from the rough ponytail he'd shoved it into that morning. "Little crew means different rules."

Sebastian huffed but pulled up a text-comm. "Sorry," he typed. "Got trapped in the percentages airlock."

A message buzzed back quicker than he expected. "K."

"Dimae? Do they have K's in Ouaeahhn?"

Sauraxen

The ship towered over Sauraxen, the height of a four story house with the legs and boarding plank extended. Just like the four story house she and – Nei! Moving on from that tunnel of thought.

Layer upon layer of space-gunk coated every iota of the ship, turning the bobbly exterior into a mass of extra textures that made the image of it swirl and vibrate in Sauraxen's perception. One section toward the rear had a different echo. Sauraxen sighed and pulled up the notes function of her wristband. "Hull breach? Name and registration missing from outer hull."

She trekked up the clattery grate ramp, all fuzzy to her perception thanks to the airflow, and into the belly of the ship. The rattle of metal set Sauraxen's hair on edge, too loud to create a clear image of the insides, too loud to hear anyone else's movements. When was the last time

Sauraxen had seen a belly-boarding plank? How old was this ship?

Lights shone from strategic points along the walls and ceiling, each a point of distortion even with how dim they were. A delicate balance to try to achieve: having a light that wasn't so bright as to interfere with Sauraxen's perception, but not so dim that a human couldn't see. Sebastian had pulled out all the stops; either that or this ship hadn't been designed with humans in mind.

Sauraxen shifted to ignore the lingering clatters of her boarding. The breath of a human at the top of the boarding plank shifted the air around him. Broad shoulders, scruffy bun on the top of his head, standing favouring one leg with his hip cocked out to one side.

"Sebastian," Sauraxen greeted.

"Hey, Raxen, thanks for coming."

"Thanks for coming?"

Sebastian laughed, air shifting to fully reveal the empty cargo bay. All corrugated metal, or possibly grates? It was hard to tell from a laugh. Stairs led up to a catwalk that encircled the entire upper layer and four doors barred the rest of the ship from view. Except the circular opening to the uppermost floor – the laugh didn't echo beyond the entrance. All the doors were well fitted and well-sealed. Had the ship been designed for species sensitive to scent? Definitely not sensitive to sound with the way it echoed and bounced around off the metal.

Sauraxen jerked when she sensed another presence. Her muscles tensed to run. The breath of the *Other Thing* didn't disturb the airflow at all. Sauraxen knew a predator when she sensed one.

As if noticing her tension, Sebastian took a step back.

His feet clanged on the metal floor. That would need fixing if Sauraxen was going to stay. "This is Dr Brruuh TeaYaBin. He's our evaluator."

"A pleasure," the predator greeted in a flat tone. Then, under his breath he muttered, "It is pronounced Brruuh," with a trill over the 'rr' that Sauraxen knew Sebastian wasn't capable of.

"This is Sauraxen of the Planet Pitzk, our engineer."

Brruuh stood and the air parted like he was a blade. "Is rare to see a wrexi off Pitzk."

"It's rare to see a wrexi on Pitzk too," Sauraxen joked, continuing on before Brruuh could respond. "Basti, I hope you know this ship is a piece of—"

"Hey!" Basti cut in. "Be nice to my baby."

"Needs some work," Sauraxen placated.

"You haven't even seen the engine room yet," Basti winced.

"I can feel it from here," Sauraxen lied.

Basti laughed. "You want the grand tour or not?"

"You're not waiting for anyone else?"

Basti pulled up a text file from his own wristband, the pixels stabbing at Sauraxen's eyes unpleasantly. She turned her face toward Brruuh, attempting to examine the being that disappeared when he stopped moving. She couldn't get much of a read on him. Something soft coated his form, sucking air into it like a muffling device. A point of unnatural stillness that she would have to learn to look for.

"Just my pilot," Sebastian said. "They'll be fine. I'm not even sure when they'll get here." It sounded more like an 'if' the way he said it, but Sauraxen kept that thought to herself.

"Okay then, give me the grand tour and explain to me

why you bought such a—" She paused to let Basti bring in a breath to argue with "— vintage vessel."

"Two words: price range."

Sauraxen laughed as she followed Basti's clanging footsteps to the door on the rear wall of the cargo bay.

"May I accompany you on the tour?" Brruuh asked from behind her.

Scales! When had he moved?

"Of course," Sebastian agreed easily. "You come up and walk with me. Raxen likes her personal bubble free of people when she's assessing."

How in the sulpherous atmosphere of Pitzk did Sebastian know that? Sure, they were friends, and no offence to Basti, but he wasn't the most aware person in the universe.

Sebastian slid the door open, a smooth, silent movement. It disappeared into the solid metal floor. Inside, one engine clicked repetitively, the others lay dormant.

Sauraxen might as well have been alone for all the attention she paid to the other people she'd walked in with. Sebastian's quiet chatter illuminated the room for her, the vibrations of it bouncing up to the second floor and back down.

The lower floor had two of the silent engines. Sauraxen shrugged off her hood to allow her senses to function at full capacity. She was alone with Sebastian and the psychological evaluator who would be living on the ship with her anyway. They would have to learn to cope with Sauraxen's appearance and how it made them feel eventually.

Sauraxen didn't like the distortion of her senses that

came with wearing the hood, but she recognised the value of the hiding her outer appearance form others. Plus a hood was a great shade for her light-sensitive eyes.

The clicking of the household engine tried to draw Sauraxen's attention. That was the one that would keep the crew alive: life support, internal gravity systems, lighting, heat, water recycling, and so on. She would have to fix the clicking but it was somewhere over her head and she had questions for Sebastian before she touched anything. "Did you test these engines yet?"

"They all turn on except the second one on the top." His voice came from over by the door, just inside but not invading, still in the low light from the cargo bay.

"Why are you hovering by the... Did you read up on wrexi customs?"

"If I'm gonna have a wrexi engineer, I'm gonna put in the work to make 'em comfy."

Sauraxen tilted her head back to convey her happiness.

"Why are there no lights in here?" Brruuh's voice rumbled through the room, illuminating the lower two engines clearly but not disturbing the air on the upper floor.

"Wrexi are sensitive to light."

"Is it not hazardous to the rest of the crew to have no lights?"

"I can add some lights that aren't too bright and don't make noise for emergencies," Sauraxen offered, trailing a hand over one silent engine. A rubber belt? Rare. That would be a serious cost to replace when it wore out, unless she could replace it with something else? Maybe she could get some ouaeahhn vines? Would that be frowned upon? "Retro anti-grav engine," she muttered.

"Ja," Sebastian agreed. "Dimae said I need to source rubber if I wanna reliably get this thing out of more than one atmosphere."

"Not straight away." She shifted to the other engine squatting on the lower floor. She tapped against it, the quiet thunk sending ripples of information up her arm. "How did you get ouaeahhn designed thrusters?"

"It came with the ship. I may not know much about engineering, but I do know somebody butchered the input."

"When did you figure that out?"

"When I was taking out the wiring for the lights in here." Sebastian's humour-filled voice bounced off the stairs next to the door. The airflow dampened on the stair tops.

"Did you carpet those?"

"Ja. They clattered something rotten. It was the best thing I could think of."

Sauraxen dashed up the stairs to the top floor, bare feet sinking into the soft carpet.

A frisson rippled up her spine. The shift of the carpet fibres under her feet revealed the two engines on the upper floor. Sensory feedback she had tried and failed to be able to explain to Basti several times over.

"The carpet is only zip-tied down," Sebastian called up.

Sauraxen made an affirmative peep but her attention had already settled on the clicking engine. Her hair expanded, allowing more airflow to reach her, to take in the internal mechanisms. Turning cogs, levering pistons, interconnected devices swirling in a dance so well-choreographed that no biological life-form could imitate. And one cog, misfiring, slightly out of alignment.

Sauraxen flipped the power over to the emergency engine. The backup that could replace any of the others – an ugly mechanism that took up most of the upper floor. Maybe she should have checked its functionality first, before possibly plunging a ship full of people into darkness. Oh well, too late now.

As the emergency engine groaned to life, Sauraxen slid one hand into the household engine and gently pushed the cog back into place. "There you go," she whispered. "Find your place, little friend."

She flicked the power back. No more click. Maybe this wasn't going to be an utter rust bucket after all. And, even if it was, at least she would get the chance to be creative.

7 Standard Days To Liftoff

Brruuh

The doorway to the engine room stood open, the door itself disappearing into the floor in a way that unsettled Brruuh – how did it get pulled back into place? He hesitated just outside the realms, peering into the top floor of the engineering bay. Brruuh might have the eyes of a cat, but even he could barely make out more than the edge of the habitation engine where it stood closest to the door.

His ears twitched with the clanging of whatever it was Sauraxen was doing in the darkness of the interior.

"If you have time," he called into the darkness. "It would be helpful to check in."

"You wanna do it in here or...?" the ethereal voice of Sauraxen called from the darkness. It should have echoed off the walls, shouldn't it? At least that would have given

Brruuh some kind of clue as to Sauraxen's location within the room. As it was he couldn't even tell what floor she was on.

"I have prepared an office in one of the unused crew quarter rooms."

Sauraxen popped into the light, like a spring out of a sofa. Brruuh flinched back, claws extending automatically. He smoothed a hand over his head, settling the raised hair there. "Apologies, your appearance was unexpected."

"You called for me."

"The format of your appearance from the darkness," Brruuh tried to clarify. Curse earth common eurean and its abundance of words beginning with S.

"Too sudden, got it. Well, lead the way, doc."

"Brruuh," he corrected, leading Sauraxen up the ladder to the Habitation deck.

"I can't trill."

"I would rather an untrilled Brruuh than 'doc'."

The converted quarters utilised the high bed frame as a desk. The pair of soft chairs Brruuh had added fit nicely in the space, even the luxuriously cushioned bipedal bimanual designed ones he'd chosen. And, of course, the hand knitted blankets on each chair were purely for the comfort of the crew, not for Brruuh. Even if the fact that he had been the ones to knit them meant they would forever carry the underlying scent of him thanks to the scent glands around his claws.

"Comfy," Sauraxen noted, running a hand over the blanket on the back of one chair. The glittering white of it matched her scales almost perfectly.

"Please take a chair."

She did as Brruuh bade; sinking relaxedly into the

armchair she'd touched.

"I read your primary evaluation. I just wanted to touch base and find out if there is anything you think I ought to know."

Sauraxen let out a series of small peeps. "Do you mean medical or cognitive-psychological?"

"I mean, what made you decide to pursue a Deep Travel Permit?" Brruuh pressed his tongue against his fangs and clarified, "A job on a Deep Travel Vessel? You do not have any attachments on planet?"

Sauraxen turned her head to one side and grumbled, "Not anymore."

"Not anymore?"

She flexed her fingers, dragging them against the arms of the chair. If she'd had more obvious claws, Brruuh might have been concerned that she would split the fabric. "My girlfriend cheated on me and we broke up."

That would explain the warning on her evaluation. Anyone making a decision like this based on recent, highly emotional changes were unlikely to want to manage this long-term, or even be able to manage something like Deep Space Travel.

Brruuh pushed aside his own personal horror at the prospect of a partner betraying someone like that. Just because harrushetti could die of heartbreak didn't mean other species would. This assignment would be challenging enough without worrying that Sauraxen could die of heartbreak at any given moment, or worse, being confronted with the possibility of crew members starting relationships with one another, let alone the possibility of them *ending* those relationships.

Thankfully the only pre-bonded group were the

monogamous human and mated YaPar harrushetti. But there was an ouaeahhn. How was an ouaeahhn supposed to manage on a ship with this few crew? Brruuh flicked to Matter's file on his datapad and made a quick note before flicking back.

"You decided to join a long-term mission after a bad breakup?"

"Not exactly?"

"Explain?"

"Liz and I... We were together for three years." Her hair started to lift like tentacles propelled by water. She took a deep breath and shifted in her chair. "Can you not look at me like that?"

"Like what?"

"So intently. You're setting me on edge."

Brruuh shifted his eyes to the datapad in his lap and added the note, 'Prey. Do not look at directly.' Not an easy thing to ask of him, especially considering Sauraxen shone like the moon reflected through ice. Were all wrexi this pale? They did dwell underground, right? He needed to do more research.

"Timeline-wise," Sauraxen said, settling into the chair again. "It goes: Liz and I got together three years ago – planet years. I got a job in a manufacturing plant as an engineer – not the dream but worth it for the girl of my dreams." She sighed. "Four planet-weeks ago, Basti approached me about joining this crew. I told him I'd think about it and get back to him. I went to discuss it with Liz. She was in bed with someone else."

Brruuh couldn't keep the horrified gasp from escaping him. In their bed? Not just a betrayal but done in their shared space? His chest actually hurt at the thought of it.

"And before you start looking into wrexi relationships, all the info you'll find is complete nonsense. There isn't really a standard for relationships on Pitzk, everything is case-by-case and agreed upon upfront with the potential for change upon discussion. So, what's important here is that Liz and I had agreed to be monogamous, and then she broke that agreement. I found her with someone else and I packed my stuff and left. Now there isn't a reason to stay at my meh job when I could do something exciting with people I like."

"People you like?"

"Basti and I were at Station-Earth 799 together for our MScs."

"The captain is not an engineer." Was he?

"No. He was in promotional fast track – MSc in Leadership and Base Ship Maintenance."

"You know any of the other crew members?"

Sauraxen laughed. "I really need to get out of engineering and see who else is here."

"I am inclined to give you the active task of that. A vessel like this cannot run with a crew who do not get on like a colony."

"Colony like expansion planets?"

"Colony like a group of cats." Not that Brruuh was experienced with colonies, but he wasn't about to share that fact with any relative strangers.

Dimae

Dimae reclined half on the desk pressed up against what should have been a window, if this weren't a DST vessel.

The bedroom-office had already been draped in fabrics and posters to disguise the ugly grey metal walls. Brown, gold, and amber swathes of soft velvet and smooth silk and harrushetti loom-work in the YaPar patterns hung up against silly human motivational posters that Dimae could never make sense of. 'It's not over when you fail, it's over when you quit' – what did that even mean and who was the strange, spiky-haired man saying it? But Dimae had long since given up trying to understand these things; it was part and parcel of being with Sebastian. A few weird motivational posters were hardly much of an inconvenience.

Sebastian leaned over the bed, tucking the sheets into tighter and tighter corners. Dimae's eyes drifted down Sebastian's back and up his legs as he watched.

"I know you're watching me," Basti drawled over his shoulder. "And I'll tell you now; you're not throwing me on this thing."

Dimae huffed and continued to watch as Basti layered freshly covered pillows on the bed.

Motivational posters aside, the hardest thing about being with a human was definitely their propensity for cleanliness – not that Dimae wanted things to be dirty, but a pile of pillows and blankets did not a nest make. A nest needed the smell and the wear, but Basti couldn't cope with 'dirty sheets' and, after all, humans did sweat.

When Basti had tried to wash Dimae's Kitten Blanket, it had nearly broken their relationship. Now the Kitten Blanket lived on a shelf in the wardrobe for Dimae to grab when he wanted or needed it. Although it had yet to be unpacked from the boxes they'd both brought aboard the ship.

Basti pulled his shirt over his head, muscles in his back rippling, hair tugged into a single unit and then freed to land around Basti's head and shoulders in dark coils. Dimae wanted to sink his hands into that hair, to pull Basti to him and rub his scent all over him.

Without turning around, Basti tossed the shirt at Dimae. "Stop huffing," he said, voice filled with humour. "I'll be done soon."

Dimae lifted the shirt to his nose, letting his mouth fall open to fully engage with the scent of his mate. "When are we planning to lift off?" he asked, mind clear enough to open a line of conversation now that he wasn't so thoroughly distracted by Basti's alluring scent and visage.

"Pilot isn't even here yet."

"Immediately after full crew, then?"

Basti hummed but didn't stop fiddling with the bed, shifting pillows and blankets this way and that. "I think I wanna give it a few days. Let everyone settle in, maybe look for a job posting, fix up the ship."

Dimae huffed out of his nose, an affirmation and judgement all in one.

This time, Sebastian did turn around. He put his hands on his hips. "What is that supposed to mean?"

Dimae chirruped, tilting his head to one side and flicking his left ear.

"I am not afraid!" Basti protested.

Dimae leaned back, a challenge for Sebastian to come forward, to reach for his own defence.

"I am not!" He stalked over. "Don't you take that tone with me."

Dimae's canines peeked out of his mouth at the aggression. He tugged Sebastian close by his belt loops. Basti slotted between Dimae's legs like it was a practised manoeuvre and, after so many years together, it might as well have been.

Dimae dragged his face across Sebastian's cheek from ear to mouth, then sealed their lips together in a kiss.

When they split for breath, Sebastian muttered a half-hearted, "I hate you."

"Because I am right or because I am—?" Dimae rumbled in search of the word.

"Because you're right *and* because you're sexy," Sebastian filled in, pressing his nose against Dimae's. "I just want it to go well."

"It cannot go well if it's not going at all. Pick a lift-off date."

"Let me see if I can get a job first, then we have a destination."

Dimae huffed again.

"Oh, shut up," Basti grumbled, rubbing his own face against Dimae's. Humans might not have the same kind of claiming scent glands in their faces that harrushetti did, but the way Sebastian's stubble dragged against Dimae's skin always sent shivers down his spine and into the tips of his ears.

"When Matter gets here, I'll set a leaving date. Give 'em a couple of days to settle in and meet everyone else. Then we'll go."

"You have continued worry they won't come?"

Basti shrugged.

Dimae let it slide. "And in the meantime?"

"In the meantime, I guess you can pick me up and throw me into your nest."

"Our nest," Dimae corrected, scooping Sebastian close to him and launching the pair of them onto the pile of pillows still lightly scented with their mingled smell.

Basti's laugh shifted to a gasp as Dimae nibbled at his throat. Purrs escaped Dimae as he shifted down Basti's bare torso.

Matter

Matter peered up at the ship, then at the docking reference, and finally at the message from Sebastian, displayed in highlighted pixels over their wristband. This was the right port. Trust Sebastian to buy a R1BB1t craft. The frog-like ship towered over Matter's head, at least as tall as a four story building with its gangly legs extended like that, and longer than most small crew crafts. How many crew quarters rooms did this thing have? Why would Basti buy a craft that needed eight to ten people to run it? What exactly was he planning to do with this ship?

Not that it mattered, Matter had signed up either way. They shifted the hover trolley containing all their worldly possessions – a box, a backpack, and a suitcase to be exact

– so it lined up with the boarding plank.

"You're finally here!" Basti cheered, jogging down the boarding plank to take the hover trolley off Matter.

"I told you I had stuff to sort before I could–"

"Ja, I know," Basti drawled. "But I was worried."

"Don't be." They nudged Basti with their hip.

"Welcome to My Baby!"

The cargo bay stretched out around Matter, an echo-worthy space that reminded Matter of every other cargo bay they had ever seen. Not a space they had any desire to spend excess time in. "You're not planning to register it as that?"

"What's wrong with it?"

Matter turned to head back down the boarding plank.

Basti grabbed them by the arm, abandoning the hover trolley to float off into the cargo bay. Matter scrambled away from his grabbing hands, a laugh bursting out of them.

"Come back here!" Basti demanded, grabbing Matter around the middle and hoiking them into his arms, and pulling them out of the sunlight eeking into the cargo bay up the boarding plank.

"Nei!" Matter squealed through their laughter.

"You're stuck with me now," Basti put on the deeper voice that always made him sound like his dad – technically both of their dads even if Matter hadn't met the man until they were an adult.

"Sebastian LeaYaPar-Jones, you put me down right now."

"Never!" He cackled. "There is nei escape."

"Free me!" Matter cried.

Metal slammed. Matter and Sebastian froze, Matter's

feet still off the ground.

A figure leaned over the catwalk, wrapped around the cargo bay about half the way between the floor and the ceiling. "You are in need of help?" the soft growl undercutting the words told Matter it was a harrushetti asking.

Matter meowed.

The figure launched over the railing, landing neatly in a crouch on the black grated floor.

Sebastian lowered Matter to the floor. "By the stars, Matter, you and stressing out psychologists."

Matter tried to look innocent. "It's a talent?"

The harrushetti emerged from the shadows. The dim sunlight that filtered into the cargo bay highlighted the grey tiger-like stripes poking out from under his clothing.

"Nei..." Matter gasped.

Dr Brruuh TeaYaBin's grey-tipped ears twitched as he made an affirmative trill-huff.

"Basti, this is the same psych– sorry, cognitivist. The one that asked me if I was going to be professional."

"Professional is the harrushetti replacement for serious in ECE. They struggle with S," Basti clarified.

"Ah. Well, like I said in our interview, I just don't take anything seriously anymore."

"Speaking of that," Basti cut in. "I want you to check in with the ship's doctor."

Matter groaned. "Come on, Basti. You know I hate doctors."

"That explains a lot," Dr Brruuh muttered under his breath.

"I concur," a voice called from over Matter's shoulder. The clipped consonants of a YaPar harrushetti speaking earth common eurean.

"Leave off Dimae," Matter grumbled. "I have my reasons."

"Reasons you won't bring me into."

"It's none of your business. Either of you."

"You must be Dr Brruuh TeaYaBin," Dimae said, ignoring Matter in favour of the other harrushetti in the room.

The pair conversed in harrushetti: meows, purrs, and chirps mixed with body-based language that Matter hadn't a hope of figuring out any time soon. Basti's eyes flicked between the two, like he followed some of what was being said but not enough of it to really understand.

Matter stuck their tongue out at him, breaking his concentration and making him snort.

Dimae switched to ECE, refocusing on Matter. "Do you consent to my providing Dr Brruuh access to your medical records?"

"Do you have to?"

"Would be helpful."

"You are allowed to tell us not to," Dr Brruuh said quietly.

Matter looked away. "Let me think about it."

"Come on," Dimae led Matter into the bright medical bay.

A pale green examination bed sat in the centre of the room, a second one tucked away in an alcove. Monitors lined the walls, quiet and dark with no patient to keep an eye on. Everything about the room made Matter expect the scent of disinfectant, but the room smelled surprisingly neutral. "How did you avoid the disinfectant smell?"

"Harrushetti disinfectant – we have sensitive noses."

Dimae tapped the medical bed. "Hop up."

Matter did as bade and let Dimae scan them.

"You are elevated, when was your last contact?"

"I literally just hugged Basti."

"Before that?"

Matter huffed. "It's been a while."

"You know you are meant to maximise contact before long journeys. How do you plan to manage this?"

"Same way I always do. I'll handle it. And my pain is fine before you ask."

Dimae scrunched up one side of his nose in a lightweight grumble. A semblance of annoyance, more performative than real, even Matter with their relatively low tele-empathic scores could tell. "Keep me informed."

"Sure thing," they called as they headed back to the cargo bay.

A thrumming bass called to them from the door opposite medi-bay. Matter shifted past Brruuh where he lingered on the catwalk stairs to let themself through the open doorway and into the darkness of engineering.

Bioluminescent mushrooms shone at them from the tops of engine blocks, cupboards, and almost everything that could be counted as a corner. Blue and yellow speckled bioluminescent mushrooms.

"Sauraxen?" Matter called into the relative darkness.

Something clattered to the floor. "Matter?"

"Axen!"

A body launched itself at Matter from the darkness, tangling them up in limbs and sensory hair.

Sauraxen

Sauraxen was almost done patching the butchered installation of the thruster engine when her wristband buzzed for her attention. She extracted herself from the machinery, wiggling out from the awkward, incomprehensible position she'd got herself into to swipe across it. Calls were always uncomfortably echoey when answered inside an engine.

Liz's pixelated and too-bright face appeared – what was it with Liz and wanting to video chat? All the other humans Sauraxen had met, befriended, or even been with had no issues with voice-only calls. Then again, Liz had always been a rule unto herself.

It had been endearing once.

"Liz?" Sauraxen asked, like an idiot. What kind of a question was that? It was clearly Liz's pixelated face, even if she hadn't been the only person who tried video calling Sauraxen.

"Saura," Liz's voice came out all pouty, the way it did when she wanted something. It rumbled over Sauraxen's skin like a soft caress, even when mildly distorted by the calling hardware. That pout wasn't just for sulking with, the amount of times those odd but all too pleasant human lips had pressed against Sauraxen's skin, whispering words that made her squirm, pressing wet kisses that left her shivering...

Sauraxen steeled herself. "I've asked you not to call me Saura."

"Come home, babe."

"Home? Where I found you in bed with someone else? That home?"

"Come on, Sauraxen," Liz huffed. "You're a non-monogamous species. I was going to tell you about it eventually."

"Eventually isn't early enough. Scales, Liz, I would have been okay with it if you'd just told me outright. But you kept it a secret and that's a trust break. I'm not coming back."

Liz's face turned sour, at least what Sauraxen could make out of it from the pixels that stabbed at her eyes. "Then what exactly are you going to do? Where are you staying?"

"I'm on a ship."

"What ship? What about your job!?"

"I quit."

"You can't just quit."

"I can. I did. I have a new job." Sauraxen gestured, hoping it was in frame enough for Liz to make out. "I'm on a ship."

"Leaving the planet is pretty fucking extreme, S."

"As is deciding to cheat. Now, if there's nothing else you want..."

"Well, if we're breaking up, what's going to happen with the house?"

If. This was so typical of Liz. Nothing was ever her fault. Everything was according to her schedule and her wants. She had wanted to be monogamous, so Sauraxen had done it. She had wanted to stay on planet, so Sauraxen had stayed. She had wanted to live in the nice, four story house, so Sauraxen had helped make it happen. "There's no if here. The breakup happened as soon as I saw you with whoever it was. There was nei coming back from that. And you can have the house. I don't care."

"I can't afford it alone!"

Sauraxen's hair squirmed against itself, rubbing like the tentacles of an anxious Kil. It plastered itself to Sauraxen's back and shoulders, a protective coating for the pain it expected. Stupid intrinsic nervous system. But Sauraxen didn't want to leave Liz in a dangerous position. She didn't want Liz to end up... Wait. This wasn't her problem anymore. Liz had more than enough ability to move if she needed to, and anyway, "Ask your new partner for help."

"Sau–"

Sauraxen swiped to hang up the call and told her wristband, "Block calls from this sender."

Her wristband peeped the affirmative and Sauraxen stalked out of engineering and up the ladder. She needed a drink.

Sebastian

Sebastian wouldn't have noticed Sauraxen entering the aufenthaltsraum, her bare feet silent against the solid metal flooring, but she hissed at the brightness of the lights.

"Sorry," Basti called, scrambling out of his chair to dim the lights.

"Sorry," Sauraxen replied.

"Why are you sorry?"

"I hate needing special treatment."

"It's not special," Sebastian argued. "Just because your needs are different doesn't make them special."

"But–"

"Don't make me start comparing your needs with the needs of other crew members."

Sauraxen pulled a box from the freezer and upended it over a plate. Several beige lumps clanked onto the plate, which she shoved into the heater. Her hair stuck up at the roots in a way that hinted at irritation. Before Sebastian could ask, she leaned her back against the kitchenette counter top and asked, "What are you doing?"

"Looking for cargo jobs."

"Job boards make me shed." She shuddered.

"Do... do you actually shed?"

"Yes."

"In one big go?"

"Don't act grossed out, I have to deal with humans' sweatiness all the time. Once, Liz left a sweaty hand-print on the door handle and I could sense it for over an hour." Her hair cuddled around her, as if it wanted to protect her from some pain.

Basti chewed his lip. "I guess it's weird for everyone."

"Hazard of a multi-species crew." There were layers to her voice that Basti wasn't experienced enough to recognise. He missed the days they were closer, those academy days where he had been able to ask what she was feeling without the bubbling anxiety about making her uncomfortable. Friendship decay hit hard, apparently. At least for Basti. Sauraxen and Matter hadn't seemed to have any of that, slipping back into the closeness they always had whenever they were around one another.

The heater buzzed. Sauraxen yanked the plate out, holding it on the very tips of her fingers and dropping it on the table with a clank. She blew on her fingers and let out a series of peeps.

"Have you ever heard of an oven glove?" Basti drawled.

Sauraxen's whole body twisted up, making Sebastian think of a face screwed up in disgust. "Fuzzy, constricting, awful!"

"Okay," Basti laughed. "Leave that with me. I'll think of something." The scent of cheese and tomato sauce sauntered around the room. "Are you eating pizza pockets?"

"I'll warn you now; they're filled with bug paste." She flicked one into her mouth, steam escaping in tendrils not unlike her sensory hair. It made her lizard-like face shift into something like a dragon from truly ancient human legend.

Basti grimaced. "I know some people – humans even – who eat bugs. I just can't handle it. They're so itchy."

"Itchy?"

"They make my throat burn, like I couldn't swallow them all in one go."

Sauraxen touched a hand to her eyes. "Sebastian, you're allergic to bugs."

"What? No, I'm not."

"Take the test."

"I don't need to take the test."

Sauraxen snickered and pressed on her communicator. "Doc? You wanna test your husband for bug allergies?" She tossed another pocket into her mouth, shooting Sebastian the equivalent of a grin, chin tilted high in the air.

"Sebastian, come down to medi-bay please," Dimae's voice rang over the ship communications system.

A yelp of pain accompanied it from the front of the ship. "Raxen?" Matter called, voice echoing down the top corridor. "Can you alter the volume of comms in here?"

"Eating," Sauraxen called back around a mouthful of pizza pocket, steam escaping in a delicious cloud.

"Put it on your list?" their plaintive voice called after a moment's pause.

Sauraxen peeped and chirped at her wristband.

Sebastian pushed to his feet, trekking to the ladder down to the cargo bay.

A feeling of weightlessness filled him as the gravity in the ladder shifted and gently lowered him to the cargo bay floor. "Sauraxen!" he yelled. "What did you do to the ladders?"

Matter

The ship whirred to life, lights sparking on the pilot's console attached to Matter's chair. The lights faded to a dim glow, bright enough to be seen but not so bright as to interfere with visibility. This place really had been retrofitted for an Ouaeahhn pilot.

The switches and dials on the wall repeated the flare of light.

Three button clicks had the rear thrusters engaged, the atmosphere breaking engine thrumming gently underneath Matter's fingers where they lay atop the console attached to their chair.

"Ready to get going?" they called over the ships comms. They didn't wait for a response before lifting the ship into motion.

The ship rattled and buzzed like an old man who had sat too long, joints creaking and cracking as he shifted to move. Four huge clunks echoed through the metal interior as the legs retracted.

The planet's gravity pulled against the ship and Matter's body, making their joints ache. They leaned sideways and flicked a dial on the wall panel. "Engage ship gravity maintenance systems," they muttered to themself. "Lessen the grav in here and..."

With a soft sight of relief, Matter sat back in the chair to guide the ship out of atmo. The refracted light blared down at them, nothing like the soothing, ever-changing swirling of the void of space.

"Just a little further..."

"Matter," Sebastian's harshest voice called out from the aufenthaltsraum, breaking the celestial peace of shifting out of a planet's atmosphere.

"What?" Matter snapped back. Basti, of all people, shouldn't be the one to interrupt this.

"Did you adjust the gravity in here?"

Fuck. "Uh... I meant to just engage it, why?"

"Because Dimae just fell over."

"Maybe he's drunk."

"Matter!"

"Okay, okay. I'll put it back." They didn't bother to bring up the difficulty of trying to steer an airborne space ship through a busy port, still in the atmosphere and gravitational pull of the planet, while leaning over to mess with the grav settings. Mental note: ask Raxen to fix grav maintenance systems so it's divided by zone rather than whole ship inclusive.

Breaking out of the final stage of atmosphere played

over Matter's vision like a sunset, pink and gold and blue and so many other colours that Matter couldn't begin to name them. Until, finally, the darkness of space loomed around them.

Matter settled back as the chair shifted to a wider angle, allowing them to lie down and look up at the void above and around them through the huge spherical window over their head. Their eyes adjusted slowly, too human to jump into coping with the pinpricks of light in the darkness immediately.

All the tension leaked out of them; the residual grumpiness at Sebastian's habit of taking his stress out on them, the discomfort of having Brruuh as their assessor again, the pain that always existed in some way in their body.

Out in the void.

Galaxies played off one another, purple and blue and stark white light. Orbital lines of planets gathered in glittering dust. Asteroid tails and noses shining in gold waves. And everything in the intricate and impossible dance of chaos and order all rolled into one. Gravitational fields pulled at Matter's consciousness, grasping for their attention.

"We are not moving?" Brruuh's voice drifted down the corridor from the aufenthaltsraum.

"In an ideal world, we wouldn't know when we were moving – it makes people a bit queasy to feel space travel." Sebastian's conversational tone carried almost as well as his harsh voice had, perfectly clear to Matter. Maybe they should consider closing the door for some quiet, but it didn't really match the ethos of the ship. Everything was open here.

"But I'm pretty sure Matter's just adjusting to being out of the atmosphere," Sebastian finished.

"You have never worked with an ouaeahhn pilot, have you?" Dimae's naturally harsher voice pinged over the metal floors.

"Nei," Brruuh answered.

"Come with me."

Footsteps clanged along the corridor, stopping outside the pilot's chamber.

Matter tried to shrug off the feeling of being watched as they laid their hands on the stellar steering shifts.

This was what they were made for.

Brruuh

Brruuh settled himself on the sofas in the aufenthaltsraum, his datapad in his lap as he flicked the pen between his claws. He'd never done an on-ship assessment. He'd read the handbook on it several times over, he'd even annotated some of it already but somehow none of that made him feel more confident in his actual task.

Matter's voice echoed down the corridor. "Basti, leave off!"

"I'm just asking."

"Ten times already!" Matter snapped back, appearing in the aufenthaltsraum and making a beeline for the coffee machine.

Brruuh swiped the datapad to get to his notes. It looked like coffee was going to end up being a conversation. Stimulants and their effect on emotions. But now wasn't the time to voice any of that.

The clanks and thumps of Matter's aggressive motions made Brruuh's ears twitch.

"You can't blame me; you knocked my husband onto the floor. I just wanna know whether to expect you to casually turn the gravity off."

"I thought it was localised."

"It wasn't."

"Which I didn't know at the time. Fuck, Basti, you're acting like my joy in life comes from bothering your husband. You really think I care that much about what he's doing?"

"I think you should care."

"Why? Because you like him? That's hardly a reason for me to care."

"Because he's my husband!"

"So fucking what? If anyone's causing tension between the two of us, it's him!"

"What did Dimae ever do to you?"

Matter's shoulders slumped; they laid their head against the cupboard door. The coffee coming out of the machine steamed and sputtered as if it wanted to add to the argument. "I didn't mean it to come out like that."

"Well it did."

Matter pulled their fresh mug of coffee toward their chest, the liquid sloshing over them and onto the floor with tiny audible splats. They grimaced.

It smelled more bitter than normal, acrid and burnt in a

way it shouldn't have coming out of a coffee specific machine. Perhaps it wasn't the coffee Brruuh smelled but the emotions washing over the room. Humans perspired under strain, and this was nothing if not a strain-worthy conversation.

"I almost didn't come here, you know that? I sat in that fucking uncomfortable IPA chair with a psych staring me down, again, as a favour to you."

Brruuh stayed very still. Some ancient, instinctive part of him wanted to calibrate, ready to pounce, but he held off. The stiller he stayed; the less likely the other two were to notice him. Matter had already complained about him being a 'psych staring them down', Brruuh hardly wanted to reinforce that image, but any movement now might break the stream of the conversation, leaving everything bottled up and ready to overflow at the least opportune moment. Brruuh knew all too well what stagnant and ever-increasing water could do to a place, bottled up feelings could cause the same levels of damage.

This was already an argument that could have been a conversation if it had happened earlier, but things weren't always that simple. And between cross-cultural faux-pas and only being one day into the vacuum...

"And for my trouble," they continued. "I've been told off over and over again. I was this close–" they gestured with a finger and thumb pinched to almost touching, the motion spilling more coffee, more like a wave than a splatter this time. It set Brruuh's fur on end. "–to not even coming after the way you talked to me. You gave me a low-ball of an offer for payment for my services as pilot and you're acting like I should worship the ground you walk on. There isn't ground here, Sebastian." They threw his name like it was an insult. "We're in space!" And with that, and the hinting traces of salt from tears unshed, such a different smell to the salt of sweat, Matter stormed from the room.

"Matter!" Sebastian yelled after them but he didn't follow, instead grabbing a cloth from the sink and wiping the coffee off the floor.

Eekingly slowly, Brruuh lowered his head and scribbled some notes on his datapad.

Day one and the arguments had started already. Matter was regretting their fraught decision to come at all, and Sebastian was apparently not paying well for services rendered. It was one thing to start a new business venture and dock your own pay, but offering less than the expected base wage for someone experienced just because you had some kind of relationship was definitely a poor show.

Sauraxen

The knock on her quarter's door was tentative, almost as if the person on the other side didn't really want her to notice. She slithered over to the door, glad she hadn't wiggled out of her clothes yet.

Matter stood on the other side, fidgeting enough to send out waves of motion that twitched the edges of Sauraxen's perception.

"What's up?"

"Can I come in?" Matter's voice came out in a whisper.

"Sure." Sauraxen stepped back, letting Matter into her cave. Typically Sauraxen wouldn't have wanted a cave of her own but with so many visual creatures on the ship needing their lights on, it was nice to have a reservedly dark space, especially since Sebastian had marked this particular door for her due to the broken lights.

A guarantee of a space with nei chance of painful illumination.

The door slid shut behind Matter, leaving them fidgeting in the room instead of the hallway.

Sauraxen slid a hand over their shoulder, the fabric of their jumpsuit rustling under her fingers. Offering comfort in the wake of Matter's obvious nerves.

Matter leaned forward, lips pressing against the side of Sauraxen's face.

Sauraxen's fingers slipped under the top of the jumpsuit and slid it easily from Matter's shoulders. It clung on their waist as Sauraxen let her palms slide down Matter's newly exposed chest.

She had forgotten how warm Matter was. A trill escaped her at the feel of it. Warm and soft and smooth. Like a human, but not. Much like everything else about Matter, as soon as you got past the first impression, it was impossible to ignore their ouaeahhn nature.

Sauraxen's fingers caught on a raised pattern. "New," she muttered.

"I've aged."

"Do you have new moves to match it?" Sauraxen teased. It had been a few years since she and Matter had come together like this. It only ever happened when they were both in the same place at the same time and Sauraxen wasn't in a closed relationship.

Matter's warm hands slid under her hair, and with a single deft flick of their fingers, Sauraxen's strappy sleeves disappeared from her shoulders and her dress puddled around her feet. "I'm sure you'll find out," Matter hummed, not bothering to shift near her ears, knowing she didn't need that, knowing her entire body was receptive to sound waves.

Sauraxen backed the two of them toward the raised bed, letting Matter land almost atop her, catching themself on their forearms with a brief hiss.

"Pain?" she murmured.

"Ignore it."

Sauraxen did as asked, hair tendrils lifting to wrap around Matter as she pushed their jumpsuit off their waist. Matter wriggled against her to kick it off.

Sauraxen gripped their upper arms tight, the patterns carved into their skin playing havoc over her hands. "Not that."

"Sorry," Matter replied.

"The wiggling is too much like..." She didn't want to say breeding, didn't want to think about eggs and hatchlings at all. Not now, not in this situation.

"I won't do it again."

Sauraxen ran her face up Matter's neck, tongue dipping out to taste the pulse points.

Matter's groan sent a wave of pleasure through Sauraxen.

Bare skin pressed against bare scales, warmth against cool. Matter was smooth outside their ouaeahhn patterning, raised like scars all over their body. Sauraxen let her fingers trace the patterns, paying particular attention to any that coaxed noises from Matter, or those delicious warm and wet bursts of breath huffed into Sauraxen's neck.

"You okay?" Sauraxen asked when they lay together after, Matter's hands still trailing over her skin.

"I'll be fine. Just a bad start."

"It's never reassuring when the start is bad," Sauraxen murmured, a poor attempt at a wrexi idiom but there was no better way to translate it without having to explain cave systems and the use of wrexi sensitivities when seeking out new locations.

Matter said nothing.

"I just ended a three-year relationship."

"Fuck, Axen, why didn't you say anything?"

"Because it wasn't relevant." Matter had pushed into a sitting position but Sauraxen pulled them back down. "Stop. You didn't pressure me into this. You never have. If I'd said nei what would you have done?"

"Stopped." The way Matter said it made it sound like there was nei other option. For Matter, there wasn't. It wasn't always the same in Sauraxen's experience. "Okay," Matter sighed. They stopped fighting Sauraxen's hands. "Do you want to tell me about it?"

"About what?"

"The relationship?"

Sauraxen thought, letting out the hum that she usually tried to keep to herself. Something about being alone with Matter always brought out the truest form of her and her expressions. Maybe it was the ouaeahhn thing. All ouaeahhn had a level of tele-empathy that affected even the most null of species. More likely it was just Matter.

Sauraxen tucked her face into the junction between Matter's shoulder and neck. "Her name was Liz," she started.

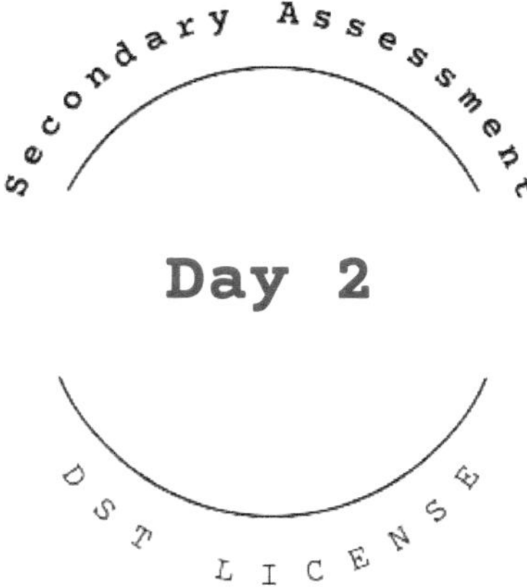

Day 2

Dimae

One day-night cycle into the assessment voyage, Dimae followed the scent of his mate from their bedroom, across the catwalk, up the ladder-turned-gravity chamber, and into the aufenthaltsraum. Sebastian's insistence on rising as soon as he woke would never make sense to Dimae.

As his eyes tracked over the room, they landed briefly on Matter, leaning their rear on the dining table, steaming mug of coffee cupped between their hands. Did they have to sit on the table like that? For all that humans were absurdly over-clean, Matter – or maybe ouaeahhn – didn't seem to have any boundaries at all.

"I always wanted a cat," Matter muttered into their coffee, obviously answering something Sebastian had said before Dimae was close enough to hear.

"You can't keep a cat on a ship," Basti replied, sleepily refilling the coffee machine. The bitter scent of caffeine already filled the space. This obviously wouldn't be Basti's first cup.

"I know; that's why I never got one. You know me, I can't stay on a planet or station for too long."

"You definitely can't keep a house cat on a ship with a harrushetti."

"Really?"

"Ja, they get all weird about it."

"How would you feel if something that sounded like a baby was kept as a pet?" Dimae cut in as he passed through the open doorway.

"Sweetie, I really don't think that would bother a human," Basti said, shifting to press a kiss to Dimae's jaw.

"What about keeping a creature you essentially evolved from as a pet?" Dimae asked.

"I mean..." Matter spoke slowly, choosing their words with care. "Humans actually do that."

"What?"

"Humans keep monkeys as pets. Not the exact ones we're descended from or anything but, ja, it would be pretty much the equivalent to a harrushetti and a house cat – potentially closer since monkeys come from Earth."

Dimae huffed, ears dipping flatter to his head. Tension crackled between him and Matter. "Do you always have an argument for everything?" The words erupted from Dimae without thought or care.

"I like to think I'm good at coming up with stuff on the fly. I don't have to have an argument prepared in advance."

Their light tone and teasing smile set Dimae's fur bristling. "You are just that argumentative?"

Matter shrugged, smile turning to an over-confident grin shot at Dimae, almost as if they dared him to retaliate.

Brruuh appeared in the hallway behind them, approaching the aufenthaltsraum, his ears perked forward with interest. Dimae turned away to crowd Sebastian in against the kitchenette counter and rub his face over Basti's face and hair.

Matter made a noise like they had a hairball stuck in their throat. "Don't be gross."

"I thought ouaeahhn were all about open displays of affection," Sauraxen's voice came from somewhere behind Dimae. Maybe the sofa area. He hadn't even noticed her.

"And being overly affectionate with anything that crosses their path," Dimae grumbled against Basti's neck.

"I'm only half-ouaeahhn," Matter grumbled.

"Ouaeahhn enough."

They huffed out a breath. "I'm gonna go check our flight path."

Dimae turned round to greet Sauraxen properly only to find her pressing her hands to the dining table with enough force that her scales rippled. "You two both need to get a handle on taking things out on Matter," she hissed.

"What do you mean?" Basti asked, shifting around Dimae to sink into a chair at the head of the table.

"I mean, you made a whole thing about not knowing when the pilot would arrive when I first got here, and then I heard the way you–" She stabbed a gesture in Dimae's direction. He flinched away from it. "Greeted them for a start, let alone this morning. And you—" She turned that stabbing gesture onto Basti. "Complaining about every tiny thing they've done that you perceive as wrong."

Neither Basti nor Dimae responded.

"Tell me this, if nothing else, did you or did you not realise that your half-ouaeahhn pilot just left the supposedly communal space to go and sit in a room *alone*?"

Sebastian's face took on an ashen sheen.

Sauraxen lifted her hands from the table. "Matter is enough ouaeahhn that they need meaningful connection in order to *survive*. They need to feel welcome and wanted and you two acting the way you were just acting..." she let out a short whine.

Dimae pressed his chin against Sebastian's head. As a medical professional he had looked up the needs of each of the species that made up this crew, but he hadn't actually worked with an ouaeahhn before.

"I don't give a shit about your internalised prejudices, Dimae," Sauraxen continued. "I know harrushetti and ouaeahhn have some serious issues with miscommunication and culture clashes, but Matter took a six week course on harrushetti culture to try and bridge that gap. What have you done?"

Dimae had expected Matter to be human. And that wasn't fair.

Sebastian

"**H**ow long have you been looking at that?" a deep, unfamiliar voice with a Harrushetti accent asked from behind Sebastian.

Basti jumped all the way out of his chair, spinning to look, getting tangled in the chair and sending it crashing to the ground with an almighty bang and clatter. "Depends how long you've been stood there."

Brruuh nabbed the datapad from the table as Basti bent to pick up the chair. "Job board?"

"Ja," Sebastian sighed. How long had he been here? He had every intention of heading to bed after Dimae. He just wanted a quick glance to see if any new jobs had popped up since the last time he had looked. That had been... twenty pages ago. He pulled the ponytail out of his hair and rubbed at his scalp. It ached from the release of the tightness of the style.

Brruuh stumbled back. "Your head is... malleable?" he squeaked.

"What? It's hair. How long did you live on an Earth Colony and you never saw anyone change their hair?"

Brruuh shook his head, eyes still wide, ears pinned back against his head.

A smile broke out on Sebastian's face. Dimae had been equally overwhelmed when he first found out about Sebastian's hair. Basti had tended toward braids back in those days and the first time he had unleashed the coils into the loose cloud around his head and shoulders, Dimae had been so enthralled that he had buried his face in it without warning. It had been Dimae's influence, the absolute joy Dimae found in Basti's freed hair, that had shifted Basti from rows of braids to the single ponytail or even just loose hair the vast majority of the time.

"Alright," he said. "Quick lowdown so you're not caught unawares next time. Matter also has malleable hair. Sauraxen doesn't, but hers is more like a limb than traditional hair."

"I know about 'Auraxen. I talked to an ex-colleague with a focus on lizardic-descendants like wrexi."

"I'm glad you're putting in the work to understand the crew. Anything you want to share or ask?"

Brruuh sat down at the table. "I continue to be concerned for Matter. As an ouaeahhn, they're..."

"Half," Basti corrected, as much for himself as for Brruuh. He couldn't blame the harrushetti for forgetting, though, especially not after this morning. Matter was good at fitting into expectation, at being what and how people needed them to be. They were so good at it that Basti hadn't even thought about what that might do to their psyche. "I know harrushetti and ouaeahhn have their long-term tensions, but you can't let that influence your assessment of them."

The tensions had begun when the two cultures had clashed over what counted as family. Because of that clash, it was one of the few cases where Inter-Planetary Alliance regulations weren't so strict. Ouaeahhn had an endless capacity for love, romance, and sex. The ease with which they embraced people into their family was like nothing Basti had seen elsewhere. Harrushetti lay on the exact opposite end of that spectrum: they were hyper-monogamous, to the extent that most of them only ever had one partner for their entire lives. Their families were insular, rarely inviting anyone else to join them; it had been tough enough to induct Basti into the LeaYaPar family when he and Dimae bonded, let alone any of Basti's family.

"I would never!" Brruuh protested.

"Not consciously, but if it's their ouaeahhn nature that is bothering you..." He trailed off, hoping Brruuh would understand what he was getting at.

By the way his ears twitched, he did. "I thought I was

meant to be the cognitivist."

"Ja, but I'm the captain. My job is as much managing my crew as it is managing the ship and our jobs." He shifted around the table, grabbing the cold and empty mug that had once contained peppermint tea from the table. "You want a hot drink?"

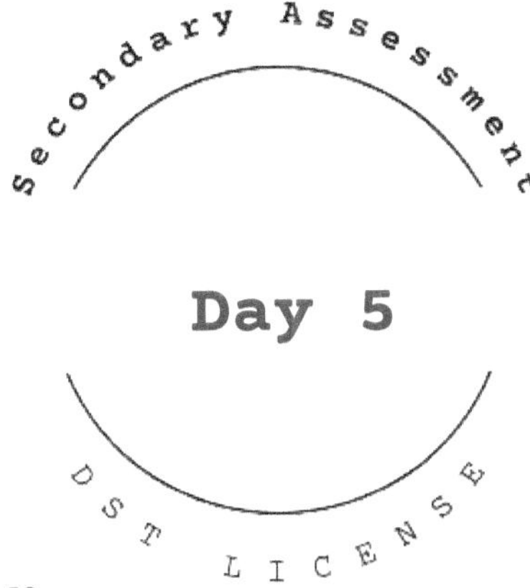

Matter

Matter had mostly contained themself to the pilot's console for the last few days, tiptoeing out only when silence coated the entire living floor of the ship. It spiked and fizzled at their skin, playing at the raised ouaeahhn patterns all over it. This was a bad plan, hiding away, not building on the relationships they had with the rest of the crew.

Ouaeahhn was a highly tele-empathic culture, the entire society and language was based on the interaction of minds and emotions as shared on ouaeahhn. It had been this way for as long as the memory persisted, and part of that was ingrained into every ouaeahhn to the extent that ouaeahhn had grown to need those connections in order to survive.

Matter, being half-ouaeahhn was more robust against being alone. But they also had to contend with human emotions, and the way human emotions would rage their way through a body. The worst times were when the emotions weren't Matter's, but that was why they wore personal shields next to their wristband.

The rejection of their last few interactions with Basti, though, still swirled in Matter's stomach like a storm waiting to explode. They didn't want to explode at him, and they didn't think they could take another blame game.

Maybe they should have listened to that instinct, that trepidation which had left them so reluctant to board the ship that they hadn't turned up until the very last minute. Maybe they should have listened to that doubting voice in their head that had warned them against working for Basti when he had railed on them about their interaction with cognitivist Brruuh.

They rubbed their face.

Cognitivist Brruuh was yet another point of tension. But at least Matter could attempt to shrug off all those awkward, stilted interactions as him doing his job. He couldn't start befriending the crew; that was outside the realms of his duties. It could even be detrimental to his duties.

Then there was Dimae...

Matter turned their attention back to the void above them, seeking comfort in the stars in the way only ouaeahhn could. The sparkling, endless possibilities of the void.

The way that... Wait. What the...?

Matter pressed on the ships comms button. "Uh... Sebastian?"

"Ja?" Basti called back from the aufenthaltsraum.

"Could you come here, please?"

Footsteps clanged along the corridor. Had Basti always been that heavy footed? "What's up?"

Matter pointed out into the void, at the spot they hadn't taken their eyes off since they first saw it. The incomplete pattern of a ship's movements.

"What am I looking at?" He peered out into space, pupils expanding to take in the darkness but unable to, not designed to see the way that Matter's were.

"There's a ship there."

"So?"

"It's not moving. At all."

"At all? Not even residual propulsion?"

"Nei."

Basti turned to face Matter, who still didn't take their eyes off the ship, as if looking away would make it disappear from their vision, like someone trying to catch a spider before it dashed under a piece of furniture. "Have you opened comms with them?"

"I wasn't sure if you wanted me to do that, or if you wanted to be in charge of it."

"I... I'm sorry, Matter. I got caught up in the harrushetti side of a theoretical argument between cultures. I shouldn't have treated you like that. I shouldn't have taken my stress out on you."

Matter frowned, shooting him the briefest of glances before their eyes darted back to the ship. Basti, outlined by the sparkling void looked the way Matter assumed he always did to Dimae. A point of attention, strong and sturdy and bold. Wide shoulders and that glorious fluff of hair, and who else knew what appealed to harrushetti.

What was he talking about? Was he trying to apologise for the way he had been treating Matter? Was this his attempt to make amends? Why now? Why in this way? And did he really think it was all fundamentally locked into their conversation about pet cats?

"That's great, Basti, but we're talking about a ship here."

Sebastian pressed his lips together. "You do comms, but I'll be here for the first one."

Matter shrugged and flicked open the inter-ship comms, searching for ships within range on IPA frequencies. They readjusted the parameters for outside IPA frequencies. Then readjusted again. "They don't appear to have a comms system."

Basti chewed his lip. "You think we should go over there? Just to make sure they're okay?"

"We could flag an IPA patrol to do that," Matter suggested. "It's not like they're going anywhere."

But even as they tried to offer alternate possibilities, an emotional spark flew off Basti, strong enough to bypass Matter's personal shields. The possibility of rescuing someone, of being like the ancient media captains he had always so admired. And the worry that, by the time an IPA patrol arrived, it would be too late for any occupant inside the ship to make it out alive.

"Flag the patrol," he said. "But I think we should go check just in case."

Brruuh

The catwalk trembled with the motion in the cargo bay, more so the further down the stairs Brruuh got. Dimae shifted around Sebastian as he pulled the pieces of the space suit into place.

Matter grumbled something about how the ship would have life support systems in place. How they had seen it still had power and that was part of why it was so concerning that it was just sat there. Sebastian and Dimae were insistent, and Matter didn't argue further. Their sideways glance at Brruuh told him their tongue-biting was for his benefit. He filed that away to make note of later.

The domed helmets were comparable to the pilot's console window, but Brruuh always found them to be incredibly claustrophobic. If Matter's grimace was anything to go by, they thought the same. At least they had some kind of sense.

"I didn't even know we had a shuttle," Sauraxen called from engineering, not emerging into the light of the cargo bay. She could see everything not contained behind a closed door anyway – at least that was what Brruuh's ex-colleague had told him.

Dimae ran his hands over each of the closures of Sebastian's space suit, ensuring the safety of his bond mate. Matter struggled with the helmet attachment on their own.

"Ja, I bought that one separately," Sebastian called back as he patted the fastening of his gloves. "The one that came with the ship was... well, it didn't have a windscreen anymore."

"What is a windscreen?" Brruuh asked.

"Glass front panel to see out of," Matter clarified offhand.

Brruuh stood and approached them. "May I?"

"Uh... sure?"

His hands pressed over the back of Matter's neck where the helmet fastenings were, solid and strong, trying not to think too hard about the vulnerability offered to him with such little concern. Kittens were scruffed on the backs of their necks, it could be infantilising for an adult, a power move by another. But Matter offered up the back of their neck like it wasn't a concern.

"There," Brruuh said, letting his hands fall back to his sides. "We do not want you dying of asphyxiation."

Matter shot him a shy smile. "Because I'm the only one who can fly?"

"Because you would be missed."

Matter's eyes brightened in that ouaeahhn way, like they were examining Brruuh as a galaxy rather than a person. They glittered Brruuh's greys and whites back at him, turning it a stunning silver. A soft smile touched their lips and Brruuh stepped back, uncomfortable with the intimacy of such a smile.

They climbed into the shuttle with Sebastian and the pair disappeared into space.

Brruuh watched even though he could see nothing but the wall that had slid back into place. His ears twitched with concern.

"It's gotta be said," Sauraxen said in a casual tone. "I think it was a weird choice to leave the prey species alone with two predators."

"Is that a real issue for you?" Brruuh asked, trailing over to linger in the lower doorway of engineering.

"I mean... kinda."

"Can you elaborate?"

"For a friend or as an assessment?"

Brruuh let out a soft trill of confusion.

Sauraxen peeped back in a way that sounded an awful lot like harrushetti gibberish. Like something just outside his understanding.

"It's the custom for wrexi to specify whether a conversation is–" She peeped again, frustration showing through the noise in a way Brruuh wouldn't have expected to be able to recognise. "Professional or personal."

"Can it be both?"

That had Sauraxen slipping into the edges of the light shining from the cargo bay into engineering.

Brruuh blinked slowly, attempting to soothe but also trying to prevent himself from becoming starstruck. Sauraxen's scales sparkled like falling snow and the wash of uncomfortable tension rippled up and down Brruuh's spine and into the tips of his ears.

"Maybe. It's just the way you present yourself – theoretical you, not you specifically – in a conversation in a professional setting is different from how you do it in a more personal setting."

"I don't know how to do things like that." How to separate the two parts of his identity.

"Wrexi are a prey species. We eat bugs and fruit and mushrooms. You trigger my predator instincts, my run response. You and Dimae both."

Brruuh nodded. "We are predators, so that makes sense." Harrushetti were obligate carnivores. They could, technically, eat foods that weren't meat and animal by-products but it didn't provide any nutritional value and it often made harrushetti ill to partake.

"I don't think I'm consciously worried about it," Sauraxen admitted, leaning against the doorway, her feet peeking into the light of the cargo bay – bare. "I think it's that instinctive thing."

"With work, you can push past that, move around it. If you wanted to."

"Do you think just spending time on the ship with the two of you will serve the point well enough?"

Brruuh thought on that before he responded. Would exposure make things better or worse? Would Sauraxen likely feel less hunted when Brruuh was around purely through the experience of his being around and not actively hunting her? Or would it compound upon itself? Would it get worse, building on each interaction? "My best idea for a plan, if you wanted to try that rather than cognitivilogical care, keep your attention on whether it improves or worsens."

Sebastian

The ship was decorated in bright whites and beehive like hexagons in various shades of pink. The lights flickered on as Matter and Sebastian stepped from the docking bay into a corridor. Plush carpets lay under their feet, nicer than anything on Sebastian's ship and not just because of the pleasant pale pink colour.

"What is this place?" Matter breathed, fogging up their helmet with the words.

"It's not anything I recognise."

Matter trailed fingers along the top of one set of hexagons, so seamlessly integrated into the wall that it couldn't have been paint. The wall rippled under their fingers, image shining and changing under their touch, nothing like the pixels that Basti was familiar with when it came to tech.

Letters Sebastian didn't recognise appeared on the wall. He stumbled back. "What the fuck?"

"I hope that's not an alarm," Matter muttered. "Any idea what language that is?"

"Not a clue."

They left the screen-wall and wandered further into the bowels of the ship. Endless pink and white corridor after endless pink and white corridor. The feeling of spinning in circles, of sinking into the plush floors.

Basti's stomach dropped. The hairs on the back of his neck stood on end and a level of breathlessness invaded his suit. He was ready to tell Matter to turn back, that the likelihood of anyone being alive here was too low to risk the pair of them, that the IPA patrol Matter had called would be far more adept at all the required search and rescue tasks.

And that was when, without any warning, the corridor opened up into a huge hexagonal chamber.

Thousands of pods coated every wall. Rows upon rows of them squished together and atop one another.

"What the fuck?" Matter whispered, once again fogging up their helmet.

Cautiously, they both approached the nearest pod. It rippled as they got close but didn't change into a screen like the wall had, instead shifting between different versions of the hexagonal pattern. Through the window in the front of it, a shadowed figure loomed, too dimly lit to make out much beyond the roundness of a head and slimness of a neck.

Sebastian shifted to look at the next one. A hole had been ripped in the side, leaving nothing contained within but dust.

The next one had cracked glass.

The next one had, much like the first, a rippling glitching display but the relative clarity of a shadowed figure contained within.

"They're cryopods?" Matter asked from across the room, having taken the opposite direction to Sebastian.

"How old is this ship?"

Matter shot him a joking smile. "You'd be better off asking someone who studied space history."

Basti couldn't muster the matching enthusiasm. "That's my point, Matter. I don't recognise any of the architecture. The mechanisms here, they're nothing like anything I studied in my history degree. These are... so far beyond what I know. Incalculably out of time."

A hiss dragged both of their attention away from the conversation. Matter zeroed in on something even as Basti couldn't begin to find the cause of the hissing.

"What's wrong?" he demanded.

"This ship is breaking apart. I think you're right. I think it's ancient and it can't hold up any longer."

"What? But it was fine." He flicked his fingers over his wristband. Even hidden beneath his space suit it responded to the motion. He pulled up the scans he's performed before they had shuttled over, the ones he had performed when the shuttle had landed. He set up a new scan; the circle of loading pixels shifting agonisingly slowly before showing everything was still good. "All the scans say we're fine."

Matter turned wide eyes to Sebastian. Their eyes glittered the way they did when Matter stared up into the void, when Matter viewed what only ouaeahhn could see in the inky darkness of space. The glitter of space dust invisible to human eyes except when reflected back.

It didn't normally happen if Matter was under an atmosphere or a roof. When they were excited, they reflected back what had excited them, shifting from human-passing with oddly purple eyes and hair into someone who could not be mistaken for anything other than ouaeahhn. And that meant the void was in here, that there was a gap in this ship somewhere that let space into it.

"Then we gotta go." He turned to retrace their steps, they had more distance to cover than he would like with a ship falling apart around them. He stopped before stepping into the corridor. "Do you think any of these people is still alive?"

The huge chamber loomed over Matter, making them look small and isolated. They looked wrong in this room and Basti couldn't figure out why. "If you want me to find out, I have to take off the helmet."

"You said the ship is gonna break apart. Matter, that's not safe. You're only half—"

But even as he spoke, Matter ignored his words and twisted the release valve for their helmet.

With space-focused eyes, they stared up into the chamber and pointed. "That one."

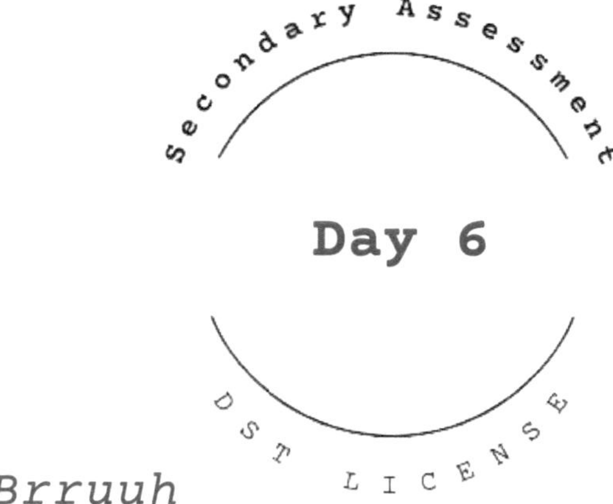

Day 6

Brruuh

Brruuh poked his head around the doorway to the aufenthaltsraum. As expected, Sebastian sat at the dining table. "Captain-Sebastian?" he ran the two words together to avoid the s at the start of a word.

Basti spun in the chair, face shifting into a smile that didn't quite meet his eyes. Perhaps he had thought Brruuh was Dimae instead.

"Could you come to my office?" Brruuh invited.

"Sure." The human followed Brruuh into his domain, taking the comfortable chair closest to the door without prompting.

"I wanted to check in regarding the discovery of the vessel and our latest addition."

Sebastian rubbed the back of his neck. "It was a lot," he admitted. "Between finding the silent ship – and I mean how scary is that? Especially since I couldn't guesstimate when it was created."

"Oh?" Brruuh prompted.

"Ja. I knew going into my space history degree that I probably wouldn't be able to use it in reality. I always wanted to be a captain of my own ship, so it didn't really matter what I studied at first. So I followed my interest in history. But to have it so thoroughly thrown into my face that there are some things about space and space history that we just don't know was..." he shuddered. "And then there was the whole thing of Matter taking off their helmet–"

"Excuse me, what?"

"Ja, that was how we found the last person alive."

Brruuh's face twisted. They had taken off their helmet? In a mystery, silent ship? They had risked their life for the potential that someone might need a rescue that they would be able to provide? The infinitesimally small chance that there was anything Matter and Sebastian could have done for any of the people that might have been left on the ship.

And yet, the part of Brruuh that had been through his own traumatic experience, his own need for a rescue, he couldn't help but wonder. Would Matter have risked their life for his?

"They used their space-vision for it," Sebastian attempted to clarify.

"Their what?"

"Their space-vision." Sebastian shifted in his seat, drawing his feet up underneath him. "Ouaeahhn have this thing where they can survive without an atmosphere for a few minutes without any issues. Then their bodies start to react to it. I dunno why. But it's super cool and super terrifying. The first time Matter did it in front of me..." he shuddered again. "But, ja, it's the whole evolutionary I-dunno-what that lets them see the way they do in the void of space. I look up and just see the light, right?"

"Right," Brruuh agreed, unsure where Sebastian was going.

"But ouaeahhn see patterns, and like, potential futures and stuff. I don't really understand it, but Matter's told me about it before. It's what makes them such good pilots, especially in uncharted space."

Brruuh let out a short affirmative chirp. He'd heard that before, that ouaeahhn were the best pilots. It had been particularly challenging to rectify since they also needed meaningful connection with their shipmates. Brruuh still couldn't quite figure what 'meaningful connection' was. The texts that talked about it were all in ouaeahhn and, even having downloaded a supposed translation technology and the IPA quickguide, he hadn't gained any clarity. When he'd put Matter's name as listed on their cognitivilogical file into the translator it has come up with: danger-movement-additionally-feeling-familiarity. And a note about the difficulty translating ouaeahhn language.

But that wasn't the point of this check in with Sebastian.

"And what is the plan now we have an unconscious person in your medi-bay?"

"Well... we let 'em wake up and then we can look into finding 'eir home."

"When you put it like that, it almost comes across easy."

Sebastian laughed, eyes crinkling at the corners. "I know it's not likely to be that simple. This person might not speak any language we can understand. They might be at war with us, or have been when they went into cryo. They probably won't hold up well to finding out the rest of their ship is gone. Stars, their whole planet or system might be gone by now. But we can't actually do anything about those possibilities yet, so I have other things to prioritise over contemplating every possible option. We'll deal with it when we get to it."

Healthy. "Keep me informed."

"You and the IPA both."

Sauraxen

The lifepod was unlike anything Sauraxen had ever interacted with before. Sleek and smooth and without any of the levers, dials, or mechanisms that Sauraxen was familiar with.

"What exactly do you expect me to do?" she asked Dimae.

"I want to check the vitals of the person inside."

"And you can't do that through the pod?"

"Apparently not."

Sauraxen trailed soft fingers over and across the pod, feeling for any uneven surfaces, anything that might suggest mechanisms within. The screens and measuring devices in medi-bay beeped and clicked, searching for patients to manage.

Sauraxen's hair rose at the root, pinning itself to her arms and shoulders, like armour wrapping around her scales. She shuddered. "Can you go? Be somewhere else?"

"Me?"

"Ja, you."

"Why?"

"You're looking at me and this thing with your predator's stare."

"I'll check the instruments." He turned away, busying himself in the corner of medi-bay, letting Sauraxen focus without the lingering fear of a predator's gaze.

Not that the logical part of Sauraxen's brain believed that Dimae – or any of the IPA species would actually try to eat Sauraxen or any other wrexi. She'd been off Pitzk and around other species for long enough to know their real reactions to a wrexi: enthralling was the word typically used. And Sauraxen could not have hated it more than she did.

But instinct spoke of the danger of predators clamping down, biting through her soft scales with their sharp teeth. And knowledge spoke of the dangers of sparkling too brightly, too much like something to covet.

Sauraxen sighed, her breath played over the pod and it folded away from the body within in ripples like water that wanted to be ice.

The body itself let out a long slow breath, as if it had been depressurised.

Dimae spun back around with such rapidity that Sauraxen actually stumbled away.

The body on the medical bed breathed, even and slow. Calm.

"Well..." Sauraxen said. "I opened it."

"Ja..." Dimae replied, equally awed. "You did. Thank you."

"Is that all you needed me for? Shall I get out of your way now?"

"I'll check her vitals."

Sauraxen let out an affirmative peep and scuttled out of the room.

The door slid easily closed behind her and she pressed her back to the wall. That poor person, out of time, out of place, and completely alone. Sauraxen could identify with that on more levels than she cared to count.

Her planet still orbited its star, her vava still lived there, she could return whenever she wanted. But most of her life she spent surrounded by people who didn't speak her language, didn't know her customs, and didn't even see the world the way she did.

Visual species littered the IPA, even the idioms often ran along the lines of visual skills; the forms were all designed to be filled out on datapads. Sauraxen always had to seek help filling those out. There were systems in place so she didn't have to find a friend to do it, but she usually did. It was easier than having to try and spell her name – not that spelling was something that was possible in wrexi languages.

She peeped into her wristband, composing an audionote home.

It might be almost impossible to visit, the atmosphere being as inhospitable as it was, but she could send her vava a note, let xem know what she was up to. Let xem know that she and Liz hadn't lasted. Connect with her family, her home, her culture in this one simple way.

And then she could go upstairs and find some proper wrexi food, take it back to her own cave, and eat it in a proper wrexi way.

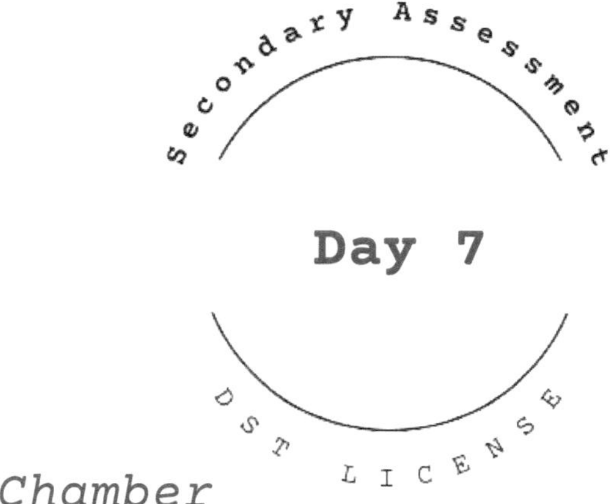

Chamber

A bland dark ceiling met Chamber when she opened her eyes. Beeping filtered into focus, the double-patterning of it mimicking Chamber's own life systems – wait, no, recording her systems?

Chamber shifted to sit up, she always thought better sat up. More bland dark walls greeted her. A cuboid space, for the most part, one rounded wall with a clinical bed pushed up against it standing out against the squareness of everything else. The bed itself was golden metal and pale green-ish surface.

Where in the name of Unity was she? And where was everyone else? She reached out, seeking the rest of her world, only finding the remnants of a bond.

A biped with strange, tufty ears sticking up off his head

tapped against a tiny screen set into one wall.

Chamber scrambled, clattering off the bed and onto the floor.

The tufty-eared biped's ears spun toward Chamber, body following the movement. His fur – or skin, it was hard to tell – matched the metal of the bed and the colour pattern on his clothing. Gold with deep and sandy brown splotches not unlike a child's drawing before the child understood the beauty of Unity.

The biped showed his teeth, ears shifting to a 45 degree angle toward Chamber. "You are awake."

Chamber couldn't explain why she could understand the words, but something in her brain clicked into knowledge. Somewhere in her species' history, they must have come across this language.

"How are you feeling?" he asked as Chamber used the bed she'd fallen off to pull herself back upright.

"Alone." The word felt weird on Chamber's tongue. They didn't have this word in her language, but it was the only one to describe the absence of anyone else. Anyone but this fluffy-eared biped. "Where are we? My we? Us?" Chamber couldn't access a way to explain.

"You were the only one left."

The only one.

Surely that couldn't be true. She couldn't be the only one. How could that be? How could Unity have been so completely destroyed? But Chamber knew. She knew who was to blame for the extinction of her peoples.

"Can you tell me your species name?" tufty-ears asked. "Your planet of origin?"

Chamber shook her head. She had no words for it. There was just Us, and everyone else was Them. Her planet had been Home and everywhere else was... well, Everywhere Else. Even the ship had been – the ship! That was where Chamber had been. Maybe she wasn't the only one left. There could be another ship. She just had to find her planet and then she could return to Unity.

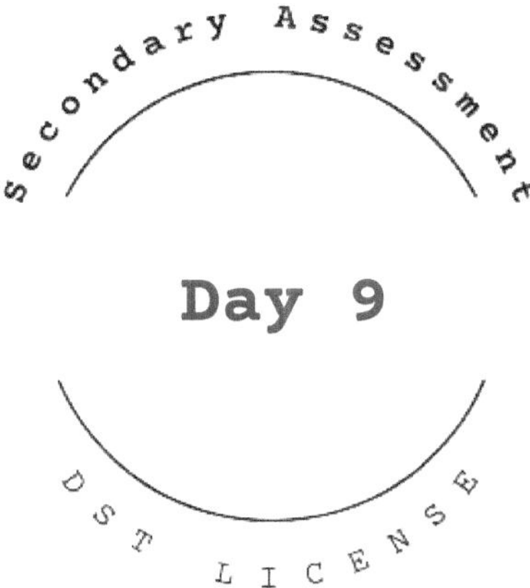

Dimae

The scent of eenya drifted down through the open hatch into the cargo bay as Dimae emerged from medi-bay. Dimae stopped to inhale. He had been intending to check in on Sauraxen, the percentages in the air didn't match her optimum consistency and he wanted to make sure she wasn't having any difficulty breathing. It was the first opportunity he'd had since Basti had brought the stranger aboard. She was finally well enough to be dismissed from medi-bay, Dimae had encouraged her to find an empty crew quarters to occupy. He'd been looking forward to getting back to regular duties, getting the opportunity to spend some time with Basti that wasn't just crashing into bed, exhausted from working with the stranger.

The twisting, enthralling scent of eenya, though, drew him up the gravity chamber and into the aufenthaltsraum.

Brruuh stood in front of the kettle, rapidly stirring a mug of eenya. His ears flicked toward Dimae but he didn't turn.

Dimae mmrp'd a greeting with his secondary vocal cords. Brruuh responded in kind and pulled another mug from the cupboard. Dimae's mug. Much like everything else he owned, it was in the YaPar colours; gold with dark sandy brown splotches that Basti always compared to leopard spots.

Without more conversation, Brruuh and Dimae sat at the dining table, each nursing their own mug of eenya.

"How are you doing?" Dimae asked in harrushetti.

"Fine," Brruuh answered in kind. "Mostly."

"You want to talk about it?"

"As a professional or as a person?"

"What?"

"Something 'Auraxen said." The use of Sauraxen's name in earth common eurean was weird in the midst of a harrushetti conversation.

Dimae noticed but was too polite to comment on Brruuh's skipping over the S at the start. How long had he been off Harrush? Dimae himself had worked hard to manage the S at the beginning of Sebastian and from there had grown more practised at the earth common eurean style of speaking – though he still avoided S-starts where possible. Brruuh not being as practised… was that just an interesting fact? Or a by-product of his history?

"About balancing personal and professional relationships," Brruuh continued in harrushetti. "I thought it was a good idea."

Dimae shrugged his ears. "Sometimes it can be both."

Dimae almost thought Brruuh wasn't going to say anything, almost thought he would keep it to himself.

"This is my first on-ship assessment," Brruuh finally admitted. "It is… more challenging than I thought it would be."

"Being in such close quarters can be a challenge," Dimae agreed. He took a sip of eenya and sighed as the flavour danced over his tongue, coating the barbs in the most pleasant way. It had been a long time since Dimae had the opportunity to partake of eenya.

"Not just that. It's also the sheer range of the crew. For so few people, there are an awful lot of backgrounds to consider."

A chuckle rattled up Dimae's secondary vocal cords.

Brruuh's ears perked, pleased by Dimae's amusement.

"I completely agree," Dimae said. "It's hard enough working on one of the huge space stations with all those personnel to cover, but at least most of them have a majority! And there's always someone to translate if you're stuck on a word."

"Right!" Brruuh agreed. "I've never spent any time this... separated from access to anyone else. I didn't realise how close you get to everyone."

"Just wait," Dimae warned, joking tone twirling in his secondary vocal cords. "Wait until Sebastian has been too busy to shower. Or when someone spills coffee grounds. It gets closer the longer we all spend here together."

Brruuh let out a rumble.

Dimae tilted his head concedingly. "I don't think it counts against you to get closer to the crew on a ship like this. We're all trained to maintain our professional distance. If I can treat my bond mate's injuries, you can assess us all." Dimae lifted his mug to his mouth and paused. "Which reminds me," he flashed his teeth, slipping into a slight YaPar colloquial tone, "Stay away from my Basti."

Brruuh held up his hands in a very human gesture of surrender. How long had he been working with humans to have picked that up? Then again, Brruuh gave off the distinct impression of someone who was ripped away from his family as too young a kit. Even if his TeaYaBin marks hadn't signified that already. Everybody on Harrush knew about the Disaster.

They each drank their eenya in blissful silence, or at least the relative silence of a ship in motion. The engines hummed gently, sound travelling easily through the open doors up to the aufenthaltsraum. The gentle thumping of both Matter and Sauraxen's respective music an undercurrent to every aspect of life on the ship. At least they were listening to the same song this time.

"I released Chamber to quarters today," Dimae said.

"Chamber?"

"The woman Basti and Matter found."

"How is she settling in?" Brruuh asked. "Any idea where she's from? Or whether she intends to stay?"

Dimae shrugged. She hadn't said all that much to him yet. He was still surprised they had been able to communicate at all. And he didn't want to overload the poor woman, her entire ship had died and she was the only one left. How did you even begin to help someone cope with that?

Again his eyes were drawn to the very specific eye-like patches on the top of Brruuh's ears that marked him as a TeaYaBin. Would this be too much for him? Living in close quarters – however temporarily – with someone else who had lost everything?

"She's getting used to being awake," he said.

"And the knowledge that she is alone," Brruuh added,

voice soft. It was aching to hear those words in Dimae's home language, a language he heard far less often than he would have liked. Alone wasn't something any harrushetti should know how to handle. But Brruuh did.

Dimae dipped his eyelids in acknowledgement.

Brruuh stared down at his drink. "It is hard to be alone."

"I never have been," Dimae whispered. "I travelled to my first off-Harrush station with my cousin. By the time I stopped working with him, I had met Sebastian."

Brruuh tilted the mug in his hands, the liquid reflecting the overhead lights onto his face. "Don't tell her you're there for her. It hurts to hear. You just have to be there. Be around. Tell her trivial things that bother you." He flicked his eyes up, twin pools of ice, keeping everything under the surface still and unreachable. "Open yourself up to her so she can do likewise."

Dimae brushed gentle fingers over his own ear, a self-soothe he thought he had grown out of. "Sebastian insists on washing our bedsheets every week."

Brruuh's whole face scrunched up, ears pinned to the sides of his head. "Why?"

"Humans do that. You would not believe how long it took to convince him to stop using the scented wash stuff."

"Is it because they perspire?" Another earth common eurean word, perspire, harsh and jarring in the melody of harrushetti.

Dimae dipped his eyelids in another yes.

Brruuh shuddered. "I can't even begin to imagine."

Dimae decided not to bring up his Kitten Blanket – Brruuh might not have one after what had happened.

Sebastian

Basti's wristband beeped with a message. He pulled the text up so it sat in pixels above his arm. 'Sorry,' it read. 'We need someone with a DST license for this job.'

Basti flicked his fingers, dismissing the message. He picked up his mug of coffee from the table and headed down to the captain's quarters.

Expecting it to be empty – Dimae having been spending all his time in medi-bay dealing with their new arrival – he stumbled when he found Dimae sat at the desk. Coffee sloshed out over Sebastian's hand. He licked it off as Dimae turned around.

A crooked, fangy smile broke out across Dimae's face. "It's rare to see you down here at this time of day."

"Ja," Basti agreed vaguely. "Are you... always here?"

"I like to use this desk as an office occasionally. Is nice to change location and have home around me. Plus, new addition."

Basti perched on the edge of the bed. "Where did you get the chair?"

"Folding chair from cargo bay."

That made a lot of sense. Basti rubbed his forehead. He probably should have thought of that. There was a stack of folding chairs tucked under one of the grates in the cargo bay that could definitely be put to use in various locations.

"What's wrong?"

Basti licked his lips. "Dimae... was this all a bad idea?"

"What do you mean?"

"I sank every credit we have into this ship because I thought there would be cargo jobs – I've worked on cargo ships before and there was always plenty of work. But I can barely keep us spaceborne. What am I gonna do if this fails?"

Dimae abandoned his work to scoop Basti into his arms, rubbing his chin on Sebastian's head, the tiny strands of fur tugging at his hair and pulling it out of the loose ponytail he'd thrown it into. "You thought there were cargo jobs because there are. Once we have our DeST license, we'll be fine. We just have to keep going until then."

"But what if I can't keep us up here that long? The full assessment takes between two standard months to two standard years."

Dimae pulled back, examining Basti with his slit-pupiled eyes. "What brought on this panic?"

"I got another job rejection."

"Maybe you better talk this over with Brruuh."

"He's our assessor! How would telling him I'm scared of failing help?"

"He's also a cognitivist. Part of his job is to help people with overwhelming feelings and gaining management abilities. I am convinced if he viewed you putting in the work to manage your –" he said something in harrushetti that Basti didn't recognise.

"Stress?"

"That. If he viewed you putting in the work to manage that, it would only reflect well in the report."

Sebastian sighed. "I guess so. It's not easy to balance building a relationship with your live-in assessor – which is super challenging on a ship this small." When all relationships turned into family, at least to bonding species like humans, ouaeahhn, and wrexi. But Dimae wouldn't understand that, harrushetti didn't work like that. He sighed again; he didn't want to talk about this anymore. "How is our newest member?"

"Awake, confused, having a hard time. Can't tell me where she's from or who her people are or were or..." he chirruped. Annoyance mixed with sadness. The frustration of a doctor who couldn't help a patient but could recognise her pain.

"Have you considered taking a break?"

"Have you?" Dimae countered.

Sebastian chuckled and set his coffee cup on the floor before wrapping his arms around Dimae and pulling him down into their nest.

Matter

The comfort of the office – or exam room as the pessimistic part of Matter's brain kept filling in – surprised them. How had Brruuh managed this? It should have looked like a weirdly laid out bedroom but it didn't. Two plush armchairs took up most of the space, the bed having been converted into a desk with a variety of ornaments clearly stuck to the surface – in case of gravity fluxes.

Matter's fingers plucked at the blanket spread over the top of the chair nearest them. The softness of the weave was surprising. What did harrushetti weave with? They didn't have sheep or goats like Earth, or fluffy moose-like creatures like on Ouaeahhn. They glanced at the silver-grey and white pattern of Brruuh's fur that so closely matched the fabric. Did they weave their own shed fur?

Matter almost laughed at the image of Brruuh brushing his own fur and storing it all in a big bag for later weaving.

Brruuh gestured to the chair. Matter clambered over it to sit on the back with their feet on the seat.

"Captain-Sebastian–" he ran the words together to avoid the S in Sebastian.

"You can call him Basti," Matter interrupted.

"That is informal."

"Everybody does, I promise you he won't mind."

"He told me you risked your life to rescue the life pod."

Ah. That. "It wasn't much of a risk. There's enough ouaeahhn in me to avoid the risk."

"Enough ouaeahhn in you?"

"Being half-ouaeahhn."

He scrunched his nose. "Half-ouaeahhn – that is a hard concept to remember, any amount of harrushetti means you are harrushetti, just as much as you are wholly whatever your other culture. You are completely both, interwoven. The idea of half..."

"It doesn't compute?"

Brruuh nodded.

Matter took a deep breath. At least he wasn't asking about the tension still crackling between them and Basti despite his apology. At least he wasn't asking about how they had felt since Brruuh had pressed strong hands against their space suit and assured them that they would be missed if they didn't come back. At least he wasn't asking how it had felt to stand on that silent ship. At least he wasn't asking about how they hadn't emerged from their room except to pilot for the last few days. At least he wasn't asking about the mysterious person they had brought back with them.

"Half's is a very human concept. Actually, it's a very human eurean concept. Ouaeahhn don't have the concept of half's, but we do have the ability to belong to several groups at once in an equal manner." Matter pulled their lip between their teeth. "If I had to choose, I'd rather you consider me human."

"You would?"

Matter nodded.

"But you grew up on ouaeahhn."

"Your pronunciation is improving."

Brruuh waited, obviously wise to this particular one of Matter's distraction techniques.

Matter rolled their eyes. "Like I've said before, people get weird about the ouaeahhn thing."

"Why do you think that is?"

"Oh... lots of reasons. But I'm not volunteering reasons for you to worry. When it comes to relevant stuff – currently relevant stuff..." Matter tapped a finger against their lips as they thought. What was relevant? Not just to this conversation but to reassure Brruuh that Matter deserved to have their Deep Space Travel assessment signed off. "Ouaeahhn wouldn't be classified as a planet to human astronomers."

"What?" Brruuh's ears twitched down.

"Ja. Humans have very specific requirements about what counts as a planet – and some serious hang-ups about Pluto. But Ouaeahhn is technically an asteroid caught in trans-spatial orbit."

"You live on a floating rock?"

"No, I live here on this ship. I'm *from* an atmospheric

floating rock."

"Okay, and what does that mean?"

"Being from a trans-orbital asteroid? Other than humans not counting it as a planet which creates some weird difficulties on some colonies? We're a mono-culture. Ouaeahhn. You can traverse the entire planet in a day and, even if you couldn't, the empathic and telepathic nature of the inhabitants allows for cross-sphere communication instantly, nei tech required."

Brruuh's stylus scrolled over his datapad. "You do not have a tele-empathic classification."

Matter pressed their lips together. "It's complicated... and variable. I'm more adept at it with other ouaeahhn, but other times I'm basically a human and just as null as one. We so align with the people we spend time with, though. Even if the people aren't tele-empaths. So, Basti and I are—" Fuck, they'd walked themself right into that discussion. The very discussion they wanted to avoid. "Adjusting. It's been a while since we've seen each other. It got more challenging to be around him after he got married – bonded – with Dimae. He didn't even invite me to the wedding. We're meant to be siblings and he didn't invite me."

"Meant to be?" Brruuh echoed.

"We share a father."

Brruuh's eyes flicked between Matter and the datapad.

"I'm guessing that's not in my profile either?"

Brruuh remained very still, like a kid caught with a hand in the biscuit tin. "Profile?"

"Psychological profile – sorry, cognitivism profile. The thing you have there with the big flashing warning sign."

"It does not flash –" he made an almost yowl. "Idiom!"

Matter couldn't help the laugh. "Look, Ouaeahhn isn't a static orbit. It floats through space and gets caught up in the strongest nearby gravitational fields, and then it shifts on. And, much like our naming convention might suggest, the people are the planet."

"I do not think I understand your point."

"We get pulled in by the brightest star, the biggest planet, the most interesting person. Sometimes it works and sometimes..." They took a deep breath, settling the flash-through of each of the times their attention had been caught by someone or something more harmful than benign. "Sometimes it gets us hurt. My point, the reason I'm telling you this, is that travelling and shifting is in ouaeahhn nature. The thing that matters are the communities we build during that travel."

"You are trying to tell me to take the warning down."

"I'm trying to tell you not to worry about me getting Space Sadness – or Galactic Depression as you would call it." At Brruuh's perked up ears, Matter laughed again. "You're not the only one who can research a culture." Because middle-belt and basin harrushetti had a harder time with starting words with the letter S than YaPar ones did.

With that, Matter stood and climbed over the back of the chair toward the door.

"Wait," Brruuh called. "I wanted to talk to you about the ship you found."

"Another time. Somebody has to keep an eye on our trajectory." They couldn't talk about this with a relative stranger anymore, and they definitely didn't want it to make an appearance in their psychological report. Everything about Matter said human because Matter had forced it to be so. It was easier if only their Ahthae knew they were ouaeahhn. If only their Ahthae knew, nobody could hurt Matter like that again.

Chamber

Chamber exited her newly claimed quarters. The doctor had told her to pick any without a name on the door, so she had chosen the one nearest to the gravity well that lifted her up to the living space on the ship.

A biped sped out of one of the in-use quarters, calling something over their shoulder. Chamber couldn't quite translate the words quickly enough to understand them. Even if she might have been able to, she was stuck, pinned to the ground.

Holographic shining skin, shimmering purplish hair pulled up into a pair of dumplings on top of their head. They should have been wearing a sheet of fabric held to their form by the sheer will of everyone else in the area but instead, this one had a khaki green jumpsuit on. Not only that, but with long sleeves hiding most of their arms to where they had been rolled up to the elbow, revealing the swirling patterns all ouaeahhn put into their skin.

"Hi," the creature said, face shifting into that teeth-bearing thing that the tufty-eared doctor had told Chamber was a smile and a sign of friendship on this vessel. "How are you feeling?"

"Ouaeahhn," Chamber snarled.

The ouaeahhn blinked slowly, eyes shifting from the sparkling reflective state to something more akin to a pool of murky water, still too many colours to name but the reflection dampened. "Um... I'm gonna go now." They edged around Chamber.

"You act as if you don't recognise me."

"Should I?"

"All your kind should!"

The ouaeahhn held up their hands, reflecting Chamber's own pink-tinged appearance back at her.

Chamber advanced. "Shae Anah. Shu Ymni."

"Ym-Tse? Ym-Shu, stranger. I am not the dangerous one here."

"All your kind are!"

The Ouaeahhn held their arms open. "You see any of my kind here? I am alone."

"Shaaya!"

"This is not the ground of Ouaeahhn, I am alone here."

A silver presence reflected off the ouaeahhn's skin, turning the Unity-pink to a swirling purple. "Is everything okay?" A voice like the doctor's asked.

"She's calling me danger," the ouaeahhn cried.

"Why?"

"Fuck if I know. Ymahs!"

"I do not know your language and I am asking her."

"That is a dangerous thing," Chamber repeated her earlier sentiments to the grey and white tufty-eared biped, sparing him the briefest of glances. "Their kind destroyed my planet! They are the reason I am here!"

The ouaeahhn stumbled backward. "What?" they breathed. Their face morphed into a horrified grimace, all open and hurt like somebody had just ripped out their insides. And Chamber had seen enough ouaeahhn with their insides ripped out in the war.

"Your people destroyed our entire galaxy." Chamber huffed out an almost laugh. "What? Did you think your asteroid planet had never been part of something larger?"

The ouaeahhn didn't say anything.

"Your innocent act won't work on me, Ym-Shu."

"What is eem-shoo?" the tufty-eared not-doctor asked, sounding out the words in an awkward way.

"It means 'you are dangerous'– like I said, Ouaeahhn is complicated. Ym is, essentially, dangerous potential. Shu is the second person pronouns, unfamiliar."

"As opposed to the familiar you?"

"Which is Hu – are we really getting into the semantics of my language right now?" They rubbed a hand over their face and refocused on Chamber. "Look, I don't know what you're talking about. When Basti and I were on your ship–"

"*You* were on my ship!?" Chamber shrieked. No wonder she was the only one left. "Ymanah!"

"I am not a dangerous home breaker!" the ouaeahhn fired back. "I am the creator of home in strange places."

Chamber spat out a breath. "And how do you make that name? How did you deserve it?"

"I originated as Ahni."

A logical sound for a young one to make. It almost came out as a sigh.

"And I grew into Ymma with time."

"You have danger in your very name."

"Potential," Ymmattrahni argued.

"If Ymaes is dangerous ones then Ymah is danger to home."

"Ymaes can be potential friends!"

Chamber let out that spit of breath again. Absurd. But that was ouaeahhn all around. Their language so basic and requiring so much emotional input and psychic signature to fully understand that they could argue almost any meaning behind their sentences.

"Please," the tufty-eared not-doctor said, footsteps clanging against the metal floor as he stepped fully out of his quarters. "Can we all take a breath. Can we all gather our calm. Come into aufenthaltsraum and we will take chairs and talk this out."

"You don't want to do it in your office?" Ymmattrahni asked.

"Not enough chairs."

The ouaeahhn almost smiled, but when they looked back at Chamber, their shoulders slumped.

Without further words, Chamber and the ouaeahhn followed the tufty-eared biped into the aufenthaltsraum.

A conference style table took up the front of the space, a wall with a variety of instruments built into it taking up almost the entire wall by the head of the table. On the opposite side sat several long padded benches with a variety of blankets and cushions coating their surfaces. The colours clashed in a way that set Chamber's already frayed nerves further on edge.

Behind what Chamber presumed was the designated living space, lay a falsified forest. Plants in more shelves than Chamber cared to count lined the entire back wall to the extent that Chamber almost could have been fooled into believing herself on a planet.

"I am Dr Brruuh TeaYaBin – you may call me Brruuh," Brruuh said as he took a seat at the head of the table.

Ymmattrahni sank into a chair of their own, their back to the false forest.

Chamber perched on the edge of the chair closest to the door.

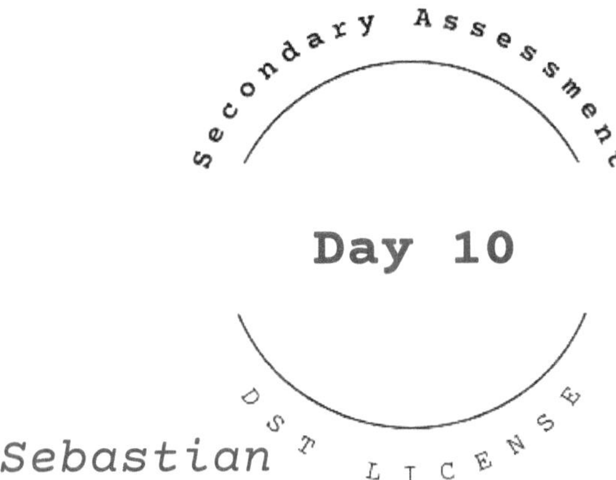

Sebastian

"Put it down," Matter demanded, slipping into the chair next to Sebastian and thunking two mugs down on the table. Had they picked up Basti's previous coffee mug? Yup. And refilled it if the coffee-chocolate scent filling the room was anything to go by. And Basti hadn't noticed anything.

"I'm just looking for cargo jobs," he said, but he let the datapad fall to the tabletop with a clatter.

"I've worked on ships a long time, Basti – longer than you for sure, and I can tell you for free that people post cargo jobs in ports, not on the boards; they want their cargo picked up fast and waiting for someone to find it on a board, travel to the planet, and pick it up takes too long. We need to land somewhere."

"But–"

"But nothing! I'm right and I'm bribing you anyway."

Basti squinted. "With what? Why? And where do you want to land?"

"With a mocha." They gestured to the coffee cup. "And I want to land on Station 24. It's thirty fuel clips from here, twenty-six if you let me turn off the gravity stabilisation in unused areas."

"Last time I let you do that, you turned gravity off on the entire floor."

"That was one time!" Matter slumped. "Come on, Basti. Please?"

"Why are you so desperate to go?"

"They're a popular trading port for ouaeahhn."

"So?"

"They're likely to have sehn."

"Which is what?"

Matter nibbled on their lip, obviously translating in their head. "Food."

"Any other reason?"

Matter blew out a long breath. "It's a multi-cultural port. They might have information about Chamber."

"I heard about your argument."

"It was hardly an argument, Sebastian. She yelled at me and called me names because of where I'm from."

Sebastian rubbed at the base of his ponytail under the hair tie. "Ja, it's not great."

Matter gave him a flat look.

"She's out of her time, Matter."

"By our estimation. We don't actually know anything about her."

"Just give it some time."

Matter huffed into their mug. "Easy for you to say, she doesn't glare at you every time she passes you. She's got a level of tele-empathy because I can literally feel her sending porcuskunk spikes at me with those glares."

"Plot in the course for Station 24," Basti conceded. It was hardly fair to expect Matter to take on that burden for an unknown length of time. Chamber's animosity toward them would have been hard enough on the small ship, but if she was sending out tele-empathetic waves, it was even less reasonable to ask Matter to suffer through.

Matter lifted their mug to their lips, inhaling the scent of coffee and chocolate and, if Sebastian knew Matter – which he did – a little chili too. "When I'm done."

A laugh broke out of Sebastian.

Matter shot him a lopsided smile. "Just because you don't know how to take a break." They shifted out of the chair, stretching their neck and hip checking Basti's chair on the way out of the aufenthaltsraum. "Drink your coffee; I'll be in my room."

Basti glanced at the now blank datapad screen before picking up the mug. Chocolate and coffee and whatever special thing Matter did to it.

He was going to have to do something about Chamber. But what could he do? The IPA patrol Matter had called hadn't got in contact for Basti's follow-up about Chamber having survived or his secondary message that she had awoken. He should have known better than to expect speed from the IPA, but still. Finding a long-lost and possibly out of time vessel should have been top priority, especially with a surviving member of the crew.

But apparently not if a tiny as yet unlicensed cargo runner was the one reporting it. Maybe they thought Basti was trying to get around the assessment period. Maybe he should ask Brruuh to send a message in. He worked directly for the IPA, maybe he'd have a slightly better chance at getting through to someone in a timely manner.

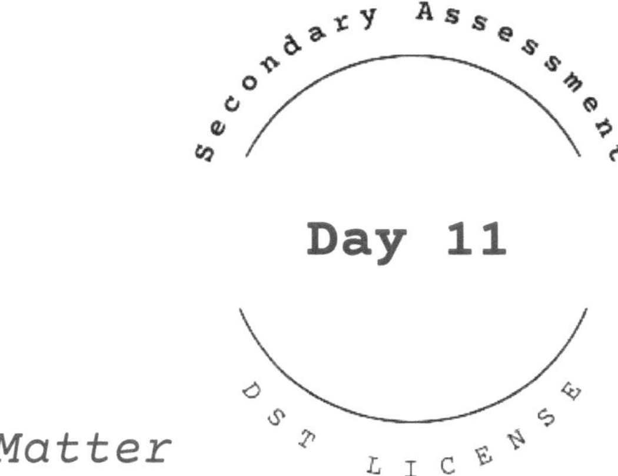

Day 11

Matter

Station 24 was built into the side of a moon whose planet had long since been stripped of all resources. So badly stripped that it had become completely uninhabitable.

The ship set down in the dusty landscape, feet sinking a little more than Matter might have liked, just for their own paranoia. It would be just their luck to get Basti's ship stuck on Station 24 with porcuskunk glares as a companion.

Why ouaeahhn traded here Matter would never know. Maybe fully ouaeahhn sight made the sand glitter in a way Matter was oblivious to, maybe it had once been close to a temporary orbit and habit turned into tradition, or maybe – if Chamber's account of her people's history with ouaeahhn was accurate – ouaeahhn had been the ones who mined the planet beyond repair.

To Matter, this moon was unpleasant and its inhabitants grew as inhospitable as the central planet around which they orbited, worsening the longer they stayed.

But if Matter wanted sehn, this was the place to look, especially if they didn't want to go all the way to Ouaeahhn. And Matter really didn't want to go all the way to Ouaeahhn.

Dimae took one look down the slightly bent boarding plank and immediately retreated to the captain's quarters with a murmuring grumble in harrushetti. Brruuh, likewise, excused himself – though more politely. Sebastian set up a folding chair at the top of the boarding plank, reminding Matter of nothing so much as an old man on a porch with a pellet shotgun.

When Matter gave him a questioning look, he leaned back in his chair. "I'm from a tropical biome, Matter. Trees, humidity, ferns, lush forests. I don't like sand. I don't like dry. And Sauraxen is that thing wiggling around out there, so she's obviously going with you, which means I gotta guard the ship."

Matter shook their head. "Okay, Basti, but if you added a shotgun, you'd turn into Jonesy."

"You take that back!"

Matter beamed. "You are your father's son."

They jogged down the boarding plank, pretending they hadn't heard Basti yell back, "He's your father too!"

When Matter's feet sank into the never-ending grit, Sauraxen extracted herself from the sand with surprising grace, sheets of gold falling from her: off her skin, out of her hair, from under the strappy playsuit she'd thrown on to appease human and harrushetti modesty standards. "Sand bath," she explained.

Matter hadn't been intending to ask but they made an affirmative noise anyway, the Wrexi equivalent of a nod.

"Market?"

"Market."

Sauraxen wrapped a shawl over her shoulders and around her hair – trying to disguise herself enough that people wouldn't stare. Wrexi were rare and coveted, after all.

A pair of ill-fitting boots slipped around on Sauraxen's feet. Did those even have laces? Why was she wearing shoes? Sauraxen had never worn shoes as long as Matter had known her. Maybe she just knew that Matter didn't care whether she submitted to majority demands or not. Did wrexi even have the concept of shoes?

The market itself wasn't too far from where Matter had parked the ship, bustling with people so cramped and crowded that Matter considered turning around and heading straight back to the ship before even truly looking around. Sehn or no sehn. Knowledge or no knowledge.

Shelters made of various materials lined up in rows. Mats covered the path but, by what glimpses Matter could get around the feet, paws, claws, tentacles, and gelatinous bodies of the visitors and traders, every mat was already coated with enough sand that there was almost no point to them.

Linking arms with Sauraxen, they headed into the crowd, wandering from stall to stall as Matter's attention shifted, drawn in by whatever shining thing or enthused stall holder. They asked generic questions about hexagonal designs and lost cryopods of people.

A basket of assorted gems sparkled in the glaring sunlight, glittering in the way Brruuh and Dimae's eyes did. Matter combed through them, searching for the right colours. Did these gems have a purpose beyond decoration?

"Hey," they looked up at the trader, loitering toward the back of the shop, well out of the way of the sun and the tracked in sand. "Do you happen to know where the ouaeahhn tend to trade?"

The slug-like being licked her eyestalks in thought. "What do you need?"

"Ouaeahhn foodstuffs."

Again she licked her eyestalks. "Maybe toward where your adorable friend went."

Matter turned, trying to locate the short, pale lizardoid in the bustling marketplace. Her shining silver hair flashed in the desert air, well outside the reach of the slug-like trader's shop.

Calling a thanks to the trader over their shoulder and abandoning the gems, Matter threaded their way through the passing customers. Ugh. All that grace when contained in a bobbly, unwieldy ship and Matter couldn't walk three steps in a marketplace without a collision.

Sauraxen disappeared into shadow. Complete shadow on a desert moon?

"Oh no. Sauraxen!" Matter called.

She didn't turn.

"Raxen!" Matter tried again, as traders with wide-brimmed hats closed the lid of the basket behind Sauraxen.

"Axen!" Matter cried, shoving past the last few people between them and the basket. A wicker basket? Really?

"Hey! Excuse me!" They stumbled out of the bustle and straight into one of the abductors, bouncing off the wide-brimmed hat. "Um, you have my friend in there."

"Nei," the abductor replied in heavily accented earth common eurean.

"Ja, you do. I just saw you shut her in there."

The abductor shook xyr hands, exoskeleton glittering like a beetle shell when the light hit it. "Nei."

"Open the basket."

"Nei."

Matter paused, almost at a loss for what to do. What could one do in a situation like this? Sauraxen was in the basket, proven even more clearly by the beetle's refusal to open the lid. Matter couldn't leave without her. They couldn't risk going back to the ship and hoping they could get Basti back here in time for him to help, before these beetles would tuck their basket back onto their ship and Sauraxen would be gone for good.

It didn't matter that it would be illegal by IPA law, Matter didn't know anything about these people, wouldn't even be able to name their species. And, if their instincts were correct, this wasn't the kind of station that took well to snitches, so none of the other stallholders would talk either.

"Ma-An, just open the basket and let me prove my friend isn't in there, if you're so insistent that she isn't."

"Nei."

"Do you know any other words!?"

"Ja. Look, human, back off or we'll call the authorities."

"You call the authorities and I ask them to investigate your 'cargo' there."

"Nice try, human, but you're an off-worlder; they wouldn't trust you for excretion."

What kind of asshole would think it was okay to abduct someone in plain view and then claim the authorities would... what kind of world would the authorities not believe an off-worlder? What kind of awful and uncommunitied society would allow such things?

"Open the fucking basket!"

The beetle shoved at Matter's shoulder. When they didn't move, he shoved again, more forceful. The other abductors approached, circling around Matter. "Sturdy for a human," one of them muttered.

Matter took a deep breath. "Give me back my friend and we can all go on with our days."

One of the beetles let out a buzz – maybe a laugh? "Make me, human." Xe tapped a hand against xyr chest. "See what your soft flesh can do to my armour."

Matter didn't often wish for more ouaeahhn skills, especially not after... but it would have been so much easier to be able to emotionally manipulate the beetles into freeing Sauraxen. It would have been much quieter to devastate the beetle people, or to persuade them oh so subtly weaving emotions into the conversation. But Matter was, for all intents and purposes and in situations like these, null. So they tightened their fists and struck out.

They knocked the hat off one beetle's head, striking with their other fist into xyr neck where one piece of xem met the other.

The beetle fell to the sandy ground.

Matter hesitated, fists still raised as the traders nearest them quieted. The hairs on the back of their neck rose at the attention. This was not the best way to pass their DeST license assessment. Then again, they'd rather fail, rather be grounded for the rest of their life than lose Sauraxen.

One of the beetles Matter hadn't punched buzzed something in xyr own language.

"I'm going to ask you one more time," Matter growled from behind clenched teeth. "Open the basket and give me back my friend."

One beetle swung open the basket, revealing a confused and mildly distressed Sauraxen, her hair swirling around her head as if caught in a wind that only existed for her.

She lurched out and attached herself to Matter's torso, legs wrapping around Matter's waist. "Let's go."

Matter turned to head back to the ship without a single further collision.

Back on the ship, Matter traded Sauraxen onto Basti, headed up to the pilots console and took the ship out of the atmosphere of Station 24. They set the ship drifting, no specific destination in mind. They leaned back in the chair, letting the swirl of the void play out over them, but even that couldn't settle the emotions jumping around inside them like a pinball.

Tears stung their eyes.

"Hey," Sauraxen called from the doorway.

Matter shifted to look at her. She held a tray with three mugs on it. The scent of coffee filled the pilot's console. Sauraxen set the tray on one lesser used surface and took her own weird wrexi drink.

Matter grabbed one of the mugs of coffee and downed its contents, letting the heat simmer and soothe their rampaging emotions. They lay back in their chair, hugging the second coffee mug close. "A wicker basket, Axen? Seriously?"

"It felt like a cave."

"You walked inside, on your own two feet you walked inside."

"I thought it was a cave!"

"In a market place?"

Sauraxen's fingers tapped against her mug, the sound of

it loud in the silent console. "Sorry."

Matter reached out a hand. "I'm not angry with you." Their fingers met Sauraxen's. Smooth warm scales against their too-human skin.

"You're hurt," Sauraxen observed. "I can smell the blood on your knuckles."

"I'll be fine."

"You should go and see Dimae."

"I can't."

"Why?"

Matter sighed and squeezed Sauraxen's fingers. Their knuckles ached where they had punched the beetle. "Because he'll know I haven't had enough contact lately. And then he'll be pissed. I just... I can't deal with that right now."

Sauraxen didn't push. She never did.

Brruuh

Brruuh crouched by the door to his quarters, claws digging into the metal. The squeal of noise it made told Brruuh it would leave marks but he couldn't bring himself to think on that. His body rumbled with tension, hot and cold all at once, endless rolls of fear and anger and more emotions rampaging through Brruuh more quickly than he could even begin to name them.

It felt like all his training in cognitivism had abandoned him as he crouched like a kitten at the edge of his private space, filled with the scent he'd built up over years on the station he'd been working on until he'd got this job. The scent had intermingled a little with the other crew aboard the ship, even with none of them having entered the room. He should be able to handle these emotions; he should be able to manage his behaviour around them.

And yet. He couldn't. He felt all too much like the abandoned kitten, unwanted, unloved, completely alone.

Except, somehow this was worse. Because he had begun to allow himself to care. Or he had begun to care through the awkward osmosis of being in close quarters with the same people for work and relaxation time. Dimae had been right; they did get closer just by physical proximity.

And now that care was battering Brruuh on all sides.

He'd smelled Matter's bloodied knuckles before they had even come into view, rushing down to the edge of the boarding plank, regardless of the sand just waiting to sink into his fur and agitate his skin. Basti had badgered him with questions, following him to the sandy edge with nothing but confusion since Brruuh had completely forgotten how to speak in anything other than Basin harrushetti.

And then they'd turned up, distant but visible. Like a single unit they had returned to the ship. Matter had handed Sauraxen over to Basti with a hard set to their jaw. She's wrapped herself around him like he was a tree she felt safe hiding within the leaves of.

Brruuh had almost followed Matter until Sebastian had touched a gentle hand to his arm and shook his head.

Sebastian had carried Sauraxen into the aufenthaltsraum, settling himself and her on the sofa,

Brruuh trailing after them.

Sebastian had mouthed, "Make drinks," over Sauraxen's head.

With his ears flat to his head, Brruuh had done as instructed, hands going through the motions by instinct he didn't know he had.

Sauraxen had told them everything: the attempted abductors, Matter having fought them off her.

Brruuh had kept it together, maintained his professional demeanour until Sauraxen had been steady enough to make drinks herself and disappear into the uncomfortably silent pilot's console – Matter not playing the music that usually accompanied their active flying.

And then Brruuh had taken himself, quietly, to his room and let himself panic.

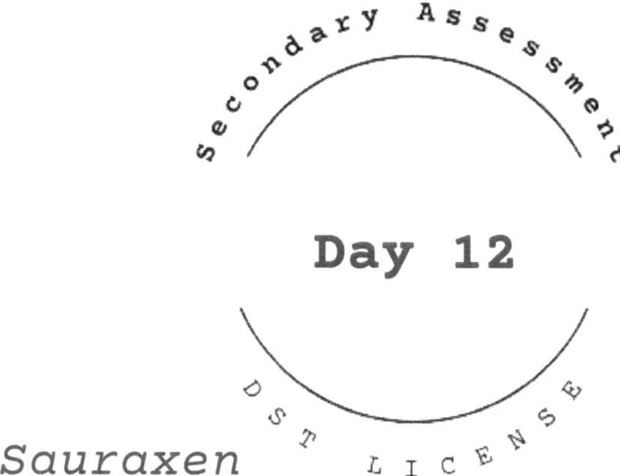

Day 12

Sauraxen

Frissons of tension buzzed through Sauraxen, making her limbs twitch until she pulled aside the curtain set that she had erected around her sleeping space. Erected was a strong word for staple-gunned into the wall, but still. It wasn't much of a cave, but it was better than the relative huge emptiness of the room without it.

Not that the room was actually huge. A bunk laid against one wall, a fold-down desk on the opposite. When the desk was down – as Sauraxen's always was – it left only a sliver of a corridor between it and the bed.

A storage container had been set into the end of the room, opposite the entry door, but Sauraxen had little use for that. Most wrexi weren't big on personal possessions and Sauraxen was no exception. After all, when you had to abandon your home regularly thanks to rock slides, personal possessions weren't high on the list of things to maintain.

When tension fizzled through Sauraxen like this, it meant something was wrong. She scrambled out from under the desk and slipped into a baggy shirt and loose shorts – having been around humans long enough to know, if not understand, their weird unspoken rules about clothing and modesty. Humans also had weird ideas about foot coverings but Sauraxen wasn't about to kowtow to that for propriety – it was one thing to wear oversized boots to wander around a marketplace, it was entirely another to attempt to wear them at home or work. Maybe if she hadn't worn the shoes she would have had half a chance at realising it was a wicker basket not a cave.

The upper corridor was dark and empty, no lights buzzed and shone to give Sauraxen a headache. Slithering down the ladder to engineering, the gravity well not activating while the ship was on sleep cycle. Snoring emanated from the captain's quarters, rattling around the cargo bay in such an illuminating way that Sauraxen couldn't assign it to anyone but Basti – something about his vocal range and resonance sent the clearest soundwaves bouncing off things.

Upon investigation, all the engines were functioning properly. Upon further investigation, the boarding hatch and shuttle cupboard were fully sealed. Upon deep investigation, which included pulling it apart and putting it back together, the kitchen systems were perfectly functional too.

Which meant Sauraxen couldn't find the problem, but the feeling of wrongness wouldn't leave her limbs.

Finally, she heaved a sigh and headed to the crew quarters door nearest to the pilot's console. The clunk of her knock sent reverberations up her arm, adding to the flittery tension.

A groggy Matter, somehow wearing their ever-present jumpsuit – the black one with no sleeves and a zip this time – slid open the door. "Raxen?" their voice was croaky with sleep.

"I can't sleep."

"Come in."

For all that Matter's quarters were an exact mirror of Sauraxen's, made up of the same parts in the same basic layout, they could not have been more different. It might as well have been an entirely different ship. The bed, set up on the bunk as was expected, had an extra mattress atop it, covered with a rumpled but intricately woven blanket. The desk was folded away into the wall with another ouaeahhn weave hung from it. A poster Sauraxen couldn't make out had been stuck on the door of the storage area, and frames that Sauraxen guessed would be filled with printed or holo pictures of Matter with friends had been hung strategically around the room. A beanbag sat, pushed up against one wall, the beans within hissing against one another like sand.

Matter sank down on the bunk, scooting across it so their back rested against the wall, their feet hanging over the edge. "What's up?"

"I don't know." Sauraxen paced the small space, eternally grateful that Matter didn't want to use their desk so she had unencumbered pacing space. "But it feels like something is."

"Talk me through it," Matter asked around a yawn.

Sauraxen explained how she had had trouble sleeping and how it had led her to check the ship for issues. "If you get a feeling like this on Pitzk, it means we need to move, that something is wrong with the cave, you know?"

"Your flight response is triggered?"

"I can't fly."

Matter broke into a sudden laugh that pressed on Sauraxen in a way that shouldn't have been calming but somehow was. "No, flight like run away, not like – never mind. Your flee response has been triggered and you can't find the cause?"

"Basically."

"Anything to do with you almost getting kidnapped today?" They lost a battle to a yawn. "Or yesterday? Whatever."

"How would it have?"

Matter shook their head. "I don't know. Maybe you'd be better off asking cognitivist Brruuh. Why didn't you go to him, anyway?"

Sauraxen peeped. "He's not comforting. You are."

"Come here." Matter held out an arm, inviting Sauraxen into the bed with them.

She sat, snuggling into Matter's warm, solid chest.

"There's a human phenomenon – basically humans developed as a predator-prey species. Predator to some, prey to others. Being prey to some gives a level of automatic panic response, APS. We call them fight, flight, freeze and fawn. Most humans typically lean toward one, but it varies. It's how early, super early, pre-farming humans protected themselves from predators. You with me so far?"

Sauraxen chirped her agreement, enjoying the way Matter's voice bounced around inside their chest and into Sauraxen where she lay on them. She'd do a lot to keep them talking, even if she couldn't begin to guess what Matter was getting at or why they knew this stuff.

"Well, humans evolved and developed and started creating settlements. The risk of predators lessened, until suddenly there was almost nei risk to most humans on a daily basis. But the APS remained."

Sauraxen hummed, encouraging Matter to continue even as their chest lifted underneath her with another yawn.

"The problem was, humans started having APS responses triggered at seemingly random times."

"Like a battery that's sparking from ill use?"

"Exactly. They called it anxiety. And they developed ways to deal with it, to help themselves. That's part of what Brruuh should do as a cognitivist."

Sauraxen chirped again. It was clear Matter had a point, but Sauraxen was struggling to wrangle the words into one.

"I think you might be experiencing the wrexi equivalent."

"We don't have that."

"How many wrexi live outside caves?"

Sauraxen hid her face in Matter's chest. They both knew the answer. It was exceedingly rare for wrexi to leave Pitzk. Most of them couldn't tolerate open spaces or direct solar light. "I don't want to be another first!"

Matter laughed.

"What do I do?"

"As far as I understand it, from my own limited experience – and again, Brruuh is the cognitivist – you locate something you find comforting. Um... when you were a hatchling, what did you do for comfort?"

Sauraxen hummed as she thought. The first few times they had needed to bail out of the cave, her vava had picked her up and cradled her close. She'd spent the rest of the night tucked against xyr chest, xyr arms wrapped securely around her scales. After that she had started being able to handle bail outs mostly by herself. But the first time a relationship hadn't panned out the way she hoped it would, it had been her vava she had turned to once again.

"Vava cuddles," she answered.

"Well," Matter said. "I'm no vava, but I can do cuddles."

Sauraxen pushed away. "Isn't that inappropriate? It wouldn't be the same as our sexual relationship. It would read more like romantic..." she trailed off, hoping Matter would understand.

Matter didn't do romance, not as far as Sauraxen had ever experienced or overheard. Not that Sauraxen was actively asking for that either. She had never pictured Matter in a relationship beyond or outside the bounds of what she shared with them – imagining, of course, that Matter would share the same kind of relationship with others.

"I'm not asking you to fuck, Axen. I'm inviting you to be comforted by me in the same respect that I seek comfort from you. My comfort looks like sex, yours looks like cuddles."

"Naked ones."

"What do you think I sleep in?"

"That jumpsuit, by what I've registered."

Matter laughed again. "I put this on to answer the door."

Sauraxen chirped, desire for comfort superseded by the question of, "Is there... anything under it?"

"I was raised on Ouaeahhn, its drapery or naught there. There's nothing on under the jumpsuit." They winked comically, shifting their entire head to Sauraxen could register it easily.

It didn't take much to wriggle out of clothing and under the blanket.

Pressing against Matter's warm, solid body, Sauraxen almost made a move, but Matter's chest rose with another yawn and Sauraxen resolved herself to settle and let them sleep. As Matter's breath slowed, Sauraxen's flee-response settled and disappeared.

Matter smelled nice, like hugs and pizza pockets – the good ones with the bug paste. How long had they smelled like that? Shouldn't she have noticed before? But the thought slipped away with Sauraxen's consciousness.

Chamber

The Ouaeahhn, dangerous-movement and family-feeling: Ymmattrahni was in the hallway when Chamber opened the door to her quarters. They froze, eyes blowing wide and eyebrows creeping together and up toward their hairline. "I'm sorry, I'll go," they said before Chamber could say anything at all.

"Wait," Brruuh called, bustling out of the aufenthaltsraum. "I wanted to talk to you–"

Ymmattrahni let out an explosive groan. "You could at least offer me coffee before you start asking difficult questions."

"We can't afford to be cavalier about you risking your life so casually."

"What's the problem? It's my life."

"That doesn't–"

"Are you about to tell me that it doesn't matter that it's my own life I'm risking? Are you about to try and convince me that how I run my life affects anyone but me? I don't have any dependents; the ship has autopilot that would get you back to the nearest IPA station safely to await a new pilot."

"You would be missed."

A wash of emotion came off Brruuh in a wave. Icy cold desperation and loneliness and fear. Chamber squinted, searching deeper, seeking her way into his mind. It was hard; anyone outside Unity was always difficult to access.

More cold, physical this time. Cold and the desperate aching loneliness that Chamber herself was feeling too. He had nobody left in the whole universe. Just like her.

She backed away from him, the emotions too raw as she retreated from her uninvited investigation.

"Brruuh, just leave it," The ouaeahhn was saying, the conversation obviously having continued while Chamber was sunk inside an un-unified mind.

"I thought ouaeahhn were supposed to be community minded," he accused.

"Why else would I have risked everything to rescue someone who doesn't even like me!?" There were clearly emotions roiling within the ouaeahhn, but Chamber couldn't feel any of them. It was like they had been wrapped within a bubble, outside Chamber's reach.

"What do you mean?" Chamber asked, despite herself.

"Matter took off their helmet to find you," Brruuh

explained.

"So?"

"Your ship was breaking apart," the captain's voice drawled. Chamber turned to find him leaning in the doorway of the aufenthaltsraum, steaming mug in hand. "I couldn't see it yet, but Matter had started to reflect space dust so there had to be a break big enough to get into whatever the room with the pods was called. And we hadn't found anyone alive yet and we were gonna leave but..." he trailed off.

"But," Ymmattrahni picked up, "there was the chance. A possibility. And I couldn't give that up. I couldn't walk away when I knew, if I just took a little risk – little, Brruuh – that I might be able to save a life."

Chamber's head was blank and empty. She didn't want to have to figure out what to feel in this situation. If her Unity was still there, she wouldn't have had to. She could have outsourced it, could have outsourced the feeling, what to say, how to react.

Instead, she stood, silent and still.

"And, for the record," they continued. "I'm sorry that you were the only one. It can't be easy. And I hope we can find your people somewhere. I didn't mean for you to be alone. I would have done anything to make that not the case. Now if we're all done having this huge heart to heart in the hallway, I was headed to the bathrooms."

And the ouaeahhn was gone.

Maybe they were right; maybe the Ym in their name didn't refer to danger but potential. But Chamber could hardly believe it. Not with her history with other ouaeahhn.

Dimae

Dimae packed up his transportable medi-kit: anti-septic for humans, gauze and bandages, small size medi-scanner with the correct profile pre-loaded on, alongside a few other standard pieces.

He didn't think Matter would need more than that, but if their knuckles were broken he'd have to convince them down into medi-bay to get that fixed. Still, the transport kit would probably be easier than trying to convince the slippery pilot into medi-bay.

"It's everybody's favourite doctor," Matter greeted from where they reclined on the sofas in the aufenthaltsraum, booted feet hanging over the arm.

"You didn't even look up."

"Didn't need to. You have a specific footfall. You just come to hang out?" They looked up from the datapad, tugging headphones out of their ears. Their eyes landed on his portable kit. "Oh..."

"I have waited as long as my duty of care will allow."

With a huge sigh, Matter pushed into a sitting position, their feet landing silently on the aufenthaltsraum floor. "Let's get it over with then."

Dimae opened his mouth in an attempt to convince them to let him but stopped. "I expected to you argue more."

"Thanks for not making me go to medi-bay for this."

Dimae pulled out his portable medi-scanner. Results started flashing up rapidly. Dual readings to compare Matter's status against that of a healthy human and a healthy ouaeahhn.

The scanner highlighted the surface damage to their knuckles and beeped when it recognised one piece of skeleton slightly askew from where it should have been.

Dimae crouched by Matter, taking their hands into his to start fixing them up. "This might hurt."

"I never noticed before, but your legs bend the opposite way to mine."

Dimae let out a trill, disinterested but affirmative. It was something he had noted about Sebastian early in their relationship.

"Do you have clothing that works with that?" Matter asked.

"What?" Dimae asked, pausing in his attempt to reset the knuckle without over-extending it – always a risk with ouaeahhn, especially one with Matter's history.

"When you crouch, your calf-equivalent sits on the floor. Do your trousers have waterproof patches for that?"

"Of course. Do... do your knees not have that?"

"Are you not familiar with Sebastian's trousers?"

A growl took up in Dimae's secondary vocal cords. He tried to push it away. They weren't actually asking. It was a Matter-ism. It was the casualness of a human or ouaeahhn talking to someone about their paramour, not someone insinuating that he wasn't taking good enough care of his mate.

"Nei," Matter clarified. "We don't have waterproof patches on the knees of our trousers – human trousers. Ouaeahhn don't really have the concept of trousers."

"They don't?" he didn't listen to the answer as he gripped Matter's left index knuckle tightly and pressed.

The yowl Matter let out triggered some base instinct in Dimae. Purrs of comfort erupted from him without any thought or intention.

Matter flopped back on the sofa, their head clunking quietly on the wall behind them.

"You okay?" Dimae asked.

"You warned me it would hurt. Can I cover my eyes with my other hand?"

The curious part of Dimae wanted to ask why, wanted to investigate the reason behind such a question. Was it that Matter just didn't like to look or was there something specific about ouaeahhn eyes that made it easier to cope with pain when they couldn't see? Was it even that they would otherwise project too much, putting Dimae at risk of being dazzled? None of it mattered, he had a patient to care for and he intended to do his duties. "For now."

Day 13

Sebastian

Basti hummed as he stirred the pot atop the cooker. It would never be as good as his papa's chili, but his attempts weren't half bad. Even if they usually ended up with Dimae scrunching his nose and huffing all the way through the evening thanks to his hatred of spice. He scooped a spoonful out of the pan. It was halfway to his mouth when his wristband beeped. He startled, chili flying off the spoon and onto the cooker backsplash, the edge of the fridge, the floor, and all down Basti's front.

"Gahh!" he tossed the spoon into the sink and pulled up the call. "Hello?"

"Hey, Kiddo."

"Papa?"

"Who else'd it be!"

Basti grinned, sinking into the chair nearest him so he could settle his arm on the table to steady the picture.

Cross-universe communications were always more pixelated and jarring than cross-planet comms, but at least it wasn't like it had once been on Earth where the video feed or sound would freeze and you might not even notice for several sentences. Not that Basti had actual experience with that, just old vids.

"I got your letter and I asked my contacts in IPA space."

"You live in IPA space, dad."

"You know what I mean!"

Basti chuckled.

"Anyway, they say the best bet for research is Station Omega Sethi, you think your pilot can get you there?"

"For sure, Matter can get anywhere."

Jonesy blinked, his easy smile disappearing from his face in the way it always did when he was surprised and trying to hide his emotions. "Matter?"

"Ja, Matter – you know, my half-sib."

"I hadn't heard from them in a while. How are they?"

In a while, that probably meant Matter hadn't called him much since their return to work. "They're great."

"You're not just saying that to keep an old man from worrying, are you?"

"Of course not, papa." He wanted to tell his papa that if he just let Matter come to him when they needed to instead of constantly pushing them to tell him everything that was wrong, they'd be more likely to come to him for exciting things too. You get it all or you don't get anything. But it was a fruitless line of conversation. He'd tried more times than he cared to count and it had never got anywhere but Basti frustrated, Jonesy confused, and Matter seeing absolutely no improvement.

It sucked.

"What are you up to that needs research into ancient things anyway? Should I have named you after your mama's favourite Old vids – that tomb robbing guy, what's-his-name Jones?"

Basti pressed his lips together to keep from laughing. "Nei."

Should he tell his papa about Chamber properly? Should he tell him everything that had happened? The ship, the pods, Matter's helmet, the way that sometimes Sebastian couldn't breathe at night because of the fear that his ship would start to break apart too? Nei. He'd worry. And what could Jonesy do from half a universe away?

"Just doing a passion project," he lied. "Found some old space junk and couldn't date it."

"You can take a refresher course in your history degree, you know?"

"I know papa, but how would I do that from my very own cargo ship."

Jonesy laughed. "Alright, alright, you got me. I dunno why you want a cargo runner in the first place but it's not for me to know. Your grampa loved working in IPA accounts, I wanted to run a farm, and you wanna do this."

"You wanted to run grandma's farm," Basti corrected.

"What's your point?"

"Nothing, never mind."

Jonesy frowned, leaning toward the camera. "What are you covered in?"

"Chili."

Jonesy laughed. "You still trying to figure out my secret family recipe?"

"I think I've landed on a better one, actually," Basti lied.

"Is that why you dumped it all over yourself?"

Basti stuck his tongue out.

They chatted for a little longer until something on the farm called Jonesy away. Basti flicked a new heading over to Matter for when they were in the pilot's console with a little note saying they were welcome to help themself to the chili he'd made, and he went back to it, starting by cleaning up the mess he'd made.

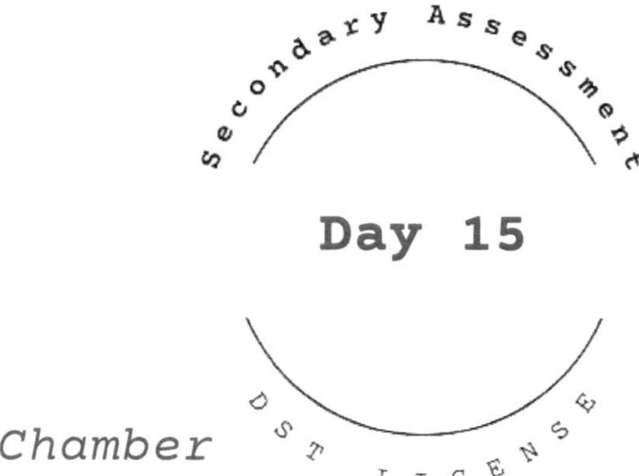

Chamber

Station Omega Sethi had been going for more years than the current standardisation knew how to count, at least according to the plaque that had been horrifically affixed with rudimentary and ugly screws.

The organisation known as the IPA – whatever that stood for because Chamber had no idea – had found it floating alone in a well maintained corner of space and had begun adapting it to their own needs.

Chamber's fingers trailed along the last remnants of the hexagons along the wall mostly covered in pieces of artwork she didn't recognise, done in various hands and various styles, each one emulating but not perfectly recreating the central piece of that section of wall. A lack of Unity could not have been more clearly displayed. All the more harsh for having cracked into the little pieces of Chamber's history and people.

To Chamber's surprise, the abused screen lit with recognition, rippling under the pressure of everything that had been affixed to it.

"Hello, Chamber. I'm sorry," it said, the words displaying under and around the art, sinking into Chamber's ears and telepathic senses all at once. The singular pronoun hurt. I. Chamber was alone and so was this AI interface.

The ouaeahhn, her unfortunate companion, put one hand over their chest, the other one flicking toward Chamber but freezing before it could make contact. Could the ouaeahhn feel her pain? At least someone could.

"We had nei idea," Ymmattrahni breathed. "It was silent when we found it. It was silent for years, generations even before we started using it."

Chamber wanted to argue, but the ouaeahhn had no reason to lie. Worse still, for the short time she had known this ouaeahhn, they had proven themself trustworthy.

"There's still parts untouched," the lizardoid said. "Deep in the centre, beyond un-openable doors. I can sense them."

Chamber scoffed. "So what if there are? Are we to stay here?"

"You can if you want," Ymmattrahni said.

"You'd like that, wouldn't you!"

"I would like to help you. I would like for you to find some semblance of what you're looking for. I would like for you to have your community back."

Chamber looked away from those spiralling, space-like eyes.

"I know it hurts."

"You couldn't possibly."

Ymmattrahni laughed but it didn't sound like an amused one. "Even if I didn't have the experience of losing out on my own community because of life events." Their hand came up to their chest again. "I feel it in here. I feel what you feel."

"Since when can ouaeahhn feel outside their own?" Chamber had known ouaeahhn in the before. They were insular then, only connecting within themselves, never with outsiders. Chamber's people, however, had been able to connect with others over time, the more time they spent with the people they met, the closer they got, the more inducted the outside got into Unity.

They smiled sadly. "Couple of thousand years."

"You have Unity?" Her chest felt empty.

Matter shook their head. "It's not like that. It's nuanced, complicated. We..." They shook their head. "We build Ahthae."

Family and the familial we. Something greater than a family, Chamber couldn't quite translate it, obviously a word newer than she was.

"Thousands of years?" Chamber trailed her fingers over the battered screen once again.

Before her current companions could say anything, the AI responded. "Yes, Chamber. I had been waiting for you for–" More numbers than Chamber could register displayed over the wall, coating the entirety of it under the pictures.

"Am I truly the only one left?"

"Maybe not," Matter offered. "Maybe your people moved like–" they cut themself off, almost choking on the word. Maybe this particular ouaeahhn wasn't so bad if they cared enough to cut off their own people just for

Chamber's comfort. "Other people have travelled away from their original planets and started new lives. Maybe you – they – your people moved and we just don't know where they are."

"And I could stay here? Learn what she knows about us?" Chamber gestured to the rippling screen.

"Or you can come with us and try to search for them. You make your own choices from here, Chamber. Whatever you choose."

"We could never have imagined a world in which ouaeahhn would offer us space. I could never have imagined it either."

The ouaeahhn shrugged, a decidedly human gesture.

Chamber looked at the rippling screen again, then back at the lizardoid and the ouaeahhn. "I will stay."

"Let us leave you with our ship's contact information, just in case. The minute you want it, we can head back and pick you up. If you want it. Ever."

Matter

Matter stared at the ceiling. Boring, bland, plain metal, almost black from age and wear. If Matter scrubbed it, would it return to the colour it had once been or was it too far gone? Maybe the colour underneath would be worse than the sad, dirty black. Maybe they should get some of those glow in the dark stars human children liked? Childish, sure, and Matter did spend an awful lot of time staring at real stars – then again glow in the dark stars were nothing like real stars.

Maybe adding extra light to the room would hinder Matter's sleep further, rather than help it.

With a final grumble, Matter flipped their blanket over one shoulder, tying a knot at their waist on the opposite side. An ouaeahhn outfit, draped fabrics, easily removed. Matter wouldn't want to wear this in front of another person – their own self-consciousness – but the likelihood of running into another person at this time of the night seemed low enough to risk it. Relative time. Ship time. Maybe that was why Matter couldn't sleep. Too human, needing a central star to create circadian rhythm. Maybe they should ask Dimae for some help with that?

Maybe it was just that they had got used to having Chamber aboard.

They headed down the corridor to the aufenthaltsraum. Sehn would have been great, but lacking that, Matter just wanted something warm to drink. Maybe someone had seeded the chamomile flowers; maybe Matter should have seeded them for themself.

Ouaeahhn thought of gardening as one of the most worthwhile pastimes a person could engage in, but Matter had never quite found the motivation for it.

Wandering through the stacks of plants, Matter started at the shifting of something white and grey. "Brruuh?" they squeaked.

Please be Brruuh and not some weird, moving, white and grey plant. Please be Brruuh and not some bugs that snuck aboard. Please be Brruuh.

"Good evening," Brruuh greeted, not rising from his crouch as he tended to some plant or other.

"You big into botany?" Matter asked cautiously, hesitating where they were. Were they disturbing him? Would he be offended by their state of dress? Harrushetti were a modest people – more modest than anyone else Matter knew of in the IPA.

When he didn't answer, Matter started to creep back out of the racks of plants. He was obviously busy. He didn't want to talk with them. They should have left him be.

"I like to care for things," he finally said.

"That's nice." Matter smiled even though Brruuh wasn't looking. "Do you know if we have any chamomile flowers growing?"

"At the back, I think, why?"

"Thought I might brew some tea, since we have nei sehn." They took two steps then stopped. "Just put any vowel in front of the s if it's too much."

"Thank you. What is e-sairn?"

"Se-hn," Matter sounded it out. "Like send without the d. Se like in ECE celebrate, and hn like a hummed sigh or even en like energy."

"That does not answer my question."

Matter laughed. "Sorry. Sehn is an ouaeahhn food-slash-drink plant." They headed to the back of the botany section to find the chamomile plant. The white and yellow flowers had bloomed close together like a tiny front lawn from an old Earth vid.

The plucked a few flowers into their palm and headed back to the kitchenette area.

"What are you doing up so late anyway?" Matter asked as the water boiled in the kettle. "And do you want a drink?"

"Harrushetti tend to rest in bursts. There is a blue box

in the top cupboard?"

Matter pulled out the box and twisted open the top to reveal an equally blue powder with a metal scoop. One scoop into Brruuh's mug – labelled as such with a series of claw marks that Matter had already asked Dimae about.

"What about you?" Brruuh asked.

"I don't sleep well. Is it just one scoop?"

"And half milk if we have any – not cow. For what reason do you have trouble resting?"

Matter shrugged, pulling open the cooler to grab some non-cow milk. They made a mental note that Brruuh's blue drink makes like a lazy milk-based hot chocolate, wanting to remember for next time.

"Might it be an ouaeahhn trait?"

"Nei. Ouaeahhn... it's hard to explain. Time on Ouaeahhn is... fluid, I guess."

"Because of the unstable nature of the orbit?"

"Exactly," Matter agreed.

"Then I am right."

"How does that make you right?"

"Fluid time means rest time is also fluid. You are trying to fit to a human rest pattern instead of allowing yourself to exist in your normal state."

Matter took a drink, letting the chamomile tea warm them. "On the other hand, when I have worked by my internal clock, it hasn't worked out any better *and* it makes working for other people almost impossible. Your burst-rests, how many of them do you plan to take during the ship's night cycle?"

Brruuh purr-chirped.

"And the activities you plan during your night-cycle activity periods, are they calm, relaxing, and low energy?"

Brruuh grumble-chirruped, all the sound coming from his secondary vocal cords.

Matter lifted their mug in salute.

"You have a point," he conceded.

"I do appreciate your concern though."

"Concern?"

"If you want to fix someone's problems, it means you're concerned about them and the trouble the problem is causing them."

"Is my job," Brruuh muttered.

Matter shrugged. "In the same way I appreciate when Dimae takes care of my injuries or illnesses, I can appreciate you having concern for my mental wellbeing. It doesn't matter if it's technically your job or not, you're actively doing it and that's nice for me."

"You have had trouble with rest for the whole of your life?"

"Ever since I was a sapling."

"Kitten?"

"Baby."

"Your parents told you this?"

Matter shifted their weight, trying to find the words to explain. "We don't really have parents on Ouaeahhn. It's complicated. We have Ahthae – family, but it's like the people we share a home with. So on Ouaeahhn that's everyone, so everyone on the planet raises saplings."

"Ah-Thay?"

"Ah meaning home or community and Thae, the family we."

"As opposed to?"

"Generic we: tsae."

"T-Say?"

Matter made an affirmative noise into their mug.

"When would you even use a generic we?"

"For a temporary group, I guess? I've never used it. Maybe colleagues and that kind of thing. It's against the value system of the language to group yourself with people you don't trust, so we have three types of singular they. Family, generic, and unfamiliar. But most people move to family pronouns pretty quick – like I said, we tend to bond."

"Must be extra difficult for you, between human pack bonding and ouaeahhn bonding."

"It's only a problem with reserved cultures. It has been an... issue with Dimae, I thought him marrying Basti would change things but..." They sighed. It should have solved the issue, as far as Matter understood harrushetti culture. Basti was their family, in both human and ouaeahhn terms, they should have been inducted into the family like Jonesy had been, but somehow it hadn't happened. Maybe there was something Matter was missing, even after the six week course.

Brruuh was watching them in that intent way he did. The way that made Matter feel like they were the only thing in the universe worth paying attention to. From someone else it probably would have made them feel special. From Brruuh, however, it felt more like an interrogation. Or being hunted.

They wanted to ask about it. Wanted to investigate Brruuh like he was a high gravity star drawing them close.

Ah. "It might prove a specific challenge for you and me. My instincts are already screaming to bond with you, since we live in the same space. But harrushetti have rules about family and I try very hard to respect that."

"The YaBin rules are less firm than the YaPar."

Something pattered against the side of the ship, a quiet noise, probably unheard by anyone else – maybe Sauraxen. It drew Matter's ever fleeting attention away from the harrushetti in front of them. "I'd love to know more some time, but I think, for now, I'm gonna head back to bed and listen to an audio-cast for a while. I've picked up rumbling from a mine-cluster nearby and I need to be awake and aware to get through that."

"Rest well."

Matter took their tea out of the aufenthaltsraum.

Brruuh's voice carried down the corridor, slipping around Matter like the soft blankets in his office. "Don't listen to anything too energising."

Matter rolled their eyes with a smile and whisper-called back, "Whatever you say, Dr Brruuh."

"And don't call me that." There was a laugh in his tone.

Brruuh

Irritation sizzled along Brruuh, lifting the fur over his scruff in a line up his head and between his ears. The scent of five people, two of whom were human enough to sweat, had burned into Brruuh's nose in a truly inescapable way.

He stalked into the aufenthaltsraum, reconsidering his opinions of Sebastian wanting to keep his bed sheets washed and clean. If this was the kind of scent build-up to be expected from as little as eighteen days, he would recommend more cleaning.

But this wasn't his ship, Sebastian wasn't his mate, and all he could hope for was that a mug of eenya would soothe his – to use an ECE idiom – ruffled feathers.

The kettle wheezed, clanked, and made a sad sort of noise. The acrid tang of burning filled the kitchen area. Brruuh's nose scrunched at the scent as he disabled the power to the entire cooking system.

Trust him to take a break and cause damage to the entire food system on the ship. How far away from the nearest repair shop were they? Brruuh really had no idea where they had travelled after leaving Station Omega Sethi.

As soon as he opened up the back it became clear what the problem was. A smoking piece was hard to ignore.

He ejected the piece in question and headed out of the aufenthaltsraum, down the gravity chamber, and into the upper floor of the engineering bay.

The bio-luminescent mushrooms shed an eerie blue glow over the room. Brruuh dilated his pupils to see as well as he could in the dimness, squinting against the heat-glow of the two running engines.

"Sauraxen?" He managed the name, even around his mouth's inability to from the s sound.

"Downstairs," she called.

Brruuh descended the stairs, feet silent on the carpeted floor. The silhouette of Sauraxen stood out by the desk tucked under the stairs. He held the mechanism out to her. "I need this wet."

Sauraxen snorted. "Does that line usually work for you?"

Brruuh stumbled back. "What?" he chuffed in harrushetti before realising Sauraxen wouldn't understand it. He waved the mechanism in front of her, at a complete loss as to how to communicate in earth common eurean.

Sauraxen's laughter only increased at his wild

gesticulating.

Something about it soothed the bristle-brush texture of his fur.

"Raxen, you in here?" Matter let themself in trough the lower door. They frowned, expression surprisingly clear even in the low light. Their eyes reflected the fluorescent-like glow of the mushrooms and the silver glitter of Sauraxen's scales. "What's so funny?"

Sauraxen took the mechanism from Brruuh's hands, cold fingers brushing against his skin sending frissons of something Brruuh couldn't name. "He said he needs this wet."

Matter snorted, shifting to face Brruuh. "Does that line usually work for you?"

"That's what I said!" Sauraxen cheered.

"Nei!" Brruuh finally managed, his secondary vocal cords rumbling under the word.

Before he could finish the thought, Matter cut in with, "If it doesn't usually work for you, why do you still use it?"

"Nei!" Brruuh cried. "The mechanism. The kettle. The engineer. The engineer wet. I need the engineer wet!"

Sauraxen and Matter cackled, Matter bending at the waist and Sauraxen's head falling back.

Brruuh huffed, folding his arms across his stomach. He had half a mind to leave them to their laughter and retreat to his office. But the thought of retreating upstairs rankled. Even if it meant remaining here to be laughed at.

"The lubricant is over here," Sauraxen finally managed, pointing to a set of drawers at the end of the desk, squashed so tightly against the stairs that Brruuh honestly couldn't tell how she'd managed to put them in there.

He pulled open a drawer only to be faced by completely

unlabelled bottles. "How do you tell what anything is?"

"By smell."

"Obviously," Matter added.

"Obviously," Brruuh muttered, lifting a can to his nose. "I don't even know is this needs oil or plasma based lubricant."

"Leave it with me," Sauraxen offered.

"Priority?" Brruuh pleaded.

"Sure thing."

"Come find me when you're done?" Matter requested. "I can wait." They let themself back out the way they came in.

"Shoo," Sauraxen ordered.

Brruuh jogged after Matter. No point in each using the gravity chamber separately if they were going the same way.

"Hey," Matter said when they reached the top level of the ship. "Anoushaah."

"If you know you need to apologise, why do you do it?" He didn't mean for it to come out so grumpy, but the build-up of scents in the living areas of the ship started burning at Brruuh's nose once again.

"I never realise in the moment. I get caught up in things. I get carried away. I get defensive. And then I see the look on your face – or someone else's." Matter sighed. "And I realised it wasn't all fun for everyone."

It reminded Brruuh of the way Matter had described ouaeahhn – the planet and the people: caught up in the nearest sparkly or gripping thing.

Matter rubbed their hands over each other, the same motion Brruuh had seen humans use to wash their hands – still weird, harrushetti just brushed their fur. They shot him a half-smile. "Better to apologise than leave someone feeling hurt and ignored. At least it mitigates the feeling ignored part, even if doesn't always work so well on the hurt."

Before they could finish turning away Brruuh asked, "You are like this with everyone?"

Matter's breath escaped them in one long blast, deflating their chest and drooping their shoulders. They looked like a wilted flower: uncared for, unaltered. "Everyone, every time."

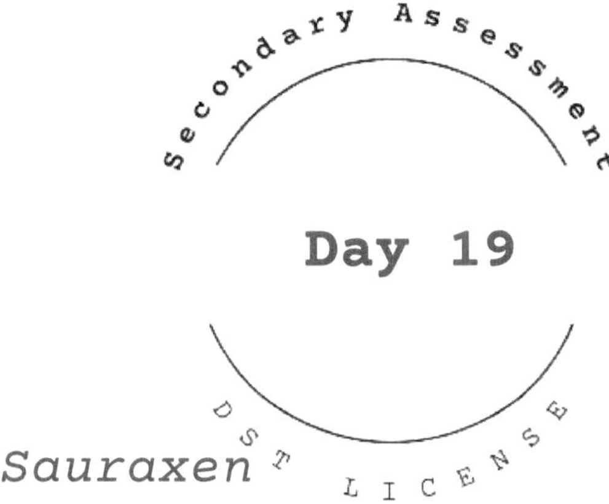

Sauraxen

Sauraxen stepped through the doorway to the pilot's console, hesitating at the edge of the room. It would be so easy to fall into the huge, encircling dome. She didn't know how Matter could stand it, the feeling of being suspended in relative nothingness. It wouldn't have been so bad in low or zero gravity, but with the gravity in here being the same as the rest of the ship – and optimised for humans and harrushetti, both of whom got weird at different gravity rates – it made Sauraxen dizzy.

"Are we anywhere near a junk yard?" she asked.

Matter laughed. "You'll have to be more specific, I don't have a catalogue of every junk yard in the universe stored in my head." They looked up into the galaxy above them.

What must it be like to be able to see out through the dome of glass? Sauraxen knew it was clear only because she had been told. Her vision didn't work like that. But then, her skill set was in fixing machinery because she could perceive it so clearly, able to peer into the inner workings of any mechanics without having to start taking it apart.

"What are we near?"

Matter listed off a few planet names.

"Wait," Sauraxen interrupted. "You think we could stop at EC.63?"

"Technically that's Basti's decision, why?"

Sauraxen held out the small piece of machinery Brruuh had brought her.

"Not gonna lie, Raxen, I don't know what that is."

Sauraxen laughed. "You saw it in this day-night cycle!"

Matter shrugged.

"It's from the kettle. Brruuh needed it wet."

"Oh."

"I've fixed it well enough but it won't last with the way this crew goes through hot drinks."

Matter swiped at the communications node on their wristband. "Basti? You want to stop off at EC.63?"

"Sure," Basti agreed. "Plot in the course."

Matter made a disgusted noise.

"What?"

"Plot in the course," they snarked. "As if I'm going to let the computer run this route. EC.63 is in a high mineral system."

"So... it's dangerous?"

"So, it's stunning. Minerals glitter like asteroid tails but better and everywhere. I wouldn't trade that view for all the worlds." They shifted around the controls. "You hanging out?"

Sauraxen grimaced. "Nei. Pilot's console gravity systems make me nauseous."

Matter detached the control panel from the chair and leaned over to flick a switch.

A joyous chirrup escaped Sauraxen as her feet lifted from the floor.

Day 21

Sebastian

The sun beat down on the dusty, desert-grass landscape. Emerald green grass hills lay to the north and east, seeming further away thanks to the solid, wet heat of the docking port.

Hat firmly set on his head, Basti strode down the boarding plank. Matter already sat at the base, basking in the sunlight as filtered through an atmosphere perfectly healthy to humanoids apart from the excess of sunlight. But Matter wasn't entirely human, so they were probably fine. Dimae had already been past, on duty to watch Sauraxen after her tale about the last time she'd been unsupervised in a junk yard and scraped right through her scales on a rusty pipe.

"Hey," Basti greeted, as if Matter wouldn't know he was there from the inescapable racket of the thundering boarding plank.

Matter, eyes still closed, turned their face to him – a wrexi smile – and gestured to his left. "Notice board."

Sebastian rolled his eyes but followed Matter's directions to peer up at the noticeboard.

The history of the planet made Sebastian's shoulders prickle. Before humans had fully mastered space travel, the eurean government had set out a law that they would not repeat the mistakes of the past, that Earth – or at least Eureans – would only claim planets that didn't have indigenous life.

EC.63 had been one of the first cryo-ship attempts, and one of the few that succeeded. From what had been visible on Earth.0, the planet was uninhabited and their presence wouldn't do any harm. So they'd sent out a ship filled with cryo-pods and frozen DNA with activators for animal and plant life.

When the ship had crash-landed, the natural inhabitants had emerged. They'd rescued the majority of the humans and started the activation process for the other lifeforms on the ship. And the Earth-creatures had had nei way to get back to Earth.

A spiky creature, black with a white stripe up its back, wandered past Basti's feet as he peered up at the noticeboard. Porcuskunk, best not to piss that off. Basti stood, frozen to the spot, as it sniffed his boots before moving on.

The noticeboard flickered from a script Basti didn't recognise to earth northern african-Xhosa, and then earth common eurean-Latinized. Notices about missing pets, docking costs, a warning about overpricing at unregistered junk yards, and some job notices. Before Basti could read them the board changed back to that unfamiliar script.

He waited; eyes fixed where the first job listing had been, for it to switch back to a script he was familiar with.

```
Job         listing:       Farm      co-ordinates
26.335x55.798xHz5   -   Galactic   cargo,   live.
Half payment upfront.

I sold some cattle to a scientist on L145.
You  collect  the  cattle,  deliver  it  to  the
scientist  and  get  the  other  half  of  your
payment. Details upon request.
```

Live cargo. Not something Basti had considered, since it usually needed feeding and left behind residue that, at the very least smelled and, at the very worst, never came out of the cracks between floor panels. But Basti was getting desperate. If he didn't have a job before his Secondary Assessment was over, it would definitely hurt his chances of getting the ship's DST.

Brruuh needed to see him work.

Basti scanned the co-ordinates with his wristband before jogging back over to Matter. The humidity had sweat running down his spine in a way that made him think of home. His younger years, dashing about the humid, forest heavy planet of EC.623 with Peggy.

"Brruuh," he called up into the ship. "Matter and I are heading out to look into a job offer."

"We are?" Matter asked from his feet but he ignored them for now.

Brruuh emerged from the ship, a lightweight scarf wrapped around his head, covering his ears.

Basti tilted his head. "You okay?"

"The hot-light." Brruuh gestured at the glaring star.

"I thought Harrush had an endless light star too?" Matter asked.

"It does," Basti confirmed. There was no such thing as a

sunset on Harrush. Even if the star disappeared as part of the planet's orbit, it shone through the centre like a lightbulb. It made sense that harrushetti didn't have long sleep cycles like humans did.

It had been quite the experience to live through when Basti had stayed with the LeaYaPars for his bonding ceremony. He'd come away with a migraine the size of a mountain from the over-abundance of light.

"Harrush is an ice planet," Brruuh clarified.

Matter huffed out a long breath. "See, and I knew that but I still asked, didn't I?"

Basti closed and locked up the ship before leading his motley crew onward. A pale tiger-striped harrushetti primed for cold environments, and a half-ouaeahhn in a jumpsuit that must have been roasting them half to death. Matter unbuttoned their sleeves, rolling the fabric up to just above their elbows, revealing the intricately detailed embellishments on their skin.

Brruuh's attention fixed on the newly revealed patterns.

"If you have questions, ask. Otherwise stop staring and watch your feet. You don't want to step on a scorpibun," Matter huffed, boots kicking up sand in a way that told Basti they were irritable.

Brruuh didn't ask any questions.

The walk to the farm led the group onto the emerald grass hills. The scent of apples exploded from each blade of grass cut by their steps.

The farm itself squatted quietly in a valley, animals too far for Sebastian to be able to make them out beyond blurred quadrupeds contained by largely rectangular fences. Basti stepped up onto the corrugated metal porch and tapped off his boots, dislodging what little sand had clung to them through the grass.

The farmer appeared before Basti had the chance to knock.

"Hi," Basti greeted the human in the wide-brimmed Stetson-like hat and overalls. "I'm Captain Sebastian LeaYaPar-Jones. I found your job on the noticeboard."

"Oh!" the farmer brushed down their overalls. "Great. I can lead the herd to your ship and provide you with enough food and cleaning bots to get you through the journey."

"If I can ask," Basti hedged. "What exactly is the herd?"

"Why, racattle snakes, of course! Best milk in all the galaxies!"

"Racattlesnakes?" Brruuh asked, squishing the words together to avoid the s.

"Sounds great," Sebastian cut in, not wanting to scare the farmer off with his lack of knowledge about how to care for such a beast. He could find it on the databanks somewhere. "I've got a couple of crew over at the junk yards–"

"Nasty business, that," the farmer mused. "Working with cold metal instead of life forms."

Sebastian hummed noncommittally. "We can't leave until they're done, but we can take your cattle whenever you're ready."

The farmer whistled and some tiny dog-shaped bots appeared to round up the cattle. While the bot-dog did its work, the farmer went over the payment plan. "You sure you're up to this?" they checked. "They're not the safest cargo."

"Of course," Sebastian lied. "My papa owns a farm; I

know what I'm doing."

As they trekked back to the ship, the farmer accompanying to ensure there was appropriate space in Basti's cargo bay for the herd, Matter leaned close to Basti to whisper, "Didn't feel like sharing that your papa's farm grows mangoes and coffee?"

"Shut up," he hissed back, trying to suppress the giddy laughter bubbling in his chest.

"That the only livestock you've worked with is the bees?"

"I'm also not telling that mama is the breadwinner of the family."

"Nor that you've been away from the farm for almost two decades?"

"Do you actually have a problem?"

"Nei."

"Then shush until we're in space."

Matter snickered.

With the cattle safely on-board the ship, and Matter back to basking at the base of the boarding plank, Sebastian turned to Brruuh and tipped his hat back. "So, you have questions."

"What is a racattlesnake?" Again he shoved the two words into one. "Why have I never heard or – or come across this creature?"

"I'm guessing you haven't heard of EC.63."

Brruuh shook his head.

Basti gave him the short version of the story the cryo-ship, the crash landing, the realisation that this planet was already inhabited. At that part, Brruuh's ears landed flat against his head. "I know." Basti winced. "But the inhabitants live on the dark side of the planet and they were gracious enough to let the humans stay on the light side."

Brruuh's secondary vocal cords chirped in the way Dimae's did when Sebastian was saying something fundamentally alien to him. "What does this have to with the beasts?"

Sebastian eyed the fluffy cow-shaped creatures shifting around in the cargo bay, trapped into their designated area by the grates that pulled up out of the floors. "During the crash, some of the DNA sequences got damaged and jumbled together. Porcupine and skunk, scorpions and rabbits, cows rattle snakes and cats – 90% of them produce the best milk most people have ever tasted, even lactose-intolerant humans can enjoy Racattle Snake milk. But 10% of them produce venom instead. They're grumpy and fluffy like cats–" Sebastian tried to cut himself off but it was too late. Grumpy and fluffy like cats, definitely the perfect thing to say to a person evolved from cats! A person evolved from cats who was doing the psychological evaluations for Sebastian's crew. And who had developed somewhat of a friendship with Sebastian's husband, who was also descended from cats. "I didn't mean that the way it came out."

"Thank you for letting me see your work, I would request to accompany on the delivery also."

Basti pressed his lips together and made an affirmative noise – kind of similar to a harrushetti chirp-yes but with only one set of vocal cords.

Brruuh disappeared up the gravity chamber and Basti rubbed his hands over his face.

A racattle snake moo-hissed.

"Oh, shut up," Basti grumbled.

Dimae

Junk yards were not Dimae's favourite kinds of places. Part of his medical training was in lesions, scrapes, and their likely infections. According to his less-than-extensive knowledge of wrexi biology, scraping through scales was tough. It lasted several sheds, indenting the flesh and making it tight and hard to move, but the likelihood of infection was low. They were a hardy bunch.

Humans were hardy in a different way. Their soft, easily breakable skin used to scare him but, from experience as well as training, when their fragile skin broke they usually didn't end up with long-term damage. And, when they did, most humans could cope and adapt. Dimae had helped humans who had lost limbs and carried on with just enough adaptations to get by.

Dimae himself, and all harrushetti, were the opposite; their skin was hard to break, there was no such thing as a bruise on Harrush, but any small injury could be fatal. Breaking skin, breaking bones, it all brought with it a high likelihood of shock. And shock always led to death for harrushetti.

He idly wondered how robust ouaeahhn were but the thought flew out of his ears as soon as he thought it.

Sauraxen chatted rapidly with the junk yard owner, who led the pair of them around the cramped paths between piles of who-even-knew what.

The sun bounced off the metal, sending spikes of brightness toward Dimae. He slitted his pupils against it, glad he was designed for seeing the world in the way he was.

The unrelenting heat and humidity, however, was far less forgivable.

"Are we nearly done?" he asked – grumbled, but he hardly wanted to admit that.

"Huh?" Sauraxen asked, turning her whole body toward him as if she had completely forgotten he was there at all. "Oh. Right." She fished something out of the bag slung across her shoulder. "Do you have a replacement for this?"

The junk yard owner took the apparatus from Sauraxen and examined it. "I think we can make something work."

"What were you two talking about if not that?" Dimae whined, secondary vocal cords rumbling like an overworked engine.

Sauraxen's head tucked close to her shoulders. "Sorry, we got carried away."

Dimae sighed. "Apologies. The heat is... difficult for me."

"You want to wait in my cabin?" the junk yard owner asked. "It's got air filters that can change the temperature."

Dimae glanced at Sauraxen.

"I'll be fine," she assuaged.

Dimae retreated to the cabin, sighing in relief at the cool, filtered air.

Sauraxen would be fine, or Dimae would have to use his portable kit to patch her up. Either way, he'd be far more useful at a temperature that didn't make him want to pant like a kitten.

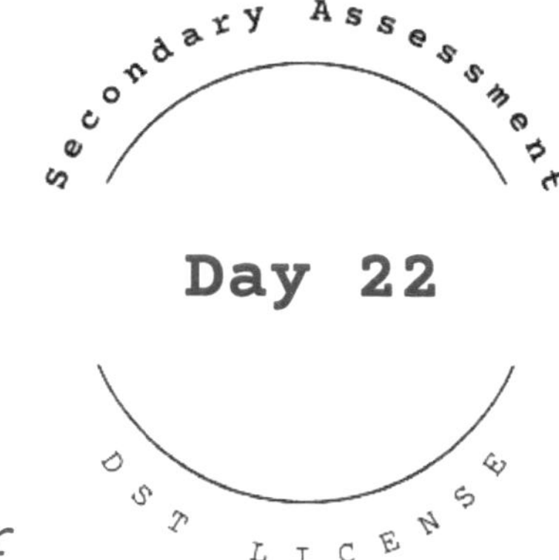

Day 22

Matter

Matter's joints ached. They felt like a person made out of elastic connections, all worn out from overuse. They rolled onto their side in the bed, pulling their blankets up to their chin and then all the way over their head.

A bad day.

One of the random ones that didn't seem to have any build-up. Matter tried to think over their latest activities beyond piloting the ship. A brief trek across a planet wouldn't have been enough to aggravate things like this, and it was too far out from when they had rescued Sauraxen on Station 24 for it to have been an emotion-based one.

Maybe they were allergic to racattle snakes.

Or maybe they were just low on contact.

They tucked their legs up to their chest. Something still wasn't clicking with Basti. Some tension still prickled, an invisible and impenetrable wall stood between them. Even Matter's jokes fell flat.

Basti was stressed and defensive – Matter could understand it, striking out on your own was hard. Leaving Ouaeahhn had been hard. Investigating their human family had been hard. Getting their pilots qualifications had been hard. But Matter knew the best bet was to lean on their Ahthae, their family, the people they were close to.

Basti apparently didn't do that.

With a huge sigh, Matter flipped the blanket back and pushed, painstakingly to their feet. They glared at the jumpsuit crumpled on the floor. That wasn't going to happen.

They pulled the ouaeahhn weave from the wall and wrapped it around themself, tucking and tying just enough to keep themself covered, and shuffled to the aufenthaltsraum.

They looked longingly at the coffee machine, groaned, and capsized onto the sofa instead. Too hard. Too much.

"Hello..." Brruuh's voice.

Matter made some kind of noise with their face smushed into the sofa cushions.

"Are you well?"

"No. I feel like shit."

"Do you want me to get Dimae?"

Did they? Would Dimae want them in medi-bay for this? Or would he offer painkillers and little else? Painkillers might be nice, actually. "Maybe..."

Brruuh spoke in harrushetti.

Matter rolled over, wriggling on the sofa so they could see him more clearly.

He lowered his wristband from where it had been near

his mouth and shifted over to the kitchenette. "Which of these foods is good for you?"

"What are you doing?"

"Making you food. That is why you are here, ja?"

"Ja."

"But it's too much for your illness?"

"It's not exactly an illness."

"But is too much?"

"Ja," they admitted. "It's too much."

"In which case, I will make and you can eat, regain your vigour, feel better."

"Coffee?" Matter asked plaintively.

Brruuh's ears twitched, giving the distinct impression of a squint, as if he wanted to ask whether that was really a good idea.

"Please?"

His shoulders and ears slumped in unison and he pulled the pot of coffee grounds from the cupboard along with Matter's mug. "Food," he insisted.

"There's chili in the cooler, Basti made it."

Brruuh chirruped, pleased.

Matter snuggled into the sofa at watched him patter around.

Dimae appeared in the doorway, portable medi-kit in hand. He pulled the scanner from it, wrinkling his nose against the scents of coffee and chili filling the room.

"Are you comfortable with tablet-based pain relief?" he asked.

Matter nodded and held out a hand.

Dimae passed over a dose. "I'll be back in four hours to give you the next set."

Brruuh approached with a bowl of chili and a mug

slightly over-filled with coffee. Matter accepted both with gratitude.

To their surprise, Brruuh pulled a blanket around their shoulders, grabbed his own food from the table, and took a seat on the sofa at a right angle to the one Matter reclined on.

He flicked fingers over his wristband until a vid started projecting onto the blank wall in front of them.

"What's this?" Matter asked.

"Comfort vid. About a young human rising above the expectations of those around them despite unfortunate circumstances."

The title appeared on the wall. "It's a rom-com."

"Your point?"

Matter smiled and snuggled into the blanket that smelled vaguely of Brruuh. "We should call Sauraxen up to watch."

"Oh? Her favoured genre?"

"Nei. But I think she'd like to be part of this anyway."

A few more flicks and mumbled words and Sauraxen launched herself through the door to the aufenthaltsraum just as the plot of the vid started in earnest.

She grabbed some snacks from the cupboard and settled on the floor under Brruuh's feet.

Wordlessly he passed down a cushion for her to sit on. She leaned her head on Matter's seat.

Matter took their pain relievers and scooped a spoonful of chili into their mouth. They should tell Basti this was his best batch yet.

"Can I try your odd food?" Brruuh asked.

"Which one of us?" Sauraxen replied, not taking her attention off the vid.

"Matter."

"Sure." Matter offered the bowl. It shook with their tenuous grasp. They set it on the arm of Brruuh's sofa. "Sorry."

Brruuh said nothing, sniffing at the bowl of chili like it was the strangest thing he had ever smelled. Maybe it was.

Tentatively, he picked up a spoonful and stuck his tongue out to taste test it before he risked putting it in his mouth.

"It tastes of hot?"

Matter nodded.

Brruuh's nose scrunched but he ate the spoonful anyway. His pupils blew wide. "This is good."

"I'll tell Basti you think so." Matter grabbed their bowl back, settling it in their lap, and snuggled further into the sofa. "But, for now, this is mine."

Brruuh made a noise that almost sounded like a protest.

Matter snickered.

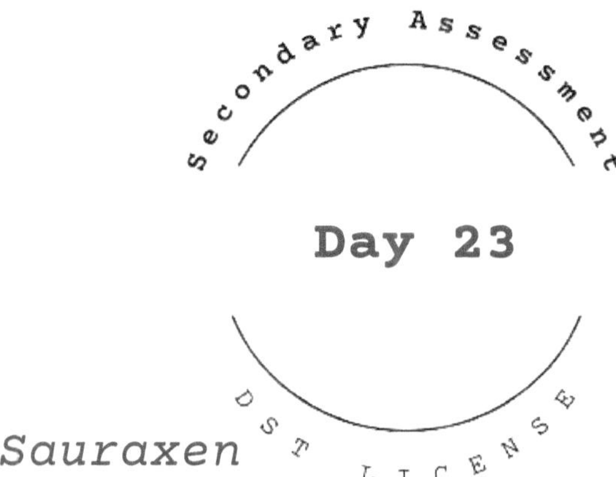

Day 23

Sauraxen

The new kettle piece from the junk yard – well, new to them – had installed easily, leaving Sauraxen with a spare piece that could be stripped for components.

She was sat atop her desk, head rubbing against the stairs every now and again, legs crossed beneath her as she detached cogs, pistons, and wires from the mechanism. Part way through, when Sauraxen had reached a particularly wonky cog that didn't want to pry free, the air by the upper door to engineering shifted.

Sauraxen ignored it. If one of the crew wanted her attention, they would call out.

A moo-eow bounced off the walls, rattling through the engines in a way that had Sauraxen on her feet before she fully registered the noise.

Stood at the open, upper door to the engineering bay was a racattle snake.

"Sebastian?" Sauraxen called.

Racattle snakes couldn't get down stairs, right? She

would be safe on the lower level, right?

The need to run rampaged through Sauraxen's limbs, but if she exited through the lower door she would emerge into the space where the rest of the racattle snakes were meant to be.

Maybe this one was just particularly skilled as escaping. Maybe the rest were still contained within the pen. But Sauraxen wasn't foolish or optimistic enough to believe that. And she definitely didn't want to emerge into a cargo bay full of free racattle snakes.

Wait. The racattle snakes were on the lower level, which meant the one lingering by the upper door had managed to get up there. How on Pitzk had it managed that?

It stepped onto the carpeted floor of engineering – shouldn't it have clunked on the floor? Didn't cows have noisy hooves?

"Sebastian?" Sauraxen tried again. It came out as a squeak. Her Danger Voice quashed by the proximity of a predator. Instinct screamed at her to run, to stay quiet and disappear into the tunnels and avoid the predator.

She tried to calm herself. There was no help available so she had to come up with a plan. What did she know about racattle snakes? The very idea of them freaked her out so badly she had always avoided mention of them. According to what she knew about cows, it should have been fine. Cats and snakes on the other path... they both ate tiny lizards and, while Sauraxen was the size of a small adult human, she was still a small lizard by instinct and that racattle snake was definitely bigger than her...

The beast approached the stairs.

Sauraxen didn't want to find out if it could descend

them. Especially not while trapped in an enclosed space.

The pieces of kettle fell to the floor, clattering deafeningly as they separated and scattered. Sauraxen bolted for the lower door.

Racattle snakes wandered about the cargo bay. Completely un-contained. They moo-eowed at each other, occasionally letting out a rattle from their scaled tails when one of the others got too close.

Sauraxen scrambled up the side of the wall, using any roughness in the old surface: lingering dirt, poor construction, damage, even the lights which pressed heat against her fingertips. She scampered up to the top floor.

Racattle snakes couldn't climb ladders, right? Surely nothing in their weird and broken DNA sequencing let them climb ladders. But the gravity well!

"Sebastian?" Sauraxen squeaked, bursting into the aufenthaltsraum.

"He's not here," Brruuh answered, turning his attention from the plants at the edge of the botany area. His ears flicked, shifting the air currents in a clear manner that none of his other movements managed. "What's wrong?"

"The– the racattle snakes are loose."

"Loose?"

"Loose. Free. Roaming. In my engineering bay!"

A rumble reminiscent of a growl escaped Brruuh as he charged for the door. Sauraxen dodged as Brruuh whooshed past her.

Tentatively she crept after him as he descended the ladder.

Brruuh held his arms wide, herding and guiding the racattle snakes that had made their way up onto the catwalk into a group and down the stairs.

Short, sharp bursts of air hissed out between his teeth had the racattle snakes skittering away from him, moo-eowing in protest as he pulled up the borders of the pen once again.

Sauraxen pressed herself to the ground to peek her whole head through the hole of the gravity well as Brruuh disappeared into engineering.

He and two racattle snakes emerged shortly after and Brruuh penned them as well, returning up the gravity well with little fanfare. Sauraxen scrambled to get out of his way, retreating all the way into the aufenthaltsraum.

"Are you well?" Brruuh asked when he stepped through the door. "Is there anything I can get to calm you?"

Her instinctive-brain still running the show, Sauraxen plastered herself to Brruuh's front, clinging tight with all her limbs and her sensory hair. "Thank you thank you thank you."

Something akin to a chuckle rumbled in his chest. "Perhaps it would be wise to extract ourselves," he suggested.

A full body shudder rippled across Sauraxen. "Stars, I thought I was going to die out there." She stumbled back. "I called but nobody came and there was nei way out of engineering that didn't go past them. There was one on the top floor of engineering!"

"They are all contained now."

"But how can we be sure? And I set up that gravity well for Matter but it will bring them up if they step into it and–"

"You are descending." Brruuh's hands landed on her upper arms, the spike of his claws a pleasant pressure against her scales. "Do we need to turn the gravity well off until we are rid of these racattle beasts?"

"Maybe... I'm loathe to do that, though. It's not fair to make two floors of the ship – and the exit at that – inaccessible to one crewmate just for the supposed comfort of another, is it?"

Brruuh let out a little trill that Sauraxen took to mean she should continue.

"I know Matter can use the ladders on a good day, but we shouldn't have to expect that they're always going to have a good day. And isn't turning off the gravity well just going to make everything bad in a new way? I'll still be down there, and I'll be alone until someone climbs all the way down the ladder to get me and–"

"You are descending again. Wait." He turned toward the open door of the aufenthaltsraum. "Matter?"

"What's up?" they called back from the pilot's console, obviously distracted.

"For how many more day-night cycles will we have the racattle beasts?"

Matter let out a long stalling noise before saying, "Should be there by relative tomorrow. Why?"

"Thank you," Brruuh called back and turned to face Sauraxen again. "I have closed the engineering doors. Perhaps take a day off."

Sauraxen peeped out a yes.

"Would you like to watch another vid with me?"

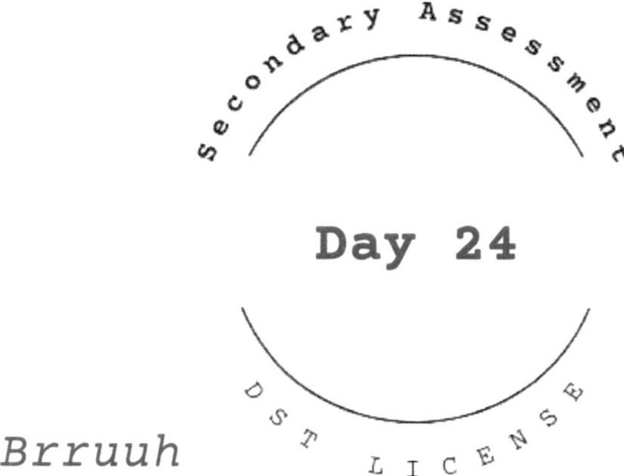

Day 24

Brruuh

White fog swirled in front of Brruuh, his pupils dilated even as his eyes narrowed to peer through it. The chilled water clung to his ears, playing havoc with his balance.

Heavy. The clingy water, the difficulty seeing. Was this planet's gravity particularly higher than Brruuh was used to or was it just the inescapable humidity? "I–" As soon as he opened his mouth wet air invaded it. "–thought we would be landing at a docking port."

"Cargo drop off is at this facility," Sebastian's voice shifted the water particles in the air, pushing them toward Brruuh. Other than the water displacement, Brruuh had no idea where the rest of the crew – or even the ship might be in this wet wilderness. "And you're the one who wanted to come."

Wanted was a strong word for the situation. And Sebastian's attitude was notably less genial since Brruuh had opened the discussion with him about the racattle snakes getting out and distressing Sauraxen. That particular discussion had quickly devolved into an argument about Sauraxen not needing the protection Brruuh would instinctively want to give.

Which had led to Brruuh questioning why exactly she wouldn't need protection from something that had terrified her so much her scales had rippled with it. And Sebastian explaining how wrexi tended to make people either incredibly protective even to the extent that they saw wrexi as pets to be cared for, all the way through to objects of sexual desire. *That* had set Brruuh's fur on end. Were all of his emotions surrounding Sauraxen so easily manipulated?

In the miasma of fog, a hand landed on Brruuh's arm. He yowled in shock, hairs standing on end and claws unsheathing. The skin of the hand in question had a holographic, reflective quality. "Matter?"

"This is why Dimae and Sauraxen stayed on the ship," Matter murmured, voice shifting the water slightly in front of Brruuh's face. Did they not know where he was or was that a purposeful choice?

He couldn't begin to explain to Matter that he needed to view Sebastian's business interactions to be an effective assessor. He couldn't begin to explain to Matter that he had already extended the Secondary Assessment portion of his job in order to view these elements at all. And he couldn't begin to open the whole conversation about racattle snakes escaping without feeling like he was betraying Sauraxen's confidence. And was all that also just because she was such a distinctly *prey* creature?

"How can you register in this water?" he grumbled, secondary vocal cords rumbling under the words.

Matter stepped closer, close enough that Brruuh could

start making out their silhouette, the twin buns on the top of their head appearing as horns in the blur. "Human eyesight, mostly. Earth.0 had a lot of foggy places."

"Earth.0," Brruuh mused.

"The original. The colonies and stations started at 1 – old computer filing tradition." They paused. "You can go back to the ship if you want."

Brruuh placed his hand over Matter's on his arm. Forward, perhaps, but this probably counted as necessary. Unlike the way he had been comforting Sauraxen, which had been decidedly less necessary and decidedly more intimate, at least for him.

"Or we can walk together," Matter suggested.

Brruuh purr-chirped his affirmative.

He let Matter lead him in a mystery direction, ears twitching to pick up on any noise through the thick dampening blanket of mist.

The clang of someone knocking on a metal door had Brruuh's claws extending into Matter's hand where he still held it on his arm. The tangy scent of human blood affixed to the endless wetness. Had he hurt them? They had barely flinched.

"Oh shoot," they muttered. "Meant to say, we're at the facility now. It's two stories above ground, cube-ish-ly shaped. Basti is knocking on the door."

Water particles shifted somewhere in front of Brruuh.

"Hi," Sebastian's voice cut through the mist. "I'm Captain Sebastian LeaYaPar-Jones. I have a delivery of racattle snakes from EC.63."

"Brilliant!" a high pitched voice replied. "Do you have herding bots or will you need assistance with transporting them to my site?"

"Assistance would be great." Sebastian's jovial tone grated on Brruuh's frayed nerves. "I think we have a herding bot but I wouldn't know how to use it."

"Let me just close up and I'll come get them." More shifting water particles before Matter shifted to lead Brruuh again.

"Human," Matter whispered. "Scientist if her – pronouns on lab coat – clothes are anything to go by. She's got her hair all loose around her face, you'd like it."

"What is that meant to mean?"

"I read that harrushetti have a fondness for loose hair. Is that not...? Is that a stereotype?"

Brruuh harrumphed but he couldn't argue. He spent more time than he cared to admit enamoured with Sauraxen's jellyfish hair.

"Anyway, we're heading back to the ship. You'll be able to see her for yourself if she comes aboard."

Sebastian and the scientist began chattering, voices carrying over Matter's low murmurs. "I'm studying the unique properties of racattle snake venom. I asked the farmer to gather all their venomous racattle snakes and send them over for testing."

"I assume you have a proper care facility for them. They're not too fond of the cold."

"Of course. I have a temperature controlled lower basement of my lab – I've been cultivating it for months while we waited for a cargo ship to transport dangerous live cargo."

"Ja," Sebastian laughed. "I won't lie, these guys gave us some trouble, didn't they Matter?"

"Oh ja," Matter joined in the laughter. "Managed to get out a time or two, you better have a super secure area."

"Hmm," the scientist muttered. "I wonder if their nature also changes with the venom production. Ah, a test for another time."

Back on board the ship, Brruuh shook off the water droplets.

The scientist was as Matter had described her: white lab coat with embroidered pronouns in blue, damp wavy grey hair that sat in line with her chin, rich brown skin with fine lines near her eyes and mouth. She leaned over the herding and care bot, flicking a few buttons to set up a series of orders.

Brruuh watched as a grinning, if slightly damp, Sebastian concluded his business. He watched as Sebastian waved the scientist off the ship with her cargo, having settled payments before releasing the racattle snakes from the cargo bay.

With business concluded, Sebastian raised the boarding plank and retreated to the aufenthaltsraum.

Matter let out a long groan and wiped their hands over their face, flicking water droplets onto the cargo bay floor.

"Galaxies, I want nothing so much as a shower right now."

"You want to solve the wet with more wet?"

They shot him a lopsided grin. "It's a temperature thing."

Brruuh flicked his ears in a nod, water splashing into Matter's face.

A shocked laugh escaped them. "That almost seemed like it was on purpose."

"It wasn't."

They squinted at him. "I'm keeping an eye on you, Brruuh."

He almost had the chance to build up legitimate concern before Matter's face shifted into humour once again and they headed up the gravity well without another word.

Brruuh hesitated at the edge of the aufenthaltsraum. He wanted nothing so much as a towel or, better yet, a hair dryer, and to hide in his room. But his assessment included keeping an eye on Sebastian's bookkeeping and records, so his wants, like Matter's, would have to wait.

It wasn't looking wonderful. Humour while trading could go well for some but, even among humans, it was often frowned upon. The expectation that the customer lead the interaction had spread throughout most of the IPA trading world.

Brruuh wiped the water from his ears as best he could. He could keep an eye on the humour thing. It wasn't a make or break issue.

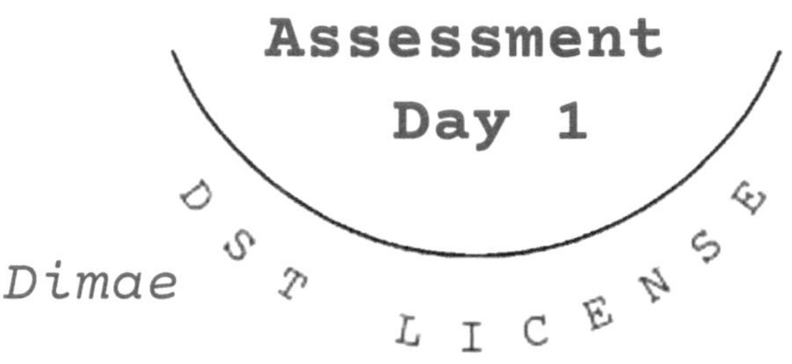

"He's gonna fail us," Basti whined, his EC.623 accent heavier with the strain pressing at his shoulders and curving his spine. He paced back and forth in their quarters, picking up pillows, squishing them, and putting them back down. More like tossing, actually, as he continued.

"He is not."

"He is. We're gonna fail and then we're gonna have to give up the ship even though we haven't even made back our investments and then we'll go back to serving on bigger ships – or at least you will. I'll have to become your tagalong husband." He flopped, face first, onto their nest, Dimae scrambling to get his legs out of the way quickly enough to avoid being landed on.

"Or worse," Basti continued. "They'll smell the stench of failure on me and we'll have to work on different ships again and never get to see each other."

Dimae dug his fingers into Sebastian's hair, scratching gently against his scalp. "That won't happen."

"How can you be so sure?"

Dimae purred to stall. How could he be so sure? He couldn't. He wasn't. He was having exactly the same anxieties as his husband. Being separated from him was the worst kind of punishment. But he couldn't tell Basti that. Not now. Not like this. Not when Basti was already so far into a spiral that he was nearing the very bottom of the metaphorical staircase and that was how people broke bones.

"He has nei reason to fail us yet," Dimae said finally.

"Yet!" Basti whined.

Dimae shut his ears and intensified his comfort purring. "We won't know anything until we meet with him."

Basti groaned into the bed.

Dimae sighed and pushed at his shoulder. "Up, please."

It only took two more prods before Basti stood, pulled his hair up into its usual pineapple, and they both headed up to the aufenthaltsraum. Basti might be the Captain, but Dimae shared ownership of the vessel with him.

Brruuh was already in one of the dining chairs when they arrived, datapad on the table in front of him as he toyed with his stylus between his claws. Discomfort radiated off Brruuh, his ears flat enough to balance a tray on.

If Dimae was running this meeting, he would rather have this conversation in a private space like his office. Performing business in the aufenthaltsraum – a space designed for relaxation, green time with the plants, and eating for the entire crew, nei privacy to be found – rankled. He had little doubt Brruuh felt the same way, even if the more human and casual crew members didn't seem to find it bothersome. But Basti didn't have an office and Brruuh's wasn't large enough for all three of them to comfortably fit.

He and Basti took the seats opposite Brruuh. Almost immediately, Basti's leg began to bounce. Dimae almost put his hand on it to stop it but, instead, folded them in his lap.

"So," Basti broke the silence, tapping his fingers on the tabletop. "What's the deal?"

Brruuh flicked the stylus across his datapad. "I have seen some positive and negative aspects of your travel habits. And your business habits." He spoke slowly, choosing each word with care.

This was it. He was going to tell them to turn around and head to the nearest IPA Station to have their ship taken away. Dimae would have left his secure, high profile ship position for nothing. Basti's reputation would be ruined. And the rest of the crew would be stranded with them on a random IPA Station, fighting for jobs once again.

"As you know," Brruuh continued. "I have had to expand this portion of your assessment by a few days. That's perfectly normal, on-vessel days do not always match with IPA days, which affects assessment lengths."

Dimae's ears started to droop despite his resolution to remain outwardly emotionless. This was a business meeting, and he was an adult. He could comport himself as such, regardless of how devastated he was at the prospect of all of Basti's worst predictions coming true.

"With all of that in mind, we will be continuing to the third part of the assessment."

The breath came out of Sebastian in a whoosh.

"What requirements are you putting forth?" Dimae asked.

"I am not able to discuss that," Brruuh countered.

Sebastian looked between the two harrushetti. "What do you mean? What does that mean?"

"It means Brruuh has put warnings on our potential DeST license. It means we have to fulfil his particular criteria or else we lose our chance."

"Okay," Sebastian drew out the word. "Is that for all of us or are there particular people you're more concerned about?"

Brruuh's ears flicked. He wasn't going to answer. A kitten-like aversion. Kittens only did that when they were learning about what would be appropriate, but Brruuh probably had a lot of kitten mannerisms he'd never learned to move on from, at least from what Dimae knew of his history.

Dimae had not missed living around other harrushetti. The rules and regulations of his homeland could be stifling, especially when compared to such a free culture as humanity. Dimae hadn't realised how human he had become in his time with Sebastian, at least not until he had started to spend time with Brruuh on this assessment.

"Is there anything you can tell us?" Dimae almost snapped.

"You need to run this vessel and your business however you want to, fighting your nature will not work in the long run."

Sebastian pushed to his feet. "Okay, well, in that case, if

you don't need anything else from us we have to get ready for Matter's birthday party."

Brruuh

Brruuh retreated to his living quarters, leaving Dimae and Sebastian in the aufenthaltsraum. That conversation would have been much more pleasant in an official workspace, without the intense worry that one of the other crew members might walk in at any moment. But there wasn't enough space in Brruuh's office for all three of them and he could hardly enter another harrushetti's nest – a bonded pair's nest at that.

And, they were right, to an extent. It was Matter's birthday and they all had to prepare for it.

Human anniversary celebrations were still a relative mystery to Brruuh. He had been to many an 'office birthday event' – ones contained within the work building, ones moved to a restaurant, ones hosted by a particular colleague at their home. Anywhere from fifteen minutes in a break room and back to work, to an event that lasted more hours than Brruuh had ever managed to spend. Some people had even returned to work the next day still in their party clothes. It didn't matter how many birthday celebrations Brruuh had attended, he had still yet to be able to explain the practise to his own satisfaction.

What he did know included cake with small fires on them – weird and gross but inappropriate to refuse,

Brruuh had learnt that one the hard way – secreted gifts from friends, family, and acquaintances, and an ancient song he would never get used to bellowed out in a series of enemy pitches all at once.

Brruuh tied the spare fabric around his gift, setting the parcel on the folded down desk in his quarters. He had been a little concerned he wouldn't be able to think of, or access, a gift in time for this event, having had little warning beyond checking through his files and discovering Matter's birth date at the top of one piece of information.

Maybe he should check to see how Sebastian planned to run this event. Had it been long enough since their conversation that Sebastian would have a handle on his emotions yet? Long enough for the bond mates to talk with each other about their feelings and plans?

He crept toward the aufenthaltsraum. The door was ajar and silence from within. He peeked inside.

Instead of Sebastian and Dimae, he found Sauraxen leaning on the kitchen counter and snacking on some brightly coloured goo with a spoon.

"Bug jelly," she answered the unverbalised question.

"You are aware of human birthday customs?" he asked, trying to pitch his voice low so it wouldn't travel around the rest of the ship. Some birthday events necessitated surprise.

"Ja," Sauraxen agreed, setting her spoon into the obnoxiously orange jelly. "Gifts, gatherings, celebration of weirdness."

"And cake with fires."

"Right. I knew I was forgetting something."

Brruuh settled his back against the wall by the door.

"What do you think of it all?"

"It's weird, right?"

"Very weird."

"I don't celebrate the anniversary of my hatching!"

"Fire-cake and gifts for not dying during the year."

Sauraxen laughed, squeaks and peeps that warmed the tips of Brruuh's ears. "Exactly," she agreed. "But it makes them so happy."

"I know." Brruuh sighed. "I hope I have chosen an appropriate gift... Have you been informed of the plan?"

"Everything's pretty much normal until dinner, then we're all eating together – Dimae is cooking – with gifts and things. You and I just have to turn up with gifts and enjoy. Apparently there was a question about whether you would want to come or not – something about a conflict of interests and too dignified to debase yourself."

"I have lived around humans for years, I am experienced with human birthdays."

Sauraxen scooped another spoonful of jelly.

Brruuh pulled out a dining chair and sank into it, leaning his chin into one hand. "What do you celebrate?"

Sauraxen tilted her head, spoon hanging out of her mouth. She swallowed. "Uh... sheds. Skin sheds – they happen every five standard years or so. We have a nice sand bath, eat some mushrooms. If we eat the bioluminescent ones, like I have in engineering, when we have freshly shed we sometimes glow."

It was easy to picture Sauraxen glowing with the same blue light as her mushrooms, skin shining from the inside out, like Harrush when you stood on the far side from the star and the light shone all the way through the ice core of the planet. Brruuh's pupils widened of their own accord and he quickly looked away. Sauraxen probably wouldn't be able to perceive pupil dilation but he didn't want her to see it anyway. Didn't want to make her uncomfortable with his desire, didn't want her to misunderstand it as predator and prey.

"What about you?" she asked, stuffing another spoonful of bug jelly into her mouth.

Brruuh's tongue poked out of his mouth a little as he thought. The scent of Sauraxen and oranges and the base undercurrent of bugs filled his mouth. "Unions," he managed. "Pair bonding, ceremonies, procreation." Procreation was hard for harrushetti. Kittens were a great triumph and gift. But he definitely should not be thinking of coupling while this close to Sauraxen. "Overcoming challenges – long winters, injuries and illnesses, resolution of disputes with others." Now that he thought about it, harrushetti would use almost any excuse for a celebration. Why had they never come up with birthdays?

"That's nice. Sometimes I wish we had more celebrations."

"Living with humans, I am convinced you've been offered that."

Sauraxen laughed again.

"My last team assigned me a birthday when I would not offer a date of my own."

Sauraxen's laughter increased.

Brruuh's heart swelled with the enthusiasm. He was sunk. He should excuse himself. He should retreat once again to his quarters. But he kept going, caught up in the camaraderie. "I warned them nei fire cake."

"Aren't harrushetti obligate carnivores?"

Brruuh tilted his head from side to side. They could

process non-meats but it wasn't a valuable nutrient source. "Pretty much."

"Then why not order nei cake at all?"

"Because there are other people who want the cake. Cake is not just for the person being celebrated."

Sauraxen's chirp sounded confused.

"Is Fire Cake!"

"Oh," Sauraxen laughed again. "Nei fire. Gotcha." She twisted the lid onto the jar of jelly and threw the spoon in the disinfector. "I'm pretty sure fire cake is going to be involved tonight. Also, it's called candles."

"I know."

"You know? Then why do you call it fire cake?"

"Fire cake is more descriptive."

Sauraxen laughed again and stroked a hand down Brruuh's arm as she left the aufenthaltsraum. Where she touched him his fur stood on end. His brain should have screamed about the inappropriateness of it all, like it had with Matter's hand on his arm guiding him through the foggy planet. Instead, his ears tingled with warmth and connection.

Matter

"Happy birthday to you! Joyeaux anniversaire! Cumpleaño Feliz! S dnyom rozhdeniya tebya!" Sebastian sang, rich voice flowing through the ancient languages in the repeating tune as Dimae revealed a deep brown cake coated in brightly coloured sugar-shelled chocolate pieces. A single lit candle stuck out of the top, slightly wonky. Not the prettiest cake in the world, but one of the most heartfelt.

Dimae set the cake on the dining table.

"Make a wish, Matter," Sebastian demanded.

"You know ouaeahhn don't make wishes," Matter teased, as they did every year they celebrated with Basti.

"Make one anyway!" he demanded, just like always.

Matter closed their eyes. *I wish I could keep this joyful Ahthae.*

They blew out the candle flame and grinned as Sebastian applauded, nudging his husband to join in. Brruuh and Sauraxen watched in amused silence.

Matter sliced into the cake before Sebastian, control freak that he was, took it off them to start handing out slices. Sauraxen sprinkled bug powder on hers. Basti didn't bother to offer any to Brruuh; instead, Dimae grabbed a bowl of what looked like ice cream from the cooler.

When the cake was finished with, Sebastian launched to his feet and declared, "Presents."

He grabbed a gift bag from behind one of the sofas.

Matter frowned. "How long has that been there?"

Sebastian laughed and dropped the bag onto the table.

Matter pulled out the item contained within. A traditional nuhn, intricate weaving of the branches to create a waterproof, dustproof container making the most beautiful patterns that would glimmer in the right light.

"Open it." Sebastian was practically bouncing on the spot.

Matter touched the top of the box, reaching out with their tele-empathic skills to encourage the box to open.

"Is that thing alive?" Sauraxen squeaked.

"Not exactly. It's basically an ouaeahhn box; it just has a lingering psychic signature."

"How?"

"Because it was requested from the tree that grew it." Inside the nuhn, leaves nestled together. Matter looked up at Sebastian and Dimae, who had clung to one another. Their eyes shone with grateful reflection, reflected back at them from the shining surface of the kitchenette behind the bonded pair. "You got me sehn?"

Sebastian beamed and nodded enthusiastically.

"Thank you."

"Moving on," Dimae insisted, pressing his nose into Basti's hair.

Matter looked down at the sehn and softly closed the nuhn.

"My go," Sauraxen said, pushing forward the small jar she'd placed on the table next to her bug sprinkles.

"It's... a jar?"

Sauraxen's shoulders drooped. "No! I worked so hard, does it not work?"

"Work?"

"Shake it."

Matter did as instructed and swirling galaxies exploded inside the jaw. Matter laughed. "This is amazing. Sauraxen, I..."

"So you can take the void with you wherever you go."

Matter leaned over the table to run their hand down Sauraxen's arm, the wrexi equivalent of a hug.

Sauraxen peeped.

To Matter's surprise, Brruuh extended his hands. A small, fabric wrapped parcel sat atop them. Where had he been hiding that while cake had happened?

With great care, Matter lifted the parcel. They undid the knot, letting the fabric fall away to reveal a knitted whale, deep blue and purple and cream with a straw sticking out of its mouth.

"Galactic whale," Brruuh clarified when Matter didn't respond.

They pressed their lips together and looked up at him, hoping the emotion wasn't showing too ouaeahhn-ly in their eyes. "You made this?"

"Ja, of course. Heartfelt."

"You made me a space whale."

"He has a pipe to take your bone marrow." Brruuh's ears had started to sink, as if he wasn't sure whether he was about to be told off.

"Brruuh TeaYaBin, Doctor of cognitivology, this is the best gift I have ever received, thank you."

"What is it?" Sauraxen bounded over, hair dancing to the music independent of the rest of her.

"It's a space whale," Matter clarified, offering Sauraxen the whale so she could fully perceive it.

"You fed him the space whale story!?" She shifted toward Brruuh, hands travelling all over the soft facade of the whale. "That's the best nonsense Matter ever came up with."

Brruuh's ears perked up. "I knew it wasn't true!"

"Of course it's true," Matter laughed, taking the whale back from Sauraxen and pointing the straw toward Brruuh while making a slurping noise.

Brruuh shoved away from the table with a squealing laugh.

Matter launched to their feet and chased him.

"Halt that!" Brruuh squealed, clambering over the arm of the sofa and into the botany area.

"Make me."

Brruuh darted around the table, laughs becoming breathless. "Leave me alone!"

Matter bounced up, over a chair, and, careful not to stand in any leftover cake, over toward Brruuh, continuing their slorping noises.

"Children, please," Dimae chided.

"He brought it upon himself," Matter insisted, pausing in the chase just long enough to look at Dimae earnestly. "He's irresistible to space whales!"

"What in the stars is a space whale?" Sebastian asked.

"They're not real," Brruuh said from near the sofas, laughter curling up his secondary vocal cords in a continuous playful chirp.

"This one is," Matter clapped back, spinning to face him with it. "And it's hungry for your bone marrow!"

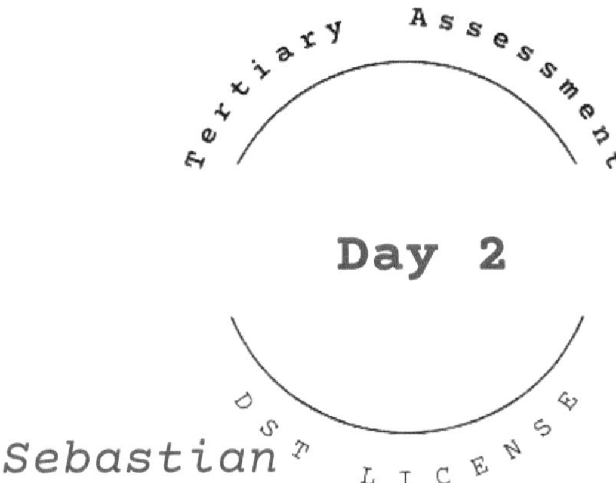

"I'm just saying," Sebastian laughed. "If she really wanted to be a singer, she could have taken lessons rather than buying herself an entire recording studio!"

"And I'm just saying," Matter mimicked. "That I don't think any amount of singing lessons would bring her up to your weird and lofty standards."

He wanted to interrupt, Peggy wasn't exactly the best singer in the world, she could just about hold a tune but her voice had nei flavour, nei enthusiasm. Basti was pretty sure she'd only bought the studio in a fit of pique or, if he was being generous, a burst of enthusiasm that wouldn't carry her very far along. But he knew what Matter would be seeing. Jealousy. Jealousy that Peggy had begun her chosen self-employed career first. Jealousy over the fact that, once again, Peggy had stolen his thunder. She always did. She always had.

They weren't close for a reason.

Basti sighed, leaning his head on one hand as Matter

turned their attention to the hissing coffee machine.

"She's your sister, Basti, cut her some slack."

The ping of Sebastian's wristband cut Matter off. They jumped at the noise, sloshing coffee all over their hand and onto the floor.

Sebastian winced. "Sorry, job alert." He rose from the sofa to grab a cloth and clean up the spilled coffee.

"Aren't you gonna check it?"

"In a bit."

"Nuh-uh. Nei." Matter clunked the coffee cups onto the table, sloshing more coffee out of them. They wrapped soft hands into Sebastian's t-shirt and pulled him toward them. "Check it now."

Sebastian laughed. "I didn't think you were so desperate for jobs. Aren't ouaeahhn all about going with the flow?"

"I'm not desperate for a job I just..." They sighed and let him go. "I just hate unchecked notifications."

Sebastian frowned. How had he not figured that out? Matter had rules about how to contact them. Time constraints, expectations, how to contact them in an emergency. He'd always assumed it was so people wouldn't feel bad if Matter took their time getting back to them. Matter and time didn't always work in a linear fashion. But this revelation implied that Matter had just turned off all notifications except those marked as an emergency.

Basti abandoned the cloth on the dining table, letting Matter clean up the secondary mess around the coffee cups. "Okay, okay." He swiped his fingers to shift the notification from his wristband to his abandoned datapad still lay on the sofa. "But it's probably just another recruitment agency."

"Recruitment agency?"

"Ja." Basti reclaimed his seat. "They post jobs for people to apply for but what they really want is for you to join their company and work under their banner. They send you jobs and you kinda have to do them nei questions asked."

Matter made a disgusted noise and set Basti's coffee on the sofa arm beside him before taking their own seat. "That's the exact opposite of the point of running your own ship."

"Exactly. But they never say in the listing that it's being run by an agency."

"So you apply and then find out when the agency emails you to try and invite you to interview."

"Pretty much–" Basti stopped short. That wasn't a message form an agency. That was a real, actual, legitimate job listing. "Matter?"

"Ja?"

"How far is Clicksphere?"

Matter hummed, shifting their head from side to side. "Maybe fifteen fuel packs?"

"Do we have that in us?"

"More than, as far as I remember. Why? What job is on Clicksphere?"

"One that pays really well." Sebastian grinned. "And you said I'd never find a job posted online."

Matter wrapped their hands around their mug of coffee. "Should I go lay in a course?"

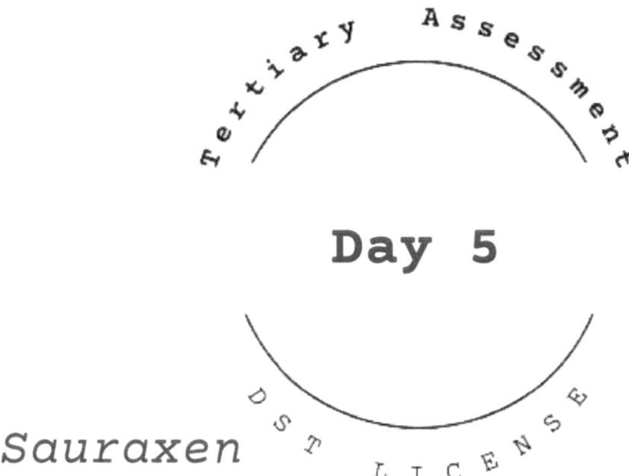

Sauraxen

Sauraxen followed Basti into the mountain-like structure, its uneven surface making Sauraxen think of stalagmites that had started to decay, leaving the underneath unstable and hollow. The glass doors swished open to allow them entry into the structure.

Carpeted floors dampened the clicking of thousands of tiny legs hitting the floor as the clickbugs clittered around the tall, mostly open structure. It reminded Sauraxen of when Basti had left a half-eaten chocolate-coated honeycomb bar in their room and the humidity had got to it, emptying the inside but leaving the exterior thoroughly packed.

The clickbugs' tidy suits – including ties, how weird, Sauraxen had never understood ties – fuzzed in Sauraxen's vision, obviously made out of some kind of wide-weave fabric that displayed like static, creating false reading all around her.

Why Sebastian had decided Sauraxen was the person to

bring was a puzzle. Sauraxen had never actually participated in a cargo pickup before. She wasn't strong or observant. And the concept of taking a bug eater into a mound-building filled with bug people... Unless that was the point? Was she supposed to be scary? These bugs were far bigger than any Sauraxen might have hunted to eat. But would they know that?

She touched a hand to her eyes as she followed Basti onto the escalator ramp. Basti stood still as the ramp moved under their feet. Some small part of Sauraxen, the part that liked to move, had prophecies of being dropped off the end of the belt into some huge carnivore's maw, or a pit where she and Basti would be ground up like bug paste in retribution for the fact that Sauraxen's breath probably still smelled like her spicy bug sprinkles.

Sebastian took Sauraxen's arm to help her navigate from one belt to another. At least he remembered that time she'd been dashing through his Earth Colony's space port and had gone sprawling across the tile. Navigating from one moving thing to another was not Sauraxen's forte.

They travelled up several floors on more conveyor belts than Sauraxen would have liked in a non-stressful environment, let alone this very stressful environment. Could these clickbugs not handle stairs? Or lifts? Or gravity chambers?

Finally, they stepped away from the belts and toward a low outcropping of the wall, maybe a desk? One of the clickbugs sat behind it. It opened its maw in a question Sauraxen couldn't understand. Nothing like the clicks contained within the wrexi languages, even if earth common eurean would have called this noise clicking too.

Sebastian shuffled around in his backpack before

pulling out a circlet that he clapped around his wrist. The disturbing clicks turned into ECE, presented in a mechanical style voice. "Do you have an appointment?"

"Ja," Basti said. "We're from the cargo ship."

"You must be Captain LeaYaPar-Jones."

"That's me, and this is my colleague, Sauraxen."

The clickbug's fuzzy form curtsied, bobbing down and up and doing something with its two pairs of hind legs. It led Sauraxen and Sebastian through a set of glass doors – did these people have anything that wasn't moulded sand or glass? Was all the glass opaque or transparent?

"Good day, Captain LeaYaPar-Jones," a different clickbug in a matching fuzzy-to-register suit spoke from behind another desk with a boxy shape atop it. Again, the translator around Basti's wrist altered the disturbing clicks into earth common eurean in its same mechanical voice, butchering Sebastian's surname in a way that would have had Sauraxen laughing in another situation. "This is the cargo."

"A single brief case?" Basti blurted.

"Ja."

"You couldn't send that through inter-planetary postal services?"

Trying to talk us out of a job, Basti?

The translator buzzed unpleasantly, sending shivers over Sauraxen's scales as it tried to come up with a translation of what the clickbug was saying. The buzz bounced off the moulded sand walls and carpeted floors – ew! Was that made out of these creatures' shed hair? Sauraxen tried to keep an open mind, but this was too much! How would she ever feel clean again knowing her bare feet had touched this much shed hair?

"It is sensitive content," the translator finally put out.

Sebastian paused, then shifted on his feet. "The listing said payment upfront."

The clickbug's stalk-antennae flicked. Irritation? Fear? "Ask–" The translator buzzed again, made a sound like a skipping disc, a cog that didn't quite catch its follow-up.

Eventually it said, "Untranslatable." The cool, mechanical voice reverberated over the glass legs of the desk and the fabric exterior of the briefcase. It registered far too much like the clickbugs' exoskeletons for Sauraxen's comfort. "At the desk outside."

Basti folded his arms, his drawl extending in the way it did when he thought he was being messed with. "I'd really rather you ask 'em to come in and we sort it all out before I even think about takin' charge of that cargo."

Again the clickbug's antennae flicked, clicking together. Still, it clattered around the desk and opened the door to call for the untranslatable-name.

Once the matter of payment was sorted, the office-owning clickbug snapped a quick, "This is a time sensitive mission."

"I know," Basti replied. "It said as much in your advert. We aim to have your cargo at its destination before the deadline occurs."

The clickbug tapped its feet on the floor. "How? We calculated how long it would take an average pilot or autopilot to arrive – accounting for hazards. There is no way you can arrive before the deadline, only upon it."

"We have a really good pilot. I'll send you a message once it's delivered."

Sauraxen followed Basti back out of the building, through the covered walkway to the docking port and onto the ship.

"Why did you want me to come?" she asked as the boarding plank sealed behind them with a thunk and a whoosh.

Basti settled the briefcase into a secure spot in the cargo bay. "You had training – you know you always take more than one person, it's a safety feature."

"Okay..." Very human thought process. "But why me? Why not Matter? Or Dimae?" Brruuh wasn't technically crew, so he would only be called to tag along with a pre-determined pair.

"Dimae is our chief medical officer; he has to stay here in case someone gets injured. Also, he's co-owner of the ship so if something happened to me–"

"Don't talk like that," Dimae's voice called from medi-bay.

"He would be in charge," Basti finished.

"That's bullshit," Matter's voice travelled down from the pilot's console as the atmo engine engaged the thrusters. "I have more training and experience than Dimae."

"And!" Sebastian shouted toward the ladder, voice bouncing around the cargo bay like a party waiting to happen. "I didn't take Matter because it's time sensitive, so I wanted to be able to hit the road as soon as possible."

"Hit the road?"

"Old human idiom. Be on the way."

Sauraxen didn't bother to ask why he didn't just say 'be on the way' – humans loved their nonsensical idioms and she'd long since accepted that she would never fully understand it.

"And," Sebastian's voice shifted to barely a whisper, skittering over Sauraxen's scales in a weirdly intimate way.

"Between you and me, the reason Clickclick is still on provisional IPA membership is that clickbugs have a huge trade on O.H."

Sauraxen's hair lifted to alertness, shifting in the safe air of the sealed ship as it passed into the void of space. O.H. Ouaeahhn Hormone.

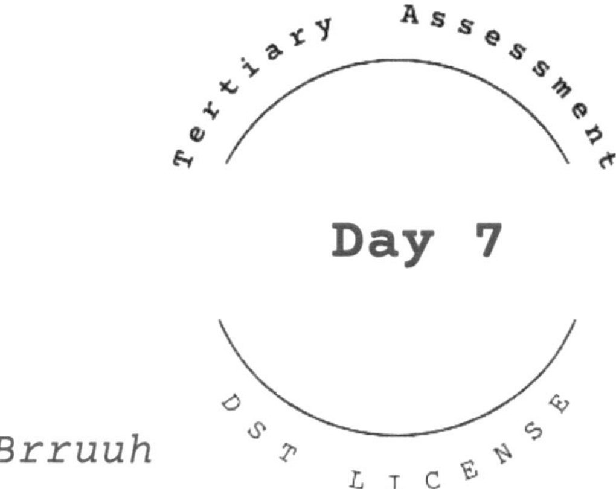

Brruuh

Brruuh extracted himself from his nest. Something had built up behind his ears – a new sensation, something he had never had before. But Brruuh was a cognitivist, he could figure this out.

For the first time in his life, Brruuh wasn't certain of what path to take. His job here was to remain neutral and assess the crew but he had to admit a growing fondness for them, particularly one specific lizardoid. Did he need to recuse himself? Should he admit to his fondness in his report? Should he keep going, pretending he held nothing but neutrality for these people?

For the first time since he was a kitten, Brruuh was starting to feel like he had some semblance of a family. A community. A place to belong. The Ahthae of which Matter had spoken.

He opened the door to his crew quarters, needing to move, to disperse the twitchiness in his ears.

A thumping drumbeat sounded from the front of the

ship – too regular to be a dangerous sound but with the door to the pilot's console open, Brruuh saw no harm in checking.

As he approached, more elements of the music made it to his ears. Earth common eurean lyrics coupled with instruments Brruuh couldn't name.

He peeked through the door, eye drawn to the source of the noise: a small purplish-red speaker sat on the control panel attached to the pilot's chair. Matter's fingers flew across the controls, twisting the ship through the debris filled space in graceful movements reminiscent of traditional harrushetti dances. The swift, athletic, and sensual shifting of pelts and patterns flowing through and around one another. Where one harrushetti would collide with another, the dance would shift from dodging to aggression and fighting. And, when it got really exciting, sparks would fly where swords and claws clashed.

Matter themself swayed side to side, like a tail calibrating balance – shifting, wiggling, rotating. How was their spine that malleable? Human spines distressed Brruuh, both from a medical perspective, and to the lingering kitten part of him.

Matter's eyes and hair glittered with the galaxies they could see out of the huge glass dome stretching above and below them, reflecting lights and swirls of colour unlike anything Brruuh had seen before.

They picked up some of the song lyrics, mumble-singing them and humming the lines between as if they didn't even realise they were doing.

Brruuh stepped back, ready to leave them to their work.

"Brruuh?"

He startled, claws extending. He rumbled a yes in harrushetti.

"If you're going to spy on me, could you at least bring coffee?"

"I'm not ps-spying!" he squeaked, stumbling over the word rather than taking the time to find a synonym.

"Or maybe a snack?" Matter said, as if Brruuh hadn't spoken. Their tone was light, even with the tiny undercurrent of strain. If they had been a harrushetti, their secondary vocal cords would have been rumbling with that tension. Now that he'd noticed it, he could see it everywhere: even with the way Matter danced, even with the graceful rush of their fingers over the controls, the muscles and tendons in their arms stood out with tension and strain.

"Coffee," he agreed, padding bare feet down the hall to the aufenthaltsraum, claws clicking lightly on the metal plates.

He pulled open the cupboard above the kettle to take out a pot of coffee. One read "Sebastian – Do Not Touch" in huge letters. Another had a swirling holographic pattern that brought forth images of warm days when the sun would glint off the snow just right to create images and mirages in the sky of Harrush. That would be Matter's. Brruuh didn't know what it was about ouaeahhn script, the lettering, the ink, maybe both, but it always created images of his favourite things about home. It had the same effect whenever he read the name plate on the door of Matter's quarters.

On the back of the tub, in plain earth common eurean, lay a list of instructions. "1 - Find a mug. 2 - Put it under the coffee spout," with a crude drawing of what that looked like. "3 - Put one (ONE, Axen!) scoop into the filter bit," another crude drawing of how to do that. "4 - Turn on machine. 5- Bring to Matter," and a little stick figure with two circles o top of its smiling face —oh, Matter with their twin buns atop their head.

Having followed the instructions, Brruuh set the filled mug to one side and flicked through the cooler drawers, looking for anything with Matter's name on it. Nothing he knew how to heat up – human food could be weird, it all had to be at different temperatures depending on some kind of system Brruuh couldn't understand at all. Maybe he should check a cupboard instead? Biscuits! He recognised those, and with no crew name on them, that surely meant they were for anyone.

He took the coffee and biscuits to Matter in the pilot's console, setting both down on the little table to the left hand side of the chair.

Matter glanced away from the window to look at him, eyes swirling in purples, golds, silvers, blues and more. The floor swayed under Brruuh's feet.

"Thanks." Matter smiled at him but their face was tight and their attention flicked back to the window over Brruuh's head.

Brruuh retreated to the door once again.

"You can hang out," Matter called. "If you want?"

"What?"

"Hang out – it's a colloquialism, it means–"

"I know what it means, it's the base of aufenthalts."

"Right, well you can. In here. If you want."

"Are you asking me to remain?"

"I'll turn off the music." Their hand flicked out to twist the volume dial until the mutters of a drum beat were all that was left. "It's just, normally you're asleep right now – everyone is, even Sauraxen and she is like a nightmare for getting to bed. So, I figure something's bothering you – gravity shifts to keep everything the right way up are messing with your internal balance, or the time limit is making you stressed, or you had a nightmare, or something..." They trailed off.

Should Brruuh confess to them about his conflicted feelings? Tell them about his attraction to Sauraxen? Anything? As a cognitivist, he knew the value of talking through issues with someone you trusted. The real question was whether he trusted Matter enough for that to be a realistic option?

"I know you probably feel conflicted because your whole job is assessing us and managing our emotions et plus, but–" they made an uncertain noise "–maybe you need someone to talk to. I got the impression from Dimae that harrushetti lean on their family a lot and..."

Brruuh didn't have a family. Not that Matter should know that. Nobody outside of Harrush knew. Unless Dimae had told them. He would probably have recognised Brruuh's surname for its unmistakable link to the YaBin disaster. Would Dimae tell such a thing?

"I haven't noticed you talking to yours," Matter finished, attempting delicacy. "And we're… Ahthae."

Brruuh shuffled to a point where he could see Matter properly, and they could have seen him if they looked away from the window. He sank to the floor, hips shifting to allow for comfort on legs that bent in a very different way to humans. "My family is gone," he admitted, surprising himself.

"My sympathies," Matter said. "That must be

particularly hard with such a family focused society."

"It was."

"Part of why you launched yourself so wholeheartedly into humanity?"

Brruuh hadn't really thought about it that way. When he was a kitten, the Galactic Awareness Lessons had included a class on humans. Humans had a tendency to pack-bond with anything – be it sentient, non-sentient, mechanical, or organic. There were tales of humans who had pack-bonded with cleaning-bots, going so far as to give it false eyes and a name. Maybe he had subconsciously picked human cognitivism because of those rumours. "Perhaps," he mused.

"Do you want to talk about what's bothering you? Or about anything?"

"Do you want that?"

Matter grabbed a biscuit and shoved it into their mouth, holding it with their teeth as they swerved the ship – it was quite unnerving to see the exterior shift so much when the internal gravity systems maintained integrity and made Brruuh feel like he wasn't moving at all. Although, at least it explained why there were no windows outside the pilot's console.

"It gets pretty lonely having to stay in here all the time." Matter bit the biscuit in half, dropped the other half on the table and chewed quickly before continuing. "It's nice to hear someone's voice – someone other than Basti coming to check," they shifted into an approximation of his accent, "How are we doing for time? What's it look like? How long until we're there? Can you go any faster?"

"I'm guessing going faster is not an option?"

"Not if I want to be useful at the end of this," Matter

joked.

Brruuh let his secondary vocal cords rumble, an approximation of a laugh, though his humour at the situation was absent. He would have a conversation with Sebastian about finding the balance between encouraging his crew and running them ragged.

Basti's experience on large, family class vessels didn't translate to a ship this size. There was nobody to replace the pilot if you wore the pilot out.

"I can't promise I'll pay you full attention," Matter said. "But, seriously, anything?"

"Wait here," Brruuh demanded, launching to his feet. He caught a glimpse of Matter's grin as he dashed into his quarters and back out.

With datapad in hand, he pulled up a harrushetti novelette and started reading.

The smile that broke out on Matter's face and the tiniest dip to their shoulders told him it had been the right move.

Sauraxen

With a frustrated groan, Sauraxen tossed the wrench across the room. It clattered from the top floor of engineering down one of the awkward side panels and onto the lower floor.

Extracting herself from where she had been half-inside the engine, Sauraxen stomped over to the door. "Sebastian?" she called in her emergency voice. It echoed neatly over the ship's tunnel-like interior, reverberating melodically in the cavernous cargo bay.

No response. Basti must be behind a shut door. That meant one of four places: medi-bay, his quarters, Brruuh's office, or Matter had got frustrated by the noise and demanded the door to the aufenthaltsraum closed.

She tried medi-bay first – start at the bottom of the ship and work up, the most efficient way. Medi-bay was completely empty.

The door to the captain's quarters was closed. When nobody answered Sauraxen's knocking she headed up the gravity well. Sauraxen had worked with enough humans to know better than to open a 'private door' – it was a weird concept for someone who grew up with only communal spaces – there was no such thing as a door on Pitzk, let alone a private one.

The aufenthaltsraum door sat closed when Sauraxen's head popped up out of the gravity well. She threw it open.

Basti, Brruuh and Dimae all started at the movement and noise. Had this aufenthaltsraum been set up as a secondary escape pod? A lockdown room? Had they not heard her coming?

That wasn't the point.

"Sebastian, I swear by the sulpherous atmosphere of Pitzk, this ship is an absolute piece of trash!"

"Hey," Sebastian chided half-heartedly, still on edge after Sauraxen's sudden appearance.

"The engine just died."

"Which engine?"

"The emergency one!"

"Oh, that's not so bad, right?"

Sauraxen laid light fingers atop the table and leaned

close to Sebastian, so close that even her terrible eyesight could make him out. "Nei, Sebastian. That's the worst possible one," she whispered.

"Why?"

"Because the emergency engine is the only thing standing between us and death."

"I don't understand."

"If the thrusters break down we'll drift and the emergency engine kicks in. If the atmo engine dies, we have pods – well, one pod and the emergency engine kicks in anyway. If the home engine dies, we lose life support except, oh ja, the emergency engine kicks in."

"As long as the other engines don't die, we'll be fine."

Sauraxen's feet joined her hands on the table. One of the harrushetti made a disgusted grumble that shivered through Sauraxen's hair, but she didn't shift her focus away from Sebastian. "It's not that simple, Sebastian. It means I can't casually turn on the emergency engine when the house engine needs to cool down. I can't swap the thrusters to the emergency engine when the mechanisms fall out of sync. And I can't continue to investigate the feedback loop that makes the comms in the pilot's console so painfully loud."

Sebastian laid one hand on Sauraxen's shoulder, a very human gesture but it translated well enough. "Tell me what you need me to do."

"I need you to..." She turned her head toward the corridor behind her, ignoring the reverberating of Sebastian's distressed noise – humans and their fixation on their own bodies being the norm, just because Sauraxen could twist her head 200 degrees around. "Matter?"

"Ja?" the pilot called, obviously distracted.

"We near any repair or junk yards?"

"Not as far as I can see."

"Any on the way to our destination?"

"I still don't have an encyclopaedic knowledge of junk yard locations, but I don't see any mineral clusters that might suggest one."

Sauraxen's muscles clenched to flee. "*At* our destination?"

"I'm gonna stop you. In this sub-orbit, there aren't any apparent junkyards. Everything broken gets stripped or abandoned to –oh fuck!–" The centre of gravity on the ship shifted with the unexpected movement and no emergency engine to back up the overburdened old home engine. Sauraxen's slightly clingy appendages stuck to the table, but the other trio in the aufenthaltsraum collapsed out of their chairs. "The void," Matter finished. "Can we close that door again now?"

"Nei worries," Basti called back, scrambling to his feet and swiping the door closed.

Everybody returned to their seats.

"We need to take a detour," Sauraxen demanded.

"Sauraxen, we don't have the pay to afford a new engine, even if this job didn't have a deadline so quickly approaching. How long can we manage?"

Sauraxen hissed, leaping off the table to pace around the room. "At a push, if we're careful... we can probably manage until we need a fuel refill."

"You're amazing. I'll try to prioritise this. Une promesse."

Sauraxen shifted out of the aufenthaltsraum, hovering in the corridor as she tried to calm a little of her desperate desire to run.

"Auraxen," Brruuh spoke quietly as he emerged from the aufenthaltsraum after her.

"Raxen is fine," she corrected.

Brruuh's ears dipped – embarrassed? Touched? "Raxen," he repeated, the way he said her nickname sent a shiver down her scales. It felt reverent. Like a wonder. Like someone finding out the name of a beautiful flower for the first time. "Can I talk with you?"

"Sure, you want to go to engineering? Or your office?"

Brruuh weighed up his options, tilting his head from side to side, fingers twitching. "Engineering?"

Engineering, Sauraxen's workspace and base of operations, rather than Brruuh's office. Either this wasn't an official talk, or it was something Brruuh thought would upset Sauraxen so much that she needed to be in her own space.

She led Brruuh down the gravity well and into engineering where she sat on her desk pressed up under the stairs. "What's up?"

Brruuh twitched, as if uncertain how to start. "I wanted to talk about your ex-girlfriend."

Sauraxen let out a groan. "You really don't need to. I don't miss Liz, I'm all better now. I've moved on."

"That is not... Really? Just, that's it?"

Sauraxen shrugged. "We don't have monogamy on Pitzk – actually we don't have relationships on Pitzk."

"You don't?"

"Nei. We have–" she paused, aware that harrushetti had serious rules about privacy in intimate relationships, even if just from talking with Sebastian about his relationship with Dimae. "Coupling interactions, but there's not really a system of long term... coupling groups."

"How are you raised?"

"Separate people. A few people come together to create eggs. When the eggs hatch, the hatchlings call out and a vava comes to care for them."

"Vava?" Brruuh echoed.

"Raising parent. It's a huge part of how we build our society. Vavas are always vavas, from adulthood at least. Everything else is fluid."

Brruuh chirped as he took that in. "We don't have gender on Harrush. We all use he/him pronouns in ECE because it was the first one listed on the translation guide and once a habit has formed it is hard to break."

"You get it then. I doubt you came down here to chat about wrexi traditions and culture, though."

"Ah, nei. Not exactly."

Not exactly?

"I wanted to talk with you about the prospect of a relationship on this type of close-quarters vessel."

"Are you worried about Sebastian and Dimae? Because they've been together so long now and I already checked the soundproofing on their quarters so –"

"Nei," Brruuh cut her off. "Not them."

Sauraxen tilted her head. "Is this about my friendship with Matter?"

"Nei, not that either." Brruuh's tongue darted out to touch his nose, giving Sauraxen the impression of when humans licked their lips in hesitation. "How would you deal with a cross-cultural relationship? How would you deal with a relationship on this kind of close quarter's vessel?"

Sauraxen tugged her legs up under herself. "When it comes to cross-cultural relationships, it's all about balance.

You each need to talk about your expectations from a relationship – nothing is normal because your foundations are so different. Then you have to agree to find a balance together. There's a lot of communication required." She lifted her hair over her shoulder, hiding her body behind its curtain. She'd tried really hard with Liz. The conversation had happened at the beginning of their relationship and then Liz had thrown her own words into her face when Sauraxen had found her in bed with someone else. "When it comes to relationships on ships like these..." She played her hands over her hair and her clothes, tracing over the tiny ridges and bumps in the fabric of her shorts. "It's hard. It's one thing to come onto the ship with a relationship that's already established, like Basti and Dimae, but starting a relationship is more complicated. The risk of it ending on bad terms is pretty high and it can be hard to be around the person after that."

Brruuh made a quiet, affirmative noise.

"Why? Are you thinking of asking Matter out?"

Brruuh's voice came out almost silent, tickling over Sauraxen's nerves. "Not Matter."

Not Matter. Who else could he be talking about? Harrushetti weren't known for managing polyamory, so he couldn't be referencing Sebastian or Dimae, or Sebastian and Dimae as a pair. Which only left... "Oh..."

"If you are not amenable to this conversation, just tell me and I will leave it and we will never discuss it again."

Almost immediately he spun on his heel to leave.

"Wait!" Sauraxen called, thinking of Brruuh's soft furred skin, of the intensity with which he observed her. Reframing their interactions up until now. She had read them as predator-prey, but he had apparently seen her as appealing.

Sauraxen was always nervous at the prospect of being attractive. Wrexi were known for being alluring in a variety of ways – even just her recent run-in with the wicker basket was enough to solidify that once again. But Brruuh didn't seem to be captivated by her appearance. He hadn't even mentioned it. And his assertion that he would leave if she wanted him to...

But what about harrushetti hyper-monogamy? She wouldn't know until they talked about it. There was no harm in a little conversation about relationships, if they couldn't meet each other's needs, surely they could take the offer back off the metaphorical table.

She let out an excited little peep, the sound echoing in the blue glow of engineering and revealing Brruuh's soft and fuzzy outline in surprisingly stark contrast as he shifted on his feet. Making himself intentionally visible to her. "I'm amenable."

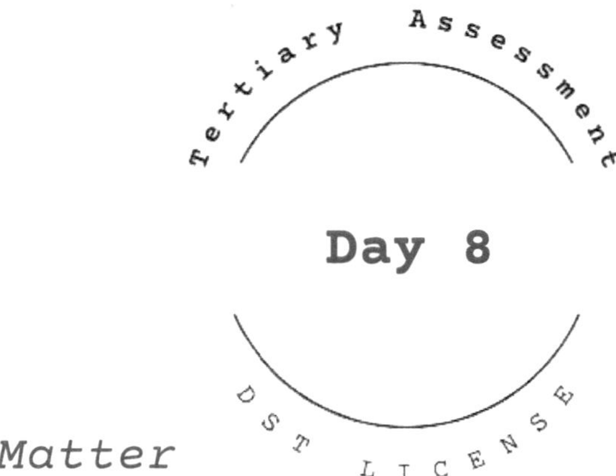

Matter

"Axen," Matter started, exhaling the word more than speaking it. They kept their hands closed by their sides, making sure not to reach out, not to cling to Sauraxen so desperately.

The blue and yellow glow of the mushrooms lit engineering only enough for Matter to make out the outline of Sauraxen. It was better this way. It was better if they couldn't see her properly. It was better if they kept their distance.

Matter had always aligned with Sauraxen fast. It was part of being best friends, and possibly part of how Sauraxen interacted with the world. Sensory output and input translated all too easily to tele-empathetic waves.

Which meant Matter knew. They knew Sauraxen and Brruuh had started something together. And they knew Brruuh was a harrushetti and that meant hyper-monogamy.

Sauraxen looked up at them.

Matter clenched their hands tighter. Reinforcing their intended boundaries.

"I just wanted to tell you..."

"Don't worry about it," Sauraxen offered into the space Matter's words had left when emotion welled too strongly against their skin.

"Don't...?"

"I know we weren't – we aren't a traditional relationship. You and I are a wrexi style thing: friends and sex. Brruuh needs a more committed style."

"I know–" The fact that Sauraxen knew Matter knew about Brruuh. This feeling was indescribably in earth common eurean, even ouaeahhn language struggled to communicate it. This connection.

"But you're okay with me and Brruuh–"

"Of course, I'm happy you're happy."

"And you're feeling like you need to officially end our sexual encounters."

"Well..."

"And I appreciate that, but it's not necessary. You and I both know how this works. We're not going to lose what we have just because we're shifting into a new style."

Matter had no words. They let out a strained attempt at a peep Sauraxen might hear as a smile – she'd shrug off the strain as just Matter not being fluent in the language – and retreated from engineering with their heart thumping so hard against their sternum it might well break their ribs.

Their vision shimmered, their joints ached. Nian, annu – they needed to contain this feeling before it burst out of them like an overfilled balloon. They needed to wash off the distress until it was all gone and they could pretend it didn't hurt anymore.

Sauraxen was right. They had shifted in and out of different styles of friendship over the years. Together and not, sexual and not. It had never felt like this before and Matter couldn't figure out what had changed. What it was about this time that left them so... empty. Alone. Yman.

Brruuh

"Matter!" Between Sebastian's yell and the pounding on the wall, Brruuh had little recourse but to emerge from his quarters. It sounded like quite the argument waiting to happen and, as a cognitivist, Brruuh was primed to intervene. Even if he had been on downtime.

Sebastian stood in the upper hallway of the ship, hammering one fist against the bathroom door.

"Fuck off!" Matter called from inside, voice muffled both by the closed door and the running water.

"Matter, you have been in there forever!"

"Yasean, Sebastian. I'll be done when I'm done!"

Sebastian didn't stop hammering.

More ouaeahhn language, its usual sighs and breaths turned hissing like an angry snake. It set Brruuh's fur on end.

The door swooshed open, releasing a cloud of steam and Matter, most of the way into their jumpsuit, chest bared for the world to see – at least the world of the ship.

Their skin glittered with water trailing over patterns raised in their skin. Brruuh had seen some of it on their arms but he hadn't realised it travelled all the way over their torso, had never anticipated seeing it disappear under a jumpsuit tied precariously at the waist with only its sleeves.

Their hair fell in a damp curtain, spirals of dripping purplish ropes. From a logical standpoint, and with Sebastian's reminder, Brruuh knew Matter had the same malleable hair as the Captain, but he had never considered what Matter's hair might look like not meticulously tied back whether in its usual pair of spheres on top of their head or the plait they sometimes wore over their shoulder.

"Some of us are working on low contact, Captain." The way Matter said captain held a series of loaded implication that gave Brruuh a clearer idea of how the empathetic piece of ouaeahhn language might work. "Showers help."

They shoved past the captain and back toward either their room or the pilot's console but froze when they saw Brruuh. They glanced down at their bared torso, water droplets still running down it.

"Sorry." They awkwardly tried to shift into the top half of their jumpsuit, the fabric clinging to their wet skin.

"It's okay," Brruuh reassured. It shouldn't have been. If Matter had been a harrushetti, or they had been on Harrush, it wouldn't have been. But Matter was an ouaeahhn. And this was a multi-species ship. And Sauraxen wore a lot less than this at her most dressed. "Can I ask...?"

"You can ask whatever you like." Matter said, distracted by wiggling back out of their jumpsuit's top with a relieved sigh.

"The markings. Are they natural or on purpose? Are they like my stripes or like a human tattoo?"

"Kinda both. We develop them over time when something important or dramatic happens that leaves an impression on us." They pointed at one on their inner forearm, a series of spirals inter-woven with one another, pointed ends sticking out, filling Brruuh's head with thoughts of the possibilities of leaving a place and all the wondrous options laid out because of it. "This is from when I left Ouaeahhn."

"Do you know when they are going to happen?"

Matter shrugged. "Sometimes you get a feeling about it, other times they surprise you."

Brruuh's eyes landed on one over Matter's heart – at least if their heart was where a harrushetti heart was. He couldn't have begun to describe the appearance of it with the way it filled him with that cold, wet feeling of drowning, of being pulled to the surface of almost freezing water by a piece of wood he shouldn't even really have had. The feeling of loss that always came with that particular memory.

Matter followed his gaze and hunched in on themself. "They're not always good memories. I should go get dressed properly."

Before Brruuh could say anything more, Matter disappeared into their quarters.

He turned to try and talk to Sebastian, only to find himself alone in the corridor. With a sigh he retreated to his rooms once again.

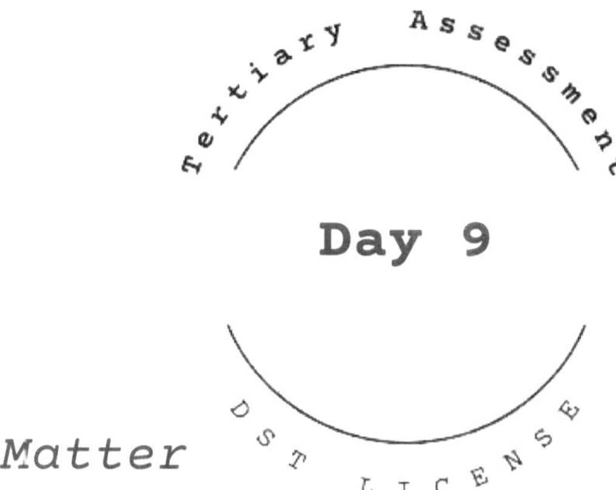

Day 9

Matter

The clunk of the legs locking in their extended position upon landing travelled up to the pilot's console in a reverberating kind of way. Matter launched out of the chair and dashed to the gravity chamber.

"Wait!" they hollered at the grind of the descending boarding plank.

Basti and Sauraxen turned from where they stood at the edge of the plank, external light sneaking through the gap to cast weird shadows across their faces.

"I gotta get off the ship, Basti. I can't sit in that chair anymore."

Sebastian chewed his lip. "You did work really hard to get us here. If Sauraxen doesn't mind."

The way he said it gave Matter the impression that he very much wanted Sauraxen to mind. The real question was why?

"You're kidding," Sauraxen snorted. "I'm still trying to feel clean after those shed-hair carpets."

"Shed-hair carpets?" Matter's eyebrows drew together.

"Time," Sebastian chided, pushing on Matter's shoulder to encourage them down the boarding plank.

Almost too quiet for Matter to hear, Sauraxen whispered, "That O.H. thing isn't going to be a problem, right?"

"I think they can pass for human well enough," Basti whispered back. "Keep guard for us?"

Matter waited at the base of the boarding plank for Basti to catch up. They could ask. They could investigate the fear Sebastian had about them being mined for Ouaeahhn Hormone again, but where would it get them? Then again, it would have been nice for him to mention that they had to pretend to be fully human.

The atmosphere of Clickglobe, the parallel planet to Clicksphere that followed the same orbit, made Matter want to sneeze.

Mountains loomed in the distance, rugged and way too much like termite hills for Matter's liking. Clickbugs were one thing but termites ate wood and ouaeahhn had evolved from trees. Between that and the O.H. problem Sebastian wasn't telling them about, leaving the ship might have been a bad idea. Too late for that now, though.

Basti lead Matter through a covered glass walkway and into a building filled with – yup, those were one-and-a-half metre tall termites dressed in business suits. Black business suits with white collared buttoned shirts and bright red ties. How weird. Matter hadn't expected to see anything weirder than Sauraxen wandering into a wicker basket – seriously, a wicker basket!

"Hello?" Sebastian called, the translator clipped around his forearm like a wide metal-ish bracelet buzzing to life and creating some kind of undercurrent of clicking attuned to the clickbugs communication wavelength. "My name is Captain LeaYaPar-Jones, I have a package from Clicksphere."

One of the termites shuffled up to Basti, looking him and Matter up and down as if disgusted. At least it went both ways. Then again, maybe it was Matter's jumpsuit – black today – or Sebastian's jumper and jeans. Maybe those weren't up to the clothing standards of this business establishment. Or even just that they weren't uniform.

If Sebastian ever tried getting Matter into a uniform, they just might quit. The last uniform Matter had worn, the zip had broken and they had needed to be cut out of it and had to pay for the privilege of getting stuck in the first place!

"Come inside," the termite-like clickbug invited, leading Basti through the glass door to the interior of what Matter was desperately trying not to call a mound.

As soon as he stepped through, the door slammed shut between them. Alarms blared, lights flashing all over the mound interior.

Matter's heart jumped into their throat. "Basti?" They asked as he spun to face them, panic coating his features.

Termites in bright red shirts with no ties or jackets surrounded Sebastian, appearing from nowhere. In their hands were some kind of weapon-like items.

"Basti!" Matter yelled, pressing up against the glass as Sebastian disappeared within the clickbug security hoard.

Dimae

Dimae didn't bother to take the time to examine the red heat of Clickglobe. The mirage-like waves of hot air didn't pull his attention away from his task even as they scorched at the hair inside his ears, leaving him even more unbalanced.

Dimae had always been skilled at maintaining his focus, rarely distracted by anything until he met Sebastian. Sebastian had changed his life.

In harrushetti stories of old, your bond mate would be the person who stopped the world for you, who set the ice under your feet melting. Dimae had never put that much stock in it, but when Sebastian Jones had appeared in his medi-bay with a huge box of supplies, muscular arms all bare and toned and the same deep brown as the splotches in Dimae's fur, it had stopped Dimae in the middle of treating a patient.

Then Sebastian had smiled. And Dimae had inhaled that smell of his. Humans always smelled salty and often perfumed. But something about Sebastian was different. It was like the whole world had narrowed to that smile and those hands and that drawl as he asked where Dimae needed the supplies.

Dimae charged down the covered path on Clickglobe to the tall building, clearly sealed off by red tape across the doors and the lack of lights on the sensors that would set the doors to open.

A communication link glowed on the door, reflecting off the glass in a way that hurt Dimae's eyes. He narrowed his pupils against it, glaring inside until one of the bug creatures approached.

"You have my husband," he snarled. The words appeared in text on the glass between him and the clickbug, a different alphabet appearing beneath them as it translated the words. "Give him back."

The clickbug skittered around on its spindly legs.

"Now!" Dimae demanded.

"I'll get a–" the translator beeped and displayed indecipherable symbols as it failed to translate the title. The clickbug skittered away.

Dimae waited so long he almost tapped on the glass with his claws to gain new attention. If he had had a tail it would have been sweeping side to side, but most harrushetti had lost their tails as they shifted to primarily bipedal walking. Basin harrushetti sometimes retained theirs thanks to the uneven footing in the Basin on Harrush.

Finally, a different but identical clickbug appeared, translator coil circling its neck, gold and elegant if somewhat clunky. It took Dimae's mind back to when Sebastian had taken him around one of the museums on some Earth Colony or other and showed him an ancient Celtic torque.

"Friend?" the new clickbug asked, the word appearing in translated text once again.

"You have my husband," Dimae repeated, secondary vocal cords thundering under the words. "Give him back to me, now."

"Sorry, friend, that won't be possible."

"Your reason?"

"He is with our security."

"Your reason?"

"He brought a weaponised piece of cargo into our mound."

"We are cargo runners, that is our job. He was employed to deliver that cargo."

"Irrelevant!" the clickbug interrupted.

Dimae's lips pulled back, revealing his sharp teeth.

"He must pay reparations."

"What reparation?"

The clickbug's antennae wiggled and its maw clicked together in a way that wasn't translated. "You can make reparations for him?"

"Only if you give him back."

"That is not how we do things."

Dimae snarled proper, fangs fully revealed as he opened his mouth, ready to smash through the glass and take his husband by force. He would not be separated from his bond mate, especially not by a puny bug with a superiority complex.

The clickbug stuttered, clacking to itself. "I'm sure something can be arranged," it finished quickly, words flashing up on the glass all at once.

The door opened and Dimae launched after the skittering bug.

Sebastian sat in a hand dug, circular room. Solid brown clay floor scuffed from hundreds of footsteps, solid brown clay walls with patterns of digging etched into every pinsect. It created a claustrophobic environment, and, despite missing the main hallmarks of most prisons, could not have been more obviously a cell.

Sebastian's hair hung loose around his head, released from the quick bun he'd thrown it into that morning. It shifted as he turned his face up at the sound of Dimae's quiet steps.

Purple had risen over his temple, across his right eye, and down his cheek.

A growl stalked up Dimae's throat at the sight even as Sebastian's bruised face broke into a crooked smile. "I knew you'd rescue me," he breathed.

Was he concussed? How could he be smiling in a situation like this?

Dimae tapped his lower lip with his tongue. Growls continued to rumble through his secondary vocal cords, layering under the whole conversation. "They require reparations."

"Alright... What reparations?"

"Cargo drop off." It had taken a lot of negotiating, but Dimae didn't want to tell Sebastian that, especially not right now. What Dimae wanted right now was to scoop Sebastian into his arms and take him back to their nest and never let him go ever again.

"We can do that."

"Nei payment."

Basti sighed, smoothing a hand over his free hair. "I guess we don't have much of a choice."

Dimae hummed.

"Will they let me out? If we agree?"

"They let me in because I agreed. I am taking you with me when I leave."

Sebastian stuck out a leg.

At first Dimae couldn't get past his bare feet. They had taken his shoes? They had taken Sebastian's shoes away from him? Why in the name of stable ice would they have done that?

And then he realised what Sebastian was directing him to was, in fact, the shackle around his ankle.

The growl overtook Dimae's voice. He grabbed the chain of it, extending his claws into the space until the chain links snapped under his grip.

He scooped Sebastian into his arms and turned to find his way out of the mound, with or without permission.

By the time he managed to get him into the covered tunnel toward the ship, Basti was more coherent and insisted on being put down so he could try to walk.

There were several piles of crates sat at the base of the boarding plank. A very red-reflecting Matter stood guard over both the crates and the ship itself. Their eyes had turned from their indescribable holographic colour that most people mistook for a fashion mod, to a full, clear reflection of the redness of the dirt and sky of Clickglobe.

Dimae didn't need to ask why Matter had lost themself to their reflective state. He'd seen it in the way they paced, the way they wrung their hands together, the way they hadn't met his eye when reporting back what had happened before Dimae had gone down to the mound itself. And then Matter had done the human thing, the thing that reinforced his continuing view of them as more human than ouaeahhn. Tears had spilled down their cheeks.

The tracks from those tears still marred Matter's face but their jaw stood out strong as they asked. "Did you agree to this?"

"You wouldn't let them on the ship?" Sebastian almost laughed.

"Nei. Not after what they pulled with you." Matter huffed. "You really think I would casually welcome their cargo after – what the fuck happened to your face?"

Basti waved a hand but didn't shift out of Dimae's supportive grip. "Just a couple of bruises. Let's get this stuff on board and get out of here."

Matter peered suspiciously at the piles of cargo crates on wheeled trolleys. "What's in it?"

"We are not to know," Dimae answered. "Part of the contract."

Matter pressed their lips together but they grabbed one of the trolley handles and wheeled the cargo up the boarding plank and into the belly of the ship.

"I promise I'll come to medi-bay later, but I gotta make sure everyone's okay and on board with the mission and stuff first. I owe my crew an explanation. At least what I can give of one."

Dimae wanted to argue. He wanted to tell Sebastian not to be so self-sacrificing. He wanted to demand Sebastian let Dimae take care of him. Both as his doctor and his husband, his bond mate. But Dimae had been pair bonded with his human long enough to know better than to say any of that. It would just make Sebastian feel guilty while he did what he felt he needed to anyway.

Sebastian worked hard to embody everything humans wanted and expected from their captains. Like his heroes from the old tele vids, he was selfless, caring, and put the crew's needs above his own happiness – and occasionally health, much to Dimae's continued and eternal stress. The amount of times Basti had made him watch those tele vids and Dimae still couldn't fully understand the Earth Common Nord'Americ accents and language.

"Okay," Dimae agreed.

Sebastian opened and closed his mouth. "I thought

you'd've made me argue that one."

"I hate those double contractions. End your use of them," Dimae grumbled half-heartedly.

This time Sebastian's smile was a little more convincing and eased the strain in Dimae just a little.

"Matter?" Sebastian called. "Once that's loaded up, I want a full crew meeting in the aufenthaltsraum to discuss what happened and the current mission plan."

Matter grumbled something Dimae couldn't understand – probably ouaeahhn language.

Dimae helped Basti up the gravity chamber and into the chair at the head of the dining table. He placed a pair of pain-killer tablets and a glass of water in front of his husband and folded his arms.

Sebastian took the medicine.

Brruuh

The call to the aufenthaltsraum surprised Brruuh, especially with it being announced over ship comms rather than just called out in loud vocalisations. It surprised him almost as much as the biting scent of pain wafting from the room.

The first thing that caught his attention was the yellowish-purple reflection over Matter's hair where it lay in a rough plait over their shoulder.

Bruises had been a surprise to Brruuh when he had begun working with humans. The idea of them made him vaguely nauseated. Broken blood vessels would probably kill a harrushetti, but the fact that they showed through human skin, and humans mostly ignored them...

Brruuh examined Matter for injuries and, when he couldn't find any, he turned his attention to the only other human on the ship. Brruuh didn't know whether wrexi were capable of bruising, but Sauraxen's inescapable rock, mushroom, and sugar scent was notably absent from the room.

A tiny, kitten-like meow escaped from Brruuh at the sight of the purple splodges coating the entire right side of Sebastian's face and disappearing down the neck of his jumper. By the scent of it, there were more, worse injuries hidden with the rest of those bruises.

"I'm fine," Basti countered, responding before Brruuh found any words to land on. "And thank you for coming."

The soft sound of feet behind him drew Brruuh away from the door. Sauraxen entered the aufenthaltsraum, pausing to take in the situation, before crawling onto the sofa in an awkward-looking but obviously comfortable for her crouch.

"Alright, crew, grab your drinks, get settled, and let's get this meeting started."

Dimae handed out mugs filled with different drinks. Sauraxen took her wide brimmed mug easily and held it up to her face. Matter took their mug with shaking hands, setting it almost immediately down on the table in front of them. Coffee sloshed onto the surface, brown liquid reflecting distorted light.

Dimae set Brruuh's mug on the dining table near where he stood and took his own seat next to Sebastian at the head of the table.

Brruuh picked up the mug and leaned against the wall near to Sauraxen.

"The last piece of cargo we were hired to transport," Sebastian began. "It was a bomb."

"What?" Sauraxen blurted.

"Ja, a bomb. On our ship. Since Clicksphere. And it set off the detectors in the building on Clickglobe." He paused, eyes tracking over to Matter who had a white knuckled grip on their mug. Basti's hand shifted up to touch the bruises on his face. "Understandably, they were annoyed..."

A quiet crunch sounded. Basti flinched.

Brruuh followed his flicking ears to the source of the noise. Coffee spread out on the table, pieces of broken mug tinkling down into the puddle of it. The sharp tang of blood intermingled with the coffee smell as the pieces that used to be Matter's mug cut into their hands.

Dimae released his bond mate's shoulder to rise and shift around the table, grabbing a small, handheld box as he moved. He set the box on the chair next to Matter and crouched, taking their hands into his own.

"As reparations," Sebastian continued, as if Matter hadn't just broken a mug with their bare hands. "They've asked us to transport the cargo currently in our cargo bay to a moon on the edge of Clickclick. That will place us really nicely on the fringes of the system, so we can move on. Does anyone have any questions?"

"What happened to your face?" Brruuh asked without thinking. He should have kept that one to himself, he knew, even if Dimae's head hadn't twisted toward him in an open-mouthed hiss. But the scents in the room were overwhelming, pain and more pain and blood and bruises.

And Brruuh had smelled all of this before when the

flood had devastated his kitten-home, the Eastern Basin. The crack of the mug breaking had been too much, far far too much like the crack of the dome.

Sebastian reached up to touch gentle fingers to his face once again. "That would be the result of their dislike of our having inadvertently brought a bomb into their midst."

"They beat you?" Again Brruuh spoke without thought, tiny squeaks escaping his secondary vocal cords.

"How barbaric," Sauraxen breathed.

"Nei need to worry." Sebastian's drawl was too present. Too forced. "I'm totally fine. Just a couple of bruises."

Brruuh's ears dipped but he didn't ask any more questions. Dimae was busy and stressed and it wouldn't do to harass the doctor by asking inappropriate questions to his bond mate. Not to mention it would be counterproductive to his job as a cognitivist.

Brruuh let out one final noise, a harrushetti half-apology for Dimae as he turned and fled the room, leaving his undrunk mug of whatever Dimae had made on the table behind him.

Sauraxen

Brruuh fled the aufenthaltsraum with a soft mewl and Sauraxen surged to her feet and over the sofa arm to follow him before she really thought about it.

"Brruuh?" she asked, outside his crew quarters door.

He let out a quiet squeak that barely travelled through

the metal door.

"Do you want to come to my room and..." Would he be offended at the suggestion? Was her room too personal? In the beginnings of their conversations about a potential relationship he'd emphasised the importance of his own personal space. But this was about hers. If he was a wrexi or even an ouaeahhn, she'd offer comfort sex, but harrushetti only fucked with serious 'I love you' levels of intimacy. So... "Cuddle?"

The door swished open. Brruuh's ears were plastered to his head. Sauraxen took him by the hand and led him into her own quarters, sitting down on the bed she didn't use and opening her arms to invite him in.

Hesitantly, Brruuh let himself sink into her. He trembled lightly and Sauraxen ran soft hands over his jumper-covered back.

"Do you want to lie down?" she whispered.

He nodded into her neck, nose surprisingly warm compared to the rest of him.

Slowly, ever so gently, Sauraxen pulled him down onto the bed. He curled up against her, nose pressed as close to her neck as he could, face shifting every now and again as he nuzzled into her scales.

His jaw opened, warm, dry tongue barely touching her scales as he inhaled.

"Scent based," Sauraxen breathed.

He made a confused noise.

"It's a joining point for us. Scent. You and I are both scent reliant species."

He said nothing, not responding to that except where his breath hitched against her scales.

"Is the talking helping?"

He nodded.

Sauraxen wracked her brain for anything to say to him, anything mundane and normal that he might be able to identify with.

"Basti was my roommate at the academy. We literally shared a room – that's a thing some people opt in for because it's cheaper than having a room to yourself. I had never been alone before, I was desperate for company. I still don't really like being alone, it's just not a thing on Pitzk." She nuzzled her chin on the top of his head. "But Basti didn't really understand that. He kept leaving stuff all over the room and being confused when I took that to mean it was free to grab. The first time I showed up for a lecture wearing one of his hoodies he got so frustrated I could feel the heat radiating off his face. Did you know humans flush when they're angry?"

She snickered. "Anyway, it lead to a serious conversation about what was and wasn't appropriate behavioural standards, according to humans. And an even longer conversation about holding aliens to human standards – or, I suppose, holding aliens to your own cultural standards. Which, by the way, was the whole reason he got a top grade on his paper in managing inter-crew disagreements."

"I wouldn't like my partner to wear another person's clothes," Brruuh murmured, voice soft, nei undercurrent from his secondary vocal cords. "In harrushetti courting – traditional harrushetti courting of old – you would offer your cloak to the person you wanted to court and you would dance for them. It was meant to represent you offering them your protection from threats and the cold – Harrush is an ice planet."

"Oh?" Sauraxen asked, lifting Brruuh's hand and playing with his fingers and the sharp tips of his claws.

"Old traditions talk about having one designated homemaker and one designated protector but most modern people disagree with that. It's a nice concept, though."

"Showing off for your potential partner?" Sauraxen teased.

Brruuh hummed.

"We don't have much by way of courting rituals on Pitzk. Like I said, relationships don't exist in any capacity I've learnt earth common eurean words for. I like them, though. Been a bit of a sucker for falling into relationships since I left the planet. Human courting is pretty boring compared to dancing for your partner."

Brruuh let out a soft hum.

"Would you want to be the dancer who offered a cloak? Or the observer who received it?"

Brruuh nuzzled impossibly closer.

Sauraxen's hair expanded, excitement, nerves, affection all spiralling through her in a way she wouldn't have expected considering what lead to them being this close to one another.

"I don' know." Brruuh's words were starting to get garbled, as if he was too tired to properly move his mouth. "Both is good."

Sauraxen smiled, tucking his head firmly under her chin, and agreed, "Both is good."

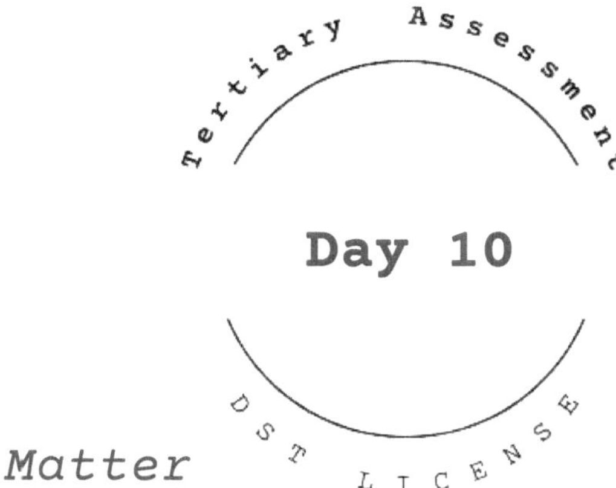

Matter

For a full day-night cycle after Basti's return to the ship, their hands hurt and their heart ached. They should have taken a break, should have gone to bed, but they didn't want to leave the ship on autopilot. Autopilot was slow, particularly so in a bustling galaxy like Clickclick with the amount of rubble, asteroids, and other shit littering the void and battering against the ships edges. Especially since the emergency engine was out of commission. Matter wanted nothing so much as to get out of Clickclick as quickly as possible. To leave it behind, to travel so far they couldn't even see the sparkling of its star.

Unfortunately for Matter's desires, the announcement of a travelling marketplace blasted over the ship's comms, its jingle loud enough that Sebastian burst into the pilot's console and asked Matter to dock.

The TM class ship looked a lot like a wide brimmed hat

with tassels where all the different ships had docked on the edge. Matter clicked in to autodock with the assistance of the docking bots.

The door creaked and squealed as it opened, the rumble of quiet voice travelling around the ship in a comforting manner as Brruuh, Dimae, Sauraxen, and Sebastian decided who was going where and who would stay behind to guard the ship.

Matter padded quietly into the aufenthaltsraum and turned on the coffee machine.

One coffee and most of the way through a plate of pasta, Matter's wristband beeped, pixels appearing over it that read "Emergency – Sebastian" in purple-red letters. They swiped their fingers over it to bring up the pixelated purple-pink version of Sebastian's panicked face.

Ripples appeared and faded behind him. He must be in the marketplace and have not put his back to the wall.

"Don't be mad," he started. "I need your help."

"What happened?"

"They took her."

"What?"

"I think I accidentally traded Sauraxen."

"You sold her!" Matter exploded.

"Just get down here!" Co-ordinates popped up where Basti's face had been.

Matter surged to their feet, abandoning their pasta plate to hammer on Brruuh's office door.

He pulled open the door, ears perked forward, attention focused toward Matter.

"I need you to come with me."

"Okay," he agreed readily. Matter couldn't have said what his internal reasoning was, Brruuh was still a mystery to them in so many ways.

"I need you to keep me from losing my temper."

Brruuh's ears twitched but Matter didn't bother to think about why. They spun and headed off the ship.

The Travelling Marketplace bustled. Each of the shops was contained within its own space, unlike Station 24 where people set up market stalls where they wanted, including blocking pathways if they so desired. It was bland and boring to look at, even with the personalised signs over each shop.

People of all kinds made their way through the spaces, shifting around each other like grain through a sieve. A kil with its many tentacles shifted around, altering shape to fit through every space it could see. A thial in full body armour to protect their vulnerable skin and aquatic breath systems stomped from place to place. And plenty of bipedal bimanual species that matched the crew Matter travelled with stood and chatted and shopped. To their left, a pah-rushi spread their wings, shaking them out in a stretch.

Sebastian stood, shifting from foot to foot, wringing his hands together, head whipping around to look for Matter and keep an eye on the shop in question.

The square entryway filled most of the shop space. The sign above it flickering in different colours and languages that Matter didn't take the time to search out for one they recognised.

"Excuse me?" they called to the trader, who hesitated in front of a door to the rear of the space – filled with all sorts of textiles, carrying devices, and an assortment of mechanical nonsense Matter couldn't figure out.

"How can I help you, friend?" the trader asked,

translator on the table in front of the register buzzing to life and humming quietly under the words.

"Give me back Sauraxen." Matter managed to keep their tone pleasant, the surprisingly comforting presence of Brruuh hovering at their shoulder giving them more confidence in their abilities than the last time they had needed to argue for the return of their best friend.

The trader shuffled, as if not understanding, even as the translator buzz continued under Matter's words.

"The wrexi," Matter clarified.

"I'm sorry, friend, the pet was offered in return for these engine parts." The trader nodded to a pile of twisted metal on the surface with the cash register.

Oh joy, a species that kept wrexi as pets. It wasn't the first time Matter had been through this. One of wrexi's most notable survival traits as a prey species was their cuteness in the eyes of anything with even half a predatory instinct. Unfortunately this led to a lot of these kinds of discussions. "She's not a pet, she's our engineer."

"Sorry, friend, the translation is bad."

Matter huffed out a breath. Okay, what could they parse out about this person's probable culture? They couldn't put a name to their species or planet. Colourful feathers and a beak-like protrusion on the front of their face – keeping a neutral expression was probably wise. The trader's claw-like hands hadn't moved, even to gesture to the machine parts – probably a low-gesture culture, then. Partial exoskeleton where there were no feathers, even Matter's ouaeahhn sturdiness wouldn't be of much use here.

Their hands fisted at their sides. "Sebastian had nei right to trade her."

The trader shuffled again. "She was not his to trade?"

"Nei."

"Then why did he offer her?"

"The translation is bad," Matter repeated the trader's earlier words back at them. "He didn't mean to."

"Sorry friend," the trader said. "But the trade is made."

The buzzing of the translator grated against Matter's teeth. They clenched their jaw and took a deep breath. "Then we trade back."

"Sorry, friend, that trade deal is nei good for me."

"You're telling me you cheated Basti into accidentally trading our engineer, who is worth more than the engine parts you got her for?"

The trader shifted. The translator buzzed loudly before stating in a cold mechanical voice. "Shrug."

Brruuh's hand landed on Matter's shoulder, grounding them in the moment, reminding them to keep calm. The pinpricks of his claws clearly stating the calmness he demanded of Matter was something he didn't, himself, feel. He stepped up beside them, his wristband glowing with use. "Oh, look," he said, a false calm facade over his words. A tight, reedy noise suppressed inside his secondary vocal cords. "A trader-review site. How many stars would I rate this interaction? Hmm. One out of seven stars. And look, there is space to talk about exactly how you cheated us and went against IPA sentient-species standards by attempting to trade an IPA protected species."

The trader's claw-like hands snapped out in an attempt to disperse the pixels. A hiss like a broken steam valve escaped them. The translator clarified "aggression."

Matter didn't flinch, but Brruuh stumbled back, letting out a brief, suppressed hiss of his own.

"Give me back my friend," Matter insisted, voice flat.

The trader hissed again but unbolted the door to the store room. Matter couldn't help but burst inside to grab Sauraxen.

The wrexi pulled Matter out into the walkway before letting herself fall into their embrace.

"You need to stop rescuing me," she whispered.

"You need to stop needing to be rescued."

Sauraxen rubbed her face into Matter's neck. "You smell like pizza pockets."

What? No. This couldn't be happening. Not now. Not with Sauraxen. Matter extracted themself from the hug, passing Sauraxen off to the safest protector available.

Brruuh wrapped a protective arm around the lizardoid as Matter spun to Sebastian. They wrapped their rage and hurt around them like a protective blanket. "Explain yourself. Now."

"We were looking for that engine part Sauraxen needed and I thought the trader meant 'does she agree' not 'trade this for her'. I'm so sorry, Raxen! Stars, this is not what you need from a captain."

"Hey, Basti, take a breath," Sauraxen said, voice soft. "It could have been worse."

"It could have been so much worse!" Matter snarled. "Come on, Sebastian, you know better than to assume human gesturing patterns. You know – how could you let this happen? You're the one always telling me to be careful with Sauraxen!"

"Matter, calm down." Sauraxen ran her fingers lightly over Matter's lower back.

They threw up their hands. "I'll be on the ship. You lot can decide what to do about the engine part. I just..." They looked at Sauraxen, still clinging to Brruuh. Their body slumped. "I'll be on the ship," they muttered again, trudging back to the docking port so they could lock themself in their cabin and have emotions alone and protected from sharing them with an entire travelling marketplace.

Brruuh

He managed to get Sauraxen back to the ship, back to her quarters before the ice core at the centre of his chest shattered into pieces. The pressure of the past few days, of Sebastian getting hurt, of this awful situation with the trader and having to step in when he saw Matter ready to lose all semblance of self-control, the fear of losing a relationship so tenuously started.

He pressed his face into Sauraxen's neck, inhaling with open mouth to let the scent of her wash over him. It was tinged with stress, but unmistakably Sauraxen.

"Never do that again," he breathed.

"I didn't *try* to do it this time," she countered.

"Nei." With a gentle hand tucked under her hair he pressed her nose to his own neck.

She nuzzled, inhaled, breath shifting his fur and sending tingles to the tips of his ears.

"Okay," she said. "I'll try. I'm not going to leave you abruptly."

The tip of his tongue pressed against her scales. The taste of her exploded in his mouth. A moan rippled up his secondary vocal cords.

Before he knew it, Sauraxen's fingers had slid under his jumper, scales surprisingly rough against the vulnerable skin of his belly.

She pressed him up against the door of her quarters, his back against firm metal, his front against soft Sauraxen.

His claws dug into the metal behind him, no doubt leaving indents. He didn't care. His whole world had narrowed to the feeling of Sauraxen's body against his.

"You okay?" she asked.

Brruuh let out an affirmative chirrup before realising Sauraxen probably wouldn't know what that meant. "Ja."

"You're shaking."

"I've never... Harrushetti are hyper-monogamous. We pick one partner and we bond mate for life."

Sauraxen pulled back. "Are you sure it's me? Do you want to stop? Am I pushing you too far?"

Without thought, Brruuh scooped a hand around the back of her neck, sliding around her hair as if it parted for him – maybe it had. He pressed his mouth against the scales of her neck once again, licking with the barbed part of his tongue.

Sauraxen shuddered under his touch, shifting into what was obviously words in a language Brruuh didn't speak.

He huffed out a pleased breath. "It's worth the risk."

It took two moves and only one hand for Sauraxen to free herself from her clothes. Her other hand not leaving his body, lingering on the small of his back just above his tailbone.

Brruuh's own clothes were far more extensive, a jumper that Sauraxen had already pushed halfway up off his stomach. Trousers tucked into boots that she hadn't gone near yet.

"You don't have to," she huffed out, words a little sharper tinged than usual, flavoured with citrus tang. "I just wanted..."

But Brruuh pulled the jumper off anyway.

Sauraxen reattached to him immediately, climbing up his body like he was a particularly inviting tree. Her legs wrapped around his waist, once again setting off sparks in his ears.

Her claws, blunter than his own, traced the lines of his stripes as she pressed her face into his neck, breath shifting fur lightly, making him squirm under her touch. She pressed harder with her claws, the juxtaposition making his knees weak.

He lurched to the bed, sinking onto it with Sauraxen firmly perched in his lap.

She pushed against his shoulders.

He fell back against the mattress. Sauraxen leaned over him, her mouth tracing lines up his stomach.

He should have felt vulnerable, weak underneath her power, in such a position: stomach exposed, a mouth near it. Instead it was like a new engine had been discovered, or brought back to function inside him. Something viscous and wanting.

Again he pulled Sauraxen by the scruff of her neck, dragging her up his body, closer to his face. His other hand gripped her hips, claws extending unbidden and pressing against her scales. They were rough, firm, unbreakable. She writhed over him and he realised he was making continuous noises with both sets of vocal cords but couldn't find it in himself to care, to quash the noises that would surely be escaping into the corridor, bouncing around the ship as all noise was wont to do.

His fangs scraped at her neck and she pressed tighter to them, letting out a hiss that almost sounded aggressive to him. But the way her body moved, the wash of scents coming off her, none of that matched a noise of aggression.

"Mine," she growled into his neck.

Brruuh saw stars.

Sebastian

Basti stared up at the drapery coated ceiling. Propped up on a mountain of pillows, his mind swirled with thoughts. While it had taken some time to get used to the sheer volume of pillows and blankets Dimae needed in order to feel comfortable enough to sleep, they had been together so long now that it seemed normal.

Dimae purred softly beside him, so deeply asleep that his secondary vocal cords were working overtime. The purr was comforting, often that was enough to coax him back to sleep even on tough nights. But tonight...

Tonight Sebastian couldn't turn off his brain.

How had everything gone so awry so thoroughly? Had buying the ship been a risky investment? His first examination of it had told him the ship needed a little repair, but he hadn't thought it was this bad.

Maybe it was Basti's fault for putting pressure on his crew. R1bb1t model ships came with eight crew quarters, not including the captain's cabin which could sleep up to five human-sized adults. Having only five total crew, if he included Brruuh – should he include Brruuh? – Either way four or five crew was anywhere between half to even just a quarter of the intended crew.

Then again, without regular, paid jobs, Basti couldn't begin to afford to up his crew numbers. He could barely afford to maintain the crew and the ship as it was. And Matter was right when they had said he had lowballed his offer to them. Let alone Sauraxen. And he wasn't even paying Brruuh, who was definitely contributing to the continuing efforts aboard the ship.

Dimae shuffled in his sleep, making a more chirrup-ey noise. Basti pressed his lips together and carefully extracted himself from the bed, freezing any time Dimae made a noise or moved. His feet landed soundlessly on the rug-covered floor.

The metal grating of the cargo bay catwalk dug into the soles of his feet as he headed toward the gravity chamber to the upper floor. Sauraxen uninstalled the energy-saving processes in it, but with the way Matter had been walking lately, perhaps that wasn't such a bad idea.

The door to the aufenthaltsraum stood ajar, as it so often did, soft light leaking into the corridor. Basti couldn't hear whoever was in there as he let himself into the room and headed for the coffee machine.

Coffee late at night when he couldn't sleep was probably a bad idea but Basti needed the comfort. He even broke out his stash of Earth Colony 623 beans. The smell enveloped the aufenthaltsraum as soon as he opened the jar, filling the space with the comforting scent of home.

"It's not good to have elevators at night," a deep rumbling voice called from inside the rows of botany racks.

Elevators also known as stimulants. "Brruuh?" As if it

could have been anyone else with that voice. "What are you doing up?"

"Harrushetti are descended from cats. Typically we rest in bursts."

Basti frowned even as he continued brewing his coffee over the stove. "Dimae always sleeps through the night with me."

"Then he has trained himself to do this for you."

"Oh," Basti said, a soft smile breaking over his face, his chest warm as if he had already taken that first sip of coffee. He poured the brewed drink into his mug. "That's sweet."

"Which creates the question." Brruuh emerged from the plants like a tiger emerging from a forest. "Why are you not resting beside him and are instead in the aufenthaltsraum with me?"

Basti leaned on the counter and blew on his coffee. "I couldn't sleep."

"For what reason?"

Basti sighed and stared into the glorious brown, fragrant liquid as white steam swirled in the air. "Stress, I guess."

"What are you distressed about?"

Basti snorted. What wasn't he stressed about. But as Brruuh waited for him to say something, as he decided it would be better to keep his concerns to himself, especially after their less than stellar Secondary Assessment, his mouth opened to spill it out to the harrushetti cognitivist. "Did I make the right choice? Should I have taken captaincy for a reputable company first? Gained some extra knowledge? Should I have waited for a higher quality ship? Should I have looked for jobs before I got my crew together?" The questions rattled out of him like coffee beans out of a can, first one, then free falling and out of control.

Brruuh sank into one of the dining chairs. "Why did you choose not to take captaincy elsewhere first?"

"What?"

"Why did you choose not to take captaincy with a reputable company first?"

Sebastian sat at the head of the table, hand wrapped around his mug. "I didn't want to spend any more time away from Dimae. It's hard to be separated – I know humans don't have the same reactions as harrushetti to that, but the bond is still there and it's more than it ever was for my previous relationships. Most companies looking for captains already have a crew. I couldn't handle asking Dimae to pause being a doctor and neither of us wanted to spend the time apart."

"Do you feel those are good reasons?"

"Absolutely."

"Would you have gained more knowledge working for a reputable company? Or are you longing for a catch-net for when you fall?"

"I guess I'll learn more if I have to catch myself... and I do like being able to make my own rules."

"Why did you purchase this vessel?"

"R1bb1ts are sturdy and this one had ouaeahhn modifications already installed. Ouaeahhn thrusters are the best – they almost never break and they provide more manoeuvrability than any other choice. It just felt right."

"Do you think you could have found a better vessel? Do you want a different one?"

"I don't want to give up my baby. And the mods

Sauraxen has installed... I wouldn't give this thing up without a fight."

"You are giving good, well thought out reasons behind your decisions. These were not impulsive or, if they were, they were foundationally based."

Basti sipped his coffee, transported for the briefest instant to his father's farm, humid air clinging to him and bugs chirping away in the night air. "I'm scared of doing a bad job."

"A bad job of what?"

"All of it. A bad job of being a captain. A bad job of running the ship. A bad job of caring for the crew. I'm scared we won't earn enough to keep running, or to even get our Deep Space Travel License, let alone actually getting out into Deep Space."

"Do not try to live in the future."

"What?"

"You are trying to live in the future. You need to live in the present. You are worried about what will come later, instead, decide what you can do now to move toward where and what you want."

"But I'm letting everyone down."

"You are forgetting important things."

"What things?"

"A captain needs to manage crew, ja. But the crew is there to help the captain too. It's a delicate eco-system. Talking of delicate eco-systems. I will get back to the plants."

Sebastian didn't watch Brruuh disappear back into the botany racks. He stared into his coffee. Maybe he should open up with the crew. Would that make things easier? Was he trying to take too much on?

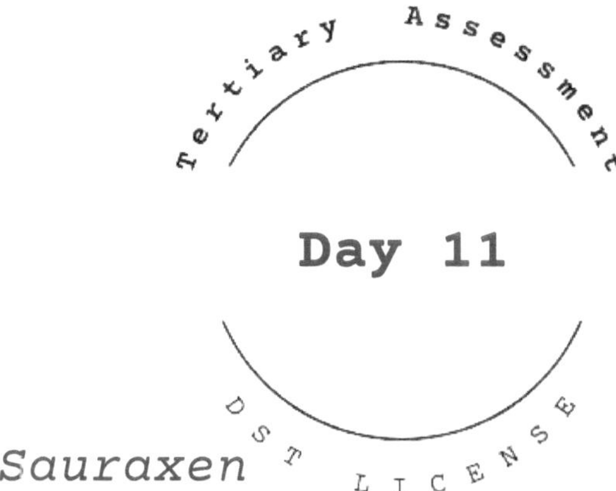

Sauraxen

The new engine part fit almost too well, bringing the emergency engine back online. Something about its quiet whirring had Sauraxen ready to run but she couldn't figure out what it was. She leaned close, knocking against it to create the right kind of echoes, laying one hand atop it as she did so for maximum possible perception. Nothing appeared to be wrong with it. She trilled at it in irritation.

"Raxen?" Brruuh called from the upper doorway.

Sauraxen abandoned the engine to meet him. She tilted her chin up in a display of happiness.

"Can we talk?"

"Of course. You want to come in?"

Brruuh stepped through the doorway and into the soft glow of the Pitzki mushrooms.

Sauraxen perched on the railing that separated the upper floor from the lower one. "What's up?"

"About the Travelling Marketplace."

"I'm fine," Sauraxen interrupted. She'd already had this conversation with both Dimae and Sebastian. Although, weirdly, she hadn't seen Matter since they stormed off.

"That is not what I was going to ask."

"Oh, it's just because I always end up having those discussions. People start to assume I can't take care of myself or that they need to hold a grudge. I know this is technically our second time going through the experience with the whole..." She rubbed the back of her neck sheepishly. "Wicker basket escapade but–"

"That is not what I was going to say either." Brruuh's laugh rumbled through her, setting her hair alight.

"I will let you talk then."

He scooped the back of her neck again, pressing his own forehead against hers. "I wanted to apologise for moving quickly and without thought."

"I enjoyed it."

"That is not the point."

His body radiated the cold of his own planet. It should have been uncomfortable to a lizard like her, but with the warm hum of engines around her it didn't matter, better yet, it was so deliciously Brruuh that the chill was somehow pleasant.

"I just need to ensure you would know to... let me down easily if you want to end what we started."

"Be gentle?" she asked, extending her spine to pull him closer and shifting her legs open so he could fit between them more neatly.

"Harrushetti can die of broken hearts. I don't want to use that to coerce you, but it's something you need to know now that we have..."

"Properly begun?" She offered, tilting her head as the thrill of pressing up against a predator mixed and mingled with the fact that it was Brruuh.

"I would never want to encourage you to do things you didn't want to."

"Oh, believe me," she whispered into his soft fur. "I want to."

A gentle rumble exploded from Brruuh's chest as Sauraxen licked her way up his neck and to his ear.

His teeth had felt so good against her scales the other day. She nibbled and nipped gently at the tip of his ear.

Brruuh's hand clenched on the back of her neck, claws extending. It should have been terrifying. But there was no fear, only the burst of pleasure-pain that made her press against him even closer.

She slipped her hands underneath the back of his jumper, tracing the patterns of his fur. "You'd left when I woke up," she accused gently.

"I–" he gasped as her hand dipped below the waistband of his trousers. "Uh, I do not rest– Raxen!"

Her nose scrunched in enjoyment at the way his heart pounded in his torso. The way his ears flicked in and out of focus.

"That's fine," she reassured. "Just wanted to make sure you knew you were allowed to stay if you wanted to."

"We have more to discuss."

"Right now?"

His teeth grazed against her scales, tongue swiping out as if to sooth it but the barbs rubbing deliciously, only adding to the sensation. "Not right now," he acquiesced.

"Good, because I have other ideas for what we could do right now."

Brruuh made a scandalised noise but his hands didn't stop moving, and the purr in his secondary vocal cords didn't pause, if anything it rumbled deeper and louder. "We are in engineering!"

"The beauty of it being dark enough for my comfort," Sauraxen whispered, pulling his jumper over his head and setting her mouth against the fur of his chest, trying to locate the source of the purr, where it rumbled the strongest against her tongue. "Is that nobody else can see in here."

"Noises," Brruuh protested.

Sauraxen huffed an amused noise. "That sounds like a you problem."

Brruuh choked back a squeal, his body turning liquid under Sauraxen's ministrations.

"Trousers?" she asked.

"Off, ja, whatever you want."

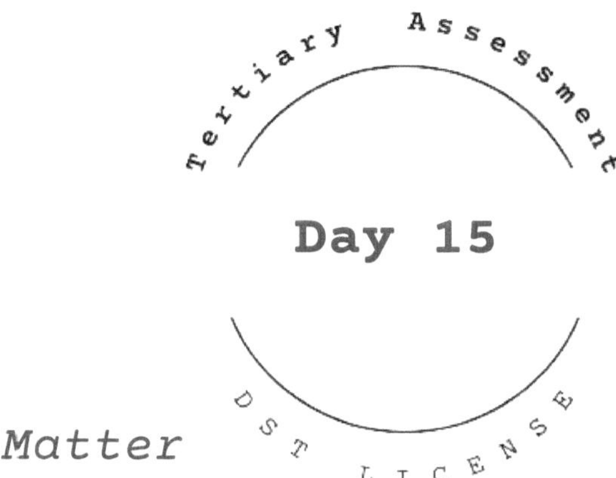

Matter

Matter rubbed at their forehead. How long had they been flying without a break? For all Matter knew it could have been five days or five hours. It was all too easy to get lost in the void. Maybe that was the human in them, or the ouaeahhn curiosity, or the combination.

They clambered out of the pilot's chair, legs shaking and joints aching under their own weight.

Matter stumbled toward the door of their quarters but hesitated before touching it. With a headache like this and this particular ache to their joints, perhaps a trip to Dimae would be a better plan. It wasn't that Matter shouldn't have let themself get caught up in flying, though they shouldn't have, it was all those things they'd been fobbing Brruuh off about since the first time they had met. Matter was running on low contact and between that and their torrid personal history...

With a heavy sigh, Matter shifted toward the gravity chamber – sure Dimae could come see them in their room, but that would make Dimae uncomfortable, it would be easier to get it over with in medi-bay.

Landing on the floor of the cargo bay had a soft groan of pain escaping Matter. They stared at the piles of cargo crates. How could they have forgotten the labyrinthine pathway of reparations crates blocking their way to medi-bay?

They stumbled forward, legs unwilling to co-operate in the wake of the sudden increase in gravity. Their eyes squeezed shut, blocking out sight that was turning to visual static, allowing the entirety of Matter's focus to fix on moving one foot in front of another. Ragged breaths rocketed around their chest.

Not far. It couldn't be far to medi-bay now. It wasn't that big of a ship.

Hot pain sliced across their hip, Matter stumbled into the corner of one of the boxes. Metal screeched as the lid shifted. Matter grabbed at it, only managing to knock it further. Ribbons of shredded paper or wood sat around metal shapes, details and registration numbers shaved off their ends in clean scratches.

"Fuuuuck," Matter groaned. "That's a lot of illegal guns."

They sank to the floor, leaning their back against the crates they'd disturbed as they flicked across their wristband to pull up comms with "Basti?"

"What's up, Matter?"

"Come downstairs please?" No need to spread the info all over the ship unless Sebastian decided it was necessary.

"I'll be right there."

They had been so close to leaving this shit-cluster behind and now who knew what was going to happen. Maybe Sebastian would want them to fly somewhere specific to sort this out. What IPA Stations were near Clickclick?

Matter slung an arm over their eyes, hiding from the lights in the cargo bay. This would be a far easier question if they could see the void. IPA stations had their own particular signature that seemed to match regardless of whether it was IPA built or not.

Ughhh. There was definitely a Station near Clickclick. There had to be, somewhere for border crossing trades to be checked.

Matter hadn't landed on an answer by the time Sebastian's well-worn boots scuffed along the cargo bay floor.

"You need help?" he drawled.

Matter pointed at the accidentally opened box.

"Fuck." Unlike Matter, he let the word out in a clipped way. "That's a lot of illegal weapons... On my ship..."

Matter rubbed their head and squinted up at Basti. "What do you want to do?"

"I guess we'll have to turn 'em into the local authorities. I'll get to researching who and where they are." He sighed. "But that's gonna be more flying with nei impending payment." He flicked over his wristband but paused before he could really get into it. "Why are you sitting on the floor? Actually, come to think of it, what were you doing opening the cargo boxes?"

"Headache," Matter said. No need to get into the full body pain that was causing it.

"You want me to get Dimae for you?"

Matter thought about saying no, thought about forcing themself to their feet and painstakingly stumbling to medi-bay, all while risking Sebastian noticing their obvious pain.

"That'd be good," they conceded.

As Basti moved away, Matter dropped their arm back over their eyes.

Next thing they knew, Dimae stood over them with a huffing breath.

"Hey, Dimae."

"What happened?"

"Can we have privacy?"

"You think you can make it to medi-bay?"

Matter glanced at Sebastian and pulled their lower lip between their teeth. "Maybe."

Dimae chuffed a laugh-like sound but helped Matter up and into his primary domain.

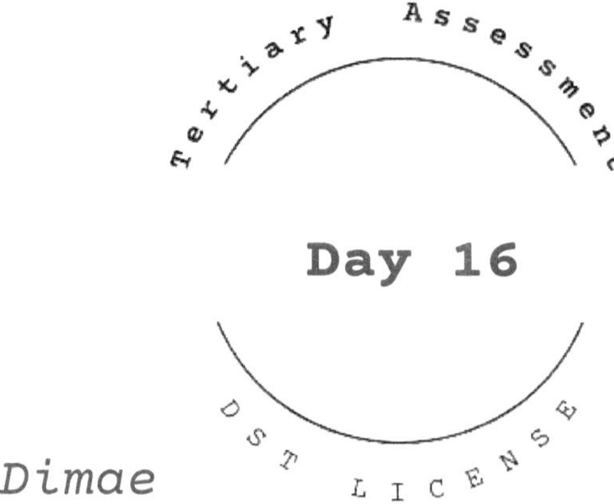

Dimae

Sebastian had, once again, taken his hair down from its ponytail, only to scoop all his hair within his hands to tie it back up. It was starting to set Dimae's fur on end.

They were both, along with Brruuh and Sauraxen, in the aufenthaltsraum at Basti's behest. Matter wasn't allowed out of medi-bay until Dimae was comfortable with the idea of them trying to move around the ship without immediately falling as their limbs ceased to function because of the pain.

As a medical professional, Dimae wanted to bring up their having been overworked to this extent to their captain but he found himself reluctant to do it when said captain was his bond mate. That was a concern in itself, something Dimae hadn't been prepared for when shifting to a ship of this size.

"Okay," Basti finally started. "We have a shit-tonne of illegal cargo in our hold. I vote going to the local authorities to turn them in. Are we all happy to do that?

Best case scenario is they take the cargo and we can get the fuck out of Clickclick."

"Sounds good to me," Sauraxen agreed.

"Ja," Brruuh seconded.

"And how are you expecting to travel to the local authorities? Or out of Clickclick at all?" Dimae asked.

"If Matter is still too ill to help–"

Dimae let out a brief hiss.

"Sorry, sweetie but on a ship this small people are going to find out when someone is sick. Anyway, I sent out a comms message asking the local authorities to meet us here."

"Wait," Dimae snapped. "You put a comms message out before asking us if we thought that was the best course of action?"

Sebastian winced and nodded.

Dimae's chest twinged. He pushed to his feet. "If you'll excuse me, there are places where I am actually needed."

"Dimae," Sebastian called after him, plaintive.

Dimae didn't turn. He couldn't bear to look at his bond mate at that moment.

Matter looked almost no better for the painkillers Dimae had prescribed. They sat, propped up against the wall of medi-bay, refusing to lie down regardless of Dimae's suggestions. Their mouth curved up into an expression almost like a smile as they cracked open an eye. Before they spoke the words on their tongue, they froze, eyebrows drawing together in a different way to the pained scrunching Dimae had been seeing over the last day-night cycle. "What's wrong?"

"You are asking me?" Dimae questioned.

Matter offered him another soft smile. "Ja, I'm asking

you. Something's up and, while I am in immeasurable pain, I still care about you."

Why? Why was it that Matter insisted on throwing those words at him? What could they possibly expect to gain from such a claim?

And yet they insisted, repeatedly that they did care.

He perched on the medi-bed next to Matter. "Sebastian."

"What did he do? Something thoughtless I bet."

"It's the little things."

"It always is," Matter sighed.

"He told everyone that you're... unwell."

Matter covered their face with their hands. "Wonderful."

"You are doing the dishonest joke."

"Sarcasm, ja."

"How are those painkillers?"

"Nice pivot," they snorted.

Dimae almost prompted them to answer the question but Matter let out a long breath.

"They're making me supremely dizzy. Ouaeahhn don't get dizzy, did you know that?"

"I did not."

"That would be lovely right about now. What else has a bug up – has you upset?"

"A bug up?"

"Idiom, cut it off because it would've upset you."

"Now I am curious."

Matter laughed. "A bug up your butt."

"You are right, that would have upset me."

Matter laughed again, letting their hands flop at their sides. "Come on, tell me so I can live through someone else's problems instead of my own."

"He called a meeting to ask what we thought was the best course of action but he had already taken the action."

"Ooft."

"Exactly. He pulled me away from my job when I actively have someone to care for and for what?" His fur bristled, ears pinning themselves back.

"Hey," Matter pushed the tips of their fingers against the side of Dimae's hand. "He's got a lot on his plate."

Dimae growled. "Idiom!"

"There are a lot of things he has to consider. There is a lot going on in his mind right now. He's stressed. He needs you."

"But I do not want to help him. He hurt me!" The pain still crunched in Dimae's chest, like a thousand shards of ice being pressed into his insides.

"Sometimes that's love."

"How would you know?" The bitter words escaped without thought.

Matter closed their eyes, leaning their head back against the wall behind them, baring their throat under Dimae's attention. "There's more to love than bond mates and romance. I know you don't think of things like this but you're all my family, my Ahthae."

"Ahthae?"

"It's an ouaeahhn word. The familiar we and Ah: home, familiar, comfort, that kind of thing. It's a complicated language. There's layers I can't even begin to explain without tele-empathy."

Ah meaning home and Thae meaning we. It made a certain kind of alien sense. The type of community bonds that came from spending time with people. Like friendship and family mixed together. "That is why you are always referring to family?"

"Ja. Our Ahthae are the people we share meaningful contact with. They are what keeps us alive."

Perhaps Matter had never meant their care as the aggression Dimae had always read it as.

"On Harrush we do not invite strangers into our colonies, our communities. A YaPar is a YaPar and if they are not, then they are not welcome in the mountainside. Even partners can struggle to find a place if they are from somewhere else." Dimae laid a hesitant hand on Matter's shoulder. "I am honoured to be in your Ahthae, even if we cannot always agree."

Sebastian

Basti watched Dimae disappear down the gravity chamber but didn't follow. His shoulders slumped but he turned back to face Sauraxen and Brruuh, trying to present himself as captain primarily, rather than a husband halfway through an argument.

"You do not appear to be confused by Matter's illness," Brruuh said cautiously.

Basti sank into his usual chair at the head of the table. "They have a chronic condition. I don't know much about the particulars of it but..."

"But?"

Sebastian sighed, resting his forearms on the table in

front of him and staring steadfastly at its shining surface. "It was years ago now." The words were soft, came out quiet. He didn't want them to travel down to medi-bay. He didn't really want it to travel inside the aufenthaltsraum either. "I got an emergency contact from a medi-centre in IPA zone 7.45E. I didn't even know where that was really."

He rubbed his face. Should he even be sharing this story?

Brruuh settled at the table, situating himself in the intimacy that Sebastian had unintentionally offered.

"It was about Matter – they had put me as their emergency contact. Stars, they looked so fragile in that bed."

The holographic sheen that marked an ouaeahhn's skin was something Matter rarely showed on normal occasions had been so prevalent that Sebastian almost hadn't recognised them at all. The animation that always accompanied Matter had been notably absent, as if all their energy was going into the shine and reflection and none into their personhood.

Basti had seen Matter sleep before, napping when they had come to visit Jonesy's farm, sharing bunks on long-haul shuttles, cheaping out on hotels and ending up sharing a single double bed between Matter, himself, and Peggy. Matter slept the same way they did everything else: animatedly. But in this green blanketed IPA medi-centre bed, Matter had been still. Silent. Tense.

"It turned out," Basti said. "That Matter had answered an ad for an ouaeahhn pilot."

"They have been qualified a long time," Brruuh murmured.

"They always knew what they wanted to do. Apparently

they used to climb everything they could to be closer to the stars." Basti could still remember the face Matter had pulled when they'd got their full pilot's license. All broad beams and eyes shining with the verdant green of EC.623, pops of red and gold dancing through them like a disco ball. They'd pulled Sebastian to his feet and danced around the room with him making zooming noises like a toddler.

"What happened?" Brruuh prompted.

"The ad was a fake." Sebastian licked his lips, but he had started this for a reason, he needed to finish it, needed to speak it out. "It was a trafficking operation. I don't... I don't know what happened but–" a broken little laugh escaped him. "Ouaeahhn are some of the sturdiest peoples in the universe. They're hard to hurt and they heal easily. But the thing is, Matter isn't all ouaeahhn."

"Humans are more fragile."

"Exactly." Sebastian tried to shrug but his shoulders felt weighed down by the cargo crates filled with illegal weapons that currently filled his cargo bay. "The rest of them got better with enough contact and time but Matter..."

"The Galactic Whale story..." Brruuh breathed.

"They won't tell me what happened and I can't bring myself to request the IPA reports on it."

Again, Brruuh let out a small distressed noise.

Sebastian let his head hang down, no longer able to hold it up under the weight of the guilt. How could he not have been there for Matter sooner? How could he not have noticed they had stopped responding to messages? He still didn't know how long they had been used like that. And now, every time their pain condition flared up that guilt ate at him. How much worse must it be to not just be in pain but to have that pain remind you every day of the worst event of your life?

"What are the lingering effects?" Brruuh asked.

"Pain, mostly. I'm not entirely sure. They're cagey about it. I barely even know what causes these flare ups."

"Lack of meaningful contact," Sauraxen's words had both Sebastian and Brruuh startling, turning to face where she still crouched on the sofa arm as she had been for the meeting. How had Basti forgotten she was there?

"What?" Basti asked.

"It's never simple," Sauraxen said. "But a lack of meaningful contact will..." She covered her mouth with one hand and ducked her head, curling in on herself.

Brruuh pushed to his feet, shifting to her side and running a soft hand over her shoulders. "You didn't know."

"It's my fault."

"How?"

"Because I didn't think ceasing our night time snuggles would hurt them but I knew continuing would hurt you."

Basti frowned. Why would Sauraxen and Matter having snuggles hurt Brruuh? And how hadn't he noticed that they were doing that?

"It isn't about what got us here, at this point," Brruuh said. "It's about what we do next."

"I guess we use autopilot for now," Basti sighed. "Give them as much time as they need–"

"We can't use autopilot," Sauraxen interrupted. "I had to take it offline for the modifications to the emergency engine."

"But Matter's not at the console so how are we moving?" Basti blurted.

"It's called–" she made a very lizardy noise.

"There is nei friction in space," Brruuh clarified. "We will continue to travel unless acted upon."

"See, I knew that." Basti dropped his head back into his hands and let out a groan. This day, this assessment could not possibly get any worse.

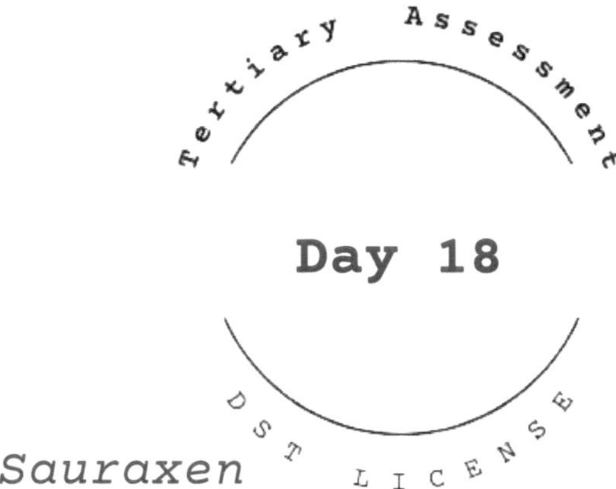

Humans, Sauraxen decided, were weird. Ultimately any species with ritual around relationships were weird but Sauraxen had been off Pitzk long enough to get used to the general idea. Humans, though, were weird.

Sauraxen watched over the top of her steaming mug of coffee as Sebastian and Dimae cuddled together on the sofa. Sebastian's face was pressed into Dimae's throat, Dimae's eyes closed to slits, his ears doing something Sauraxen couldn't understand. The undercurrent of his quiet purrs filled the space.

Basti's lips curved into a smile against Dimae's fur. Dimae murmured something in response, hand shifting from the back of the sofa to wrap around Basti's shoulders.

Humans would couple with anyone. Same base number of limbs or different. Same coupling methods or not. Same mental format or otherwise – the sheer volume of humans

Sauraxen knew in relationship with people who didn't use spoken language to communicate. None of these potential barriers seemed to bother humans.

Sauraxen could understand scratching an itch – to use an earth common eurean expression – with whoever was handy. It was the relationship part that still eluded her to an extent. And it had been bothering her ever since she and Brruuh had started their relationship. She had thought she was doing okay with Liz, up until the whole cheating fiasco. But being monogamous by choice was a far different thing than monogamy by necessity like Brruuh. And then there was Matter to factor in.

Sauraxen considered Matter her best friend and yet she'd been so distracted by Brruuh, caught up in his needs that she had neglected her best friend. What kind of a person did that make her?

But knowing that didn't solve the problem of what to do from here. How to be a good friend and a good partner. How to balance her needs against those of the people she cared most about. How to make the need for monogamy and the instinct to be non-monogamous fit together. How to make this work with someone who was so... well, Alien.

Brruuh settled into the dining chair at 90 degrees to Sauraxen, having handed Matter their own cup of Sauraxen-made coffee where they reclined on the sofa not occupied by the necking pair. Under the table, his leg brushed against hers. He nursed his own mug, flowers floating on the top of the liquid inside.

"Would you ever want kids?" she asked the room.

Brruuh choked on his flower-drink.

Sebastian and Dimae jerked out of their bubble.

And on the other sofa, Matter snorted. Answer enough.

"Uh... I never gave it much thought," Basti admitted. "And I don't think there's such a thing as adoption on Harrush."

Dimae shook his head. "I knew bonding with you wouldn't allow for a traditional family unit." He shrugged, his ears moving in the same motion. "I have nei qualms about that. Maybe we can explore it later, if it's something you want."

And with that sorted, all eyes turned to Brruuh. His ears pressed against his head. "I have nei family to fold them into."

"What about you, Sauraxen?" Sebastian asked, as if Brruuh's answer had made any sort of sense.

"I'm not a vava."

"That's a raising parent, right?" Brruuh clarified.

"Ja."

"What does that mean?" Sebastian asked.

"Wrexi come in three flavours. Two kinds of Creators – who can swip-swap but there needs to be at least one puzzle piece pair to do the creating part," she wiggled her fingers. "And vavas – raising parents. The find hatchlings and raise them."

"How do they find them?"

"When hatchlings hatch they can walk, so they just walk and cry until somebody comes for them. Vavas are the ones who naturally respond to the cry."

"You just let these babies wander around alone and crying!?" Sebastian gasped.

"Obviously, what else would they do?"

"Does nobody else respond?"

Sauraxen tilted her head in a shrug. "Evolutionarily it doesn't bother us to hear them."

"To be clear, you wouldn't be upset, distressed, bothered at all to find a crying child?" Brruuh asked.

"I'm not a monster; I know mammals don't work like that! If a kid asked me for help I'm not going to refuse or anything, just like if an adult asked me for help I wouldn't refuse. It's just not in my genetics to respond to a crying child. Sorry my DNA has upset you all so much." The last sentence came out bitter as unsweetened coffee.

"I had to learn to respond to crying children too," Matter murmured. "On Ouaeahhn, if anyone needs anything it's tele-empathetically communicated. There is nei such thing as a crying child. You all need to remember that these things aren't as simple as your instincts want them to be. My instincts want you all to start communicating via tele-empathy. Sauraxen wants us to turn off the lights. Brruuh and Dimae want everyone to have malleable ears for ease of non-verbal communication. Not to mention, from what I've heard, Dimae would only want to help a YaPar child anyway."

Dimae bristled, fur standing on end, his purrs turning deeper. Sending Sauraxen's muscles tensing, ready to run.

"My *point*," Matter spoke with force. "Is that you can't expect an alien to be anything less than alien."

Sauraxen turned her focus to Brruuh once again. And wasn't that just the crux of her issue...

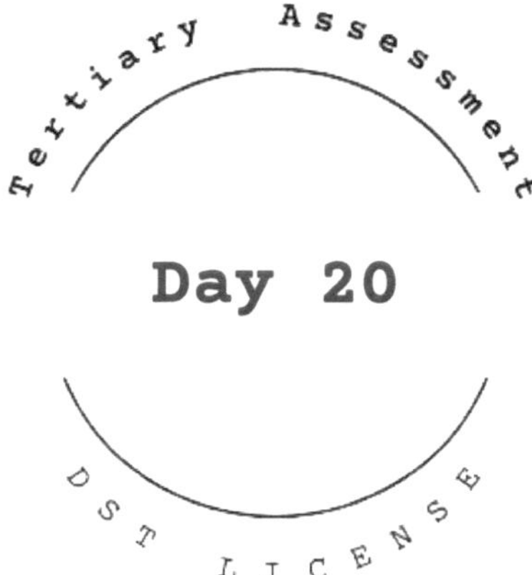

Brruuh

The Clickclick authorities set off Brruuh's predatory instincts. They looked up at him with their antennae-eyes, the stalks twisting independently of each other, always at least one trained on Brruuh as the others swivelled around the cargo bay.

Brruuh's shoulders twitched to calibrate for pouncing on the bug people but he kept himself still.

Clickclick wasn't a member of the IPA, unwilling to let go of their residual hostility toward Harrush, as well as their own propensity for infighting – as proven by the initial bomb escapade. But they were an official IPA trade galaxy, which was why Basti had been allowed to trade within the orbit and to trade over the border.

As the evaluator for the ship, and the only crew member with active and direct connections with the IPA central systems, it made sense for Brruuh to accompany

Sebastian while he spoke with the local authorities. Especially when taking into account that his face still held remnants of bruising.

"That is illegal cargo," one of the clickbugs said, words buzzing through the translator strapped to Sebastian's forearm.

"That's why I told you," Sebastian agreed. Tension lined his face and held his shoulders rigid.

The spokesbug clicked at some of the others to bring the cargo off the ship, then said to Sebastian, "We need a favour of you."

"Excuse me?"

"In response to this issue."

"I'm not sure how things work in this corner of the universe, but where I'm from the authorities don't ask for favours when someone brings them proof of a crime."

"We know there are pirates operating in the area, on the fringes of the galaxy. We need someone outside the IPA and Clickclick authorities to do this."

"We are not a battleship or crew," Sebastian protested.

"That is exactly the point. We will take this illegal cargo and dispose of it, in return we need you to take our baited cargo and let the pirates board your ship, to steal it. Then we catch them."

"Again," Sebastian said with forced patience. "We aren't a battle ship or crew. We're a simple cargo running operation. This is a completely inappropriate ask."

The spokesbug focused all of its eyestalks on Sebastian, making the human flinch.

Brruuh's fur bristled at the implicit threat.

"I wouldn't want to have to report you for transporting illegal cargo across our space, and without a license..."

"Are you threatening me?"

The spokesbug pulled a pad into its hand-like appendages. "Of course not. I just think it would be easier for everyone if you do as we ask."

"I'm the one who brought you this illegal cargo!"

"Or did we stop your ship for a random search and find it?"

Matter

The rubble of Clickclick was starting to get to Matter. What should have been a brief cargo mission, no more than a few days was turning into and endless back and forth. It might not have been so bad, even with the pain flare, but for the continuous rattle of useless space debris hitting against the ship.

Nian, this whole thing was a mess. And Matter couldn't quite battle the guilty feeling that they should never have agreed to come at all.

An unfamiliar ship appeared in Matter's peripheral vision. They jerked to one side, pulling the ship with them. Too many nose trails for the rubble, Matter hadn't seen them coming.

The ship hovered in Matter's periphery. Following? Why? What could be drawing them toward Basti's ship?

The hit rocked the ship, the gravity maintenance systems flicking in and out of functionality, making Matter feel like a car going too fast over a hill. Weightless but only for a few seconds.

What the…?

Matter flicked open external comms. "Hello? Please communicate. Why are you attacking?"

No response.

Matter swerved out of the way of the next attack. The quiet clunks of rubble hitting the ship turned to a thunderous clankering.

Fuck. Who were these people? What did they want? Matter didn't have the wherewithal to deal with both trying to communicate and avoiding further attacks. They flicked open cross-ship comms. "Someone want to talk to these – fuck, shit, Ma-An!" Another attack, blasting over the ship.

Electrical.

The jolts of overload shot into Matter where they touched the controls. Their arms spasmed, muscles locking, freezing them in place as sparks blasted through them. If they had been human it might have killed them. It would certainly have damaged their heart. Was Matter that human?

Their teeth clacked together. Jaw tight.

Something down the corridor in the aufenthaltsraum slammed to the floor with a heavy bang. Matter wanted to go check. Was it a crew member? A botany rack? Brruuh would be so sad if the plants were damaged.

They tried to wrench taught, rebellious muscles into use. To no avail.

No. No no no. This couldn't be happening.

Not again.

They couldn't be helpless like this again.

The pilot's console around them started to shine with the light from the stars. Panic released adrenaline in humans, but Matter wasn't human. And they didn't have adrenaline.

The attacking ship shifted to the front of Matter's bubble. The sleek, dark screen of its front window stared at Matter. It smiled in the face of their agony.

It shifted past and the clunk-thunk of a boarding tunnel latching into the ship accompanied the exhaustion of limbs released from shocking tension.

Matter's vision faded as their body shut down without their consent.

It couldn't go through that again.

Sauraxen

The house engine's pistons crashed at a speed Sauraxen really wasn't happy with, desperately trying to compensate for repeated shifts in gravity while also fighting to maintain atmospheric shielding. What was happening that Matter felt the need to shift around with such violence?

Something buzzed on the lower level, cross-space comms probably. Who was calling who? Maybe there had been a near miss, someone with an unskilled pilot failing to notice Basti's little cargo runner. Unless there was an issue with the registering system that would make the ship appear on other people's scanners?

Another miniscule shift in gravity made Sauraxen's gut wrench.

Matter's voice crackled over comms. "Somebody want to talk to these – fuck, shit, Ma-An!"

Something buzzed through the ship. The light spilling through the open door to the cargo bay flickered.

Steam burst from the directional engine, blasting through the grated floor. Sauraxen leapt away from the suddenly wet carpet, gripping onto the railing with her fingers.

Her scales screamed for attention. Hot. Burnt?

Over the ship comms came the distorted, teeth-clenched scream of pain.

Matter!

Sauraxen shouldn't have felt the clunk-thunk of a boarding tunnel attaching to the side of the ship. But with the underlying rumble of the engines working to get back into some semblance of order after... whatever had just happened, not unlike a quake on Pitzk, Sauraxen's internal sensors were on overdrive.

She could barely walk with the burns and it wasn't her job to check on potential boarding, and the engines needed her attention. But still. She latched onto the wall and snuck her way into the cargo bay.

She emerged just in time to register the last of the saw slicing through the outer hull of the ship.

Blurry-shaped quadrupeds in space suits emerged from the roughly cut hole. They spoke in a language Sauraxen didn't recognise as they grabbed hold of the boxes of cargo, dragging them to the boarding tunnel and loading them through the hole.

She may not have understood the words, but nobody could mistake the jovial tone. They were pleased with themselves. Pleased to have hurt Matter enough to make them scream. Pleased to have possibly stranded the ship in Clickclick space. Pleased to have torn a hole in the ship that might leave them with no atmo left.

Wrexi were a natural prey species. Even in modern, high-tech era, they still had to be wary of predators wanting to eat them, wary of natural disasters that would wipe them out, wary of the multitude of other concerns prey species had to contend with. Unlike humans, wrexi only had the instinct to run. No freeze. No fight. Every instinct should have been screaming at her to run, just like it had with the racattle snakes. But where could she go? Floating in space with enemies, predators on her ship. Where could she escape to?

So Sauraxen did something she'd never before done.

She launched herself at the blurry strangers, loosing a huge hiss as she landed.

They shrieked and screamed. One lashed out, arm slamming into Sauraxen's face.

She hit the wall, or maybe one of the crates. Her sensors overloaded with pain. Her awareness fled.

Sebastian

Sebastian forced his eyes open. Something pressed against his head, against his ribs, and against his hip. The pain that accompanied the pressure had thoughts of fractured bones flittering hazily through his brain.

Little pieces of white like snowflakes on the red lakes of Mars after they'd adjusted the atmosphere. Marshmallows floating in the top of a hot chocolate on the porch at his father's farm. The white petals of a coffee flower peeking out of the dense green leaves.

Why was everything so blurry?

He tried to get his hands underneath him, to push to his feet, or at least his knees. He crashed back to the floor, face smashing against the metal with a crack.

He turned his head to one side with a groan.

What had happened here? Why was he on the floor? Why was he so injured?

Slowly his vision cleared to reveal the aufenthaltsraum, chair legs invading like tree branches caught in the wind. Beside him, huddled in a ball and trembling, lay Dimae.

"Dimae?" Basti croaked.

No response.

Ignoring the way it pulled at his injuries, at his probable breaks, Basti dragged himself toward his husband. His heart thundered in his chest.

Pain in his hip screamed for attention, as if Basti was trying to tear himself in two. Basti clenched his jaw against the pained noises that ripped out of him, fingernails digging into the metal floor like claws.

Dimae never got hurt. Harrushetti were hard to injure.

But, unlike ouaeahhn, they didn't recover easily.

Shock could kill a harrushetti.

Dimae didn't stir at Basti's pained noises. Didn't respond to anything going on in the room around them.

Sebastian stretched his arm out, not quite close enough to reach.

His fingers dropped to the floor, clanging against the metal.

The edges of his vision darkened, black storm clouds rolling in to overtake the sky. And, as hard as Basti fought against it, they swamped him and dragged him back under.

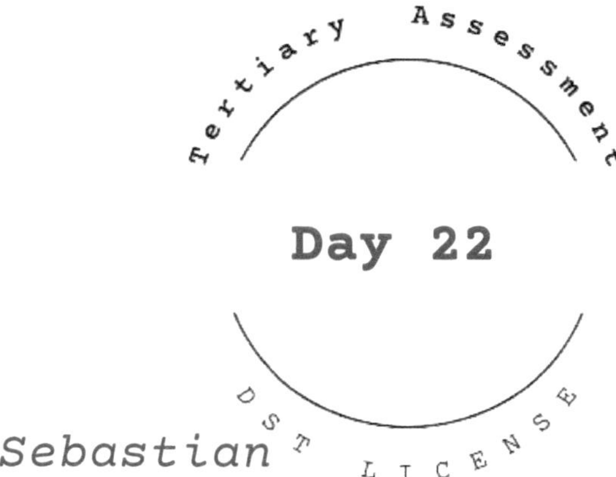

Sebastian

Sebastian's head ached. His whole body ached. As if someone had taken sandpaper to his skin and muscles. Like a hangover on steroids.

He dragged his eyes open to find himself staring up at the circular lights on the ceiling of medi-bay.

What was he doing in medi-bay? It made sense with the pain, but what... When had he come down here? And, if he was in medi-bay, what was the hard metal floor digging into his tailbone rather than the moulding soft cushion of a medi-bay bed?

Achingly, Basti pushed himself into a sitting position. A quick splint held his wrist in position, the awkward hook-and-loop closure curling back on itself where it wasn't secured. The pale peach supposed skin tone that never seemed to match anyone's actual skin tone made the bruises trailing beyond the edges of the splint all the more evident.

A shallow groan escaped him as his hip protested the

new position. Using his good hand and the conveniently placed metal medi-bed frame, he pulled himself to his feet.

These injuries were severe. More severe than any Basti had experienced before. And where was Dimae? Because Dimae would never have used a quick splint, preferring to custom make each recovery device so it moulded perfectly to the correct healing position, so nobody ended up with crooked bones that needed resetting later. It was a harrushetti necessity.

Harrushetti couldn't afford the risk of rebreaking a bone.

Basti's eyes landed on the medi-bed he'd used to pull himself to his feet. It was occupied. The green blanket pulled up to cover most of the patient within.

"Dimae?" Basti breathed, hands beginning to shake.

His husband's fur stood in matted clumps. Frizzy in a way Basti had never experienced before. The elegant leopard spots broken with the clumps. His breaths were shallow, nostrils flaring as if he couldn't quite manage to draw in the air he needed.

The sound of it echoed, huffing and squeaking in tandem with someone behind Basti.

He glanced over his shoulder to find Brruuh in much the same shape as Dimae. Fur matted, breaths short. But, unlike Dimae's whose face was so uncomfortably neutral, Brruuh's face was twisted in a mask of pain.

Tears choked up Basti's throat as he turned back to his husband. He ran soft fingers over Dimae's face, following the fur pattern up his nose and over his eyebrows to the tips of his ears. Brushing a thumb over his cheekbones.

The fur felt just as wrong as it looked. Usually it was thin, a soft downiness, but not too different from the texture of a human's eyebrow. Now, though, it felt like real fur, as if it had grown longer in the... however long this had been going on. Maybe it had. Fuck, Basti should have paid more attention to harrushetti healthcare systems.

He couldn't bear the thought of leaving Dimae in this state, could barely stomach the idea of trying to walk with whatever had happened to his hip, but he needed information, and nobody in medi-bay was about to give him any.

He could come back once he had them. He would have to, between his own injuries and... He glanced back at Dimae one last time before venturing out.

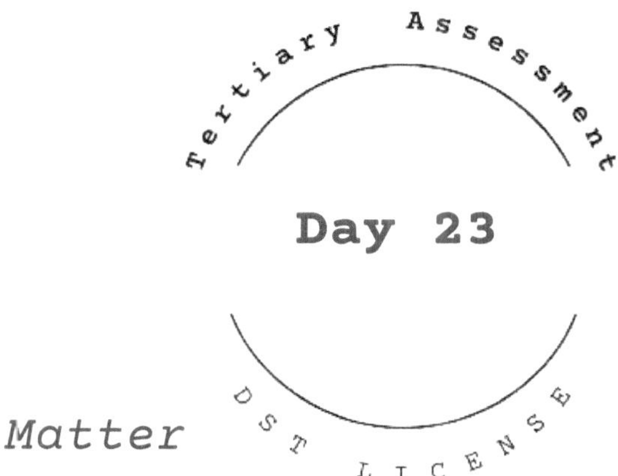

Matter

Matter stepped through the ajar door to medi-bay. Basti had set up a folding chair next to Dimae's bed, pushed from its normal spot in the centre of the room, up against one wall for ease of access to both beds.

A gold and brown peacock feather patterned blanket lay over Dimae's body, matted fur and off colour skin revealed where the blanket didn't cover his hands and face.

Basti's head hung down, as if someone had set his spine to sleep mode and he couldn't pull himself up. His hair needed a wash from how many times he'd run his hands through it, curl clumps broken up into frizz. It sat in a generous cloud around his head.

"Basti?" they prompted quietly. If he was sleeping they would leave him to it.

When he didn't respond, Matter's attention flicked to the medi-screen above Dimae's head, as if they could read it. All those graphs and lights and technical terminology. Matter wasn't even first aid trained. It had taken a lot of work and effort to get the three crewmates to medi-bay at all. They'd never been more grateful for hover trollies and the gravity chamber.

If it had been any other time, any other situation, even if it was just that everyone was healed up and they were all sitting around over hot drinks and talking about it, it might have been funny to think of proud Brruuh all crumpled up on Matter's hover trolley, like so much luggage. As it was the memory was just painful.

Matter had prioritised Basti. Brruuh and Dimae were obviously in bad shape, worse shape than Matter could manage to help with. They'd dragged Basti into medi-bay, set his hip back into its socket and slapped a restorative patch on it, set the bones in his wrist and used the quick splint Dimae had advised Matter wear to fly when their wrist hurt. His poor nose was too much for Matter to handle. He'd had to reset that himself after he woke up.

Brruuh and Dimae had gone into the beds, each one pressed up underneath the scanners so they could keep an eye on them, start potentially administering advised medications. Matter had pressed acceptance buttons for lack of any other options.

Finally, and utterly exhausted, they had gone to check in on Sauraxen, only to find her lying on the floor of the cargo bay.

Matter shook their head. This was no time to ruminate on any of that.

They flicked an equally useless glance at Brruuh. The white blanket from his office was tucked up around his face, just where Matter had put it when Basti said harrushetti healed better with the scent of their home and family around them. They could have got him something from his bedroom but they doubted overstepping boundaries would help, even in as extreme a situation as this.

His paler fur showed the matting to a greater extent. Or maybe he was worse. Hopefully, the office blanket would be enough.

It had to be enough.

Sebastian lifted his head, eyes red-rimmed from the combination of tears and lack of sleep.

Matter offered the bowl. "I brought you some food."

He took the bowl, draining the soup in one long gulp. Matter took the bowl back and ran a hand over his shoulder. His distress sizzled through them from the contact.

What a wonderful time to sync their tele-empathy with the rest of the ship.

They retracted their hand and shuffled out of medi-bay. They replaced the bowl onto the hover trolley and made their way to engineering. They set a bowl of scaldingly hot pizza pockets on the desk and stretched as high as possible to set a second one halfway up the stairs. It would have to be high enough because they couldn't face the idea of any extra walking. "Food."

Sauraxen didn't respond. She was busy. Matter could hear her clinking inside one of the engines. It was enough. It had to be.

They took themself and the now empty soup bowl back up to the top floor, allowing for one brief glance at the pilot's console.

The ship was dead in the water. The attack had gutted their thrusters. They were all lucky to have even one working engine, luckier still that it was the home engine, the one that would keep them alive. Even if it was floating in the middle of nowhere.

Retreating from their useless domain, Matter let themself into the aufenthaltsraum. They couldn't fly, but they could take care of their shipmates, their Ahthae as best they could. That included Brruuh's plants. He would be so sad to wake up and see all his hard work gone to waste.

They flicked the coffee machine on as they passed.

Maybe Chamber had been right. Maybe Matter was a dangerous thing. Maybe they did destroy the feeling of home wherever they went. After all, this home had been destroyed under their control.

Basti was out of commission, too distraught at the state of his husband, even if he hadn't been injured beyond walking. Any energy he had to work was entirely settled on medical care, since he was the only one of them with any kind of medical training. Field medicry didn't do much in the face of this, though.

Sauraxen was working herself to exhaustion to try and get the thrusters back online, butchering the broken engines in a desperate attempt to make one work.

And Matter... was at a complete loss.

What did a pilot do when they couldn't fly?

The scent of coffee filled the room as Matter spritzed the plants with each of the individual bottles stored on their racks.

They needed a plan. Something beyond waiting for Brruuh and Dimae to get better. Something quicker than hoping Sauraxen's skills would show through and get them an engine.

But what could Matter do? They were a pilot first,

foremost, and pretty much entirely.

They emerged from the botany racks to grab their coffee, slipping fingers through the handle to prevent risk of dropping it from their still weakened hands.

The scented steam and warmth offered some semblance of comfort as Matter sank onto one of the sofas, relief washing through their aching body.

What a shitty time to have had a flare up.

They checked the timer on their wristband. Time up. They pulled the painkillers from the pocket of their sleeveless jumpsuit and tossed a dose into their mouth.

Poor Basti was managing with no painkillers of his own because of Matter's need. But someone needed to be semi-functional, and Matter was more used to working in pain. They could do *something,* surely.

Okay, making a plan from start to finish was getting them nowhere. What was the ultimate end point they wanted? A destination? Someone to call.

Should they contact the authorities who had taken the illegal weapons? How would they find the contact details?

Basti's datapad lay on the table where it had been abandoned during the attack. The yellow tape reading 'captain' had started to peel at one edge.

Matter stretched to grab it.

Password protected.

"Dimae?"

"Access denied."

"Bond mate?"

"Access denied."

"Husband?"

"Access denied."

"Ugh," Matter groaned. Come on! They should be able

to get this! They pushed at the peeling tape, lips twitching to smile. Basti had always been obsessed with yellow, for at least as long as Matter had known him. Yellow clothes, yellow blankets, yellow devices. It was nei wonder he'd fallen for Dimae with his gold fur.

He even carried a packet of pineapple cubes everywhere, hardboiled sweets that were supposed to taste of pineapple but always seemed to taste of nothing so much as sugar. But Basti would try anything if it said it tasted like... "Pineapple."

"Access granted."

The information provided by the Clickclick authorities stared up at Matter.

"Take this baited cargo toward the edge of Clickclick, via the sphere-moon where the pirates tend to hit. Allow the pirates to take the cargo."

Rage sizzled in Matter's stomach.

How could Sebastian have agreed to that? How could he have put them all in danger like that? And look what had happened! Now a ship of five might die in the middle of a system full of so much trash that they would never be found again.

Matter took a deep breath and looked away from the screen.

Nei. There was nei purpose to this rage right now. They could rail at Sebastian later. After they had a plan.

There was nei going back to the Clickclick authorities.

Where else could they go?

The plain walls of the ship pushed against Matter, boxing them in.

They shifted off the sofa and into the pilot's console. They lay on the floor and stared up into the void. They had always thought better under the stars.

"I am never trusting a debris-filled system again," they muttered as they tried to focus past the rubble bouncing off the domed window.

"What do we need?" They let the words shift between ouaeahhn and earth common eurean. "Maou – Wrexi are excellent engineers but their planet is inhospitable on the surface. Too much for Ahthae to manage. Too much for broken engines. Ahya? But how could we get to anyone, EC.623 is too far. What's closer? EC.775, but Carlo lives there. Avoid if possible. EC.116? Shaayman, Lina, though. Do I have to have so many exes in useful places?"

They pushed up enough to drink some coffee, pausing as their attention caught on a particularly silver piece of galactic dust. Ymshuma? A comet nose?

Ym. If they could reach that, they could tail it with almost no power needed at all. But they'd be beholden to its destination. Potential for a dangerous movement indeed.

Matter tried to pull their eyes away from it, but the silver of it reminded them of Brruuh's eyes and weavings. Brruuh dying in their medi-bay.

"Get focused, Matter!"

The comet's nose glittered in a way that was completely impossible to ignore.

"Where are you going, ymshuma?"

Past Clickclick. Catching in the gravity of the sparkle system, – not friendly to outsiders. It would bounce off their shields just like that precursor dust was doing now that Matter had found it. And land in...

Matter scrambled into the pilot's chair. Never mind inter-stellar thrusters, if they could get into that comet's path it would push them!

They engaged the atmo engine. The whole ship rattled and shook with the motion of it. This really wasn't designed for galactic use. But it jumped into high speed, battering through the debris like a river through rocks, carving a path that would leave a scar.

"What the fuck, Matter?" Sauraxen's broken, tinny, and deafening voice screeched through the ships comms.

"I have a plan!" Matter called back.

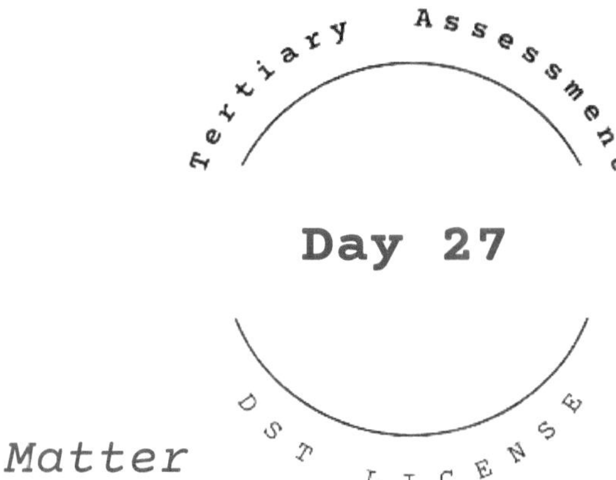

Day 27

Matter

The fringes of harrushetti space shone in a different way than most other systems. Every system was unique, but something about harrushetti space stood out as particularly unlike the others. Maybe it was the cleanliness.

Like most first-time space explorers, the harrushetti had left things in their orbit and in the orbit paths of their system. But, once they had perfected space travel they had spent the time and resources cleaning up after themselves, leaving their system relatively pristine. They even had a fining system for unlicensed junk.

The ship thundered and rattled as Matter forced it out of the comet's path and into a steady orbit of Harrush with only the rear thrusters designed for use inside an atmosphere.

That journey had been far faster than was strictly safe or sensible. If anyone had been in their path it would have been a completely decimating collision.

Matter sat up in their chair, composing themself as best they could. Their hair was up in its space buns, even if it was unpleasantly unwashed. Turned out their showers didn't work anymore.

Their jumpsuit was buttoned up to the collar. They pulled their legs underneath them to keep from leaning back by accident as they opened the communications link to Harrush's system-wide service.

The planet itself shone as bright as its star, refracting the light in a silver rainbow outward, where it played out on the other galactic bodies in the system. A light show put on specifically for Matter.

Some small part of them wanted to explore the history presented by the refraction – the way a slash revealed a scar through the planet's centre, how mountains made different shadows to flora.

But now wasn't the time. And the people of Harrush might not be quite so interested in the idea of it.

The connection beeped, buzzed, and finally answered in automated Centralised Harrushetti. That was okay, because Matter had already set up translation on their wristband. That it was unpleasantly loud was also something Matter had done their best to account for.

With a brief sigh, Matter began to explain. "My name is Ymmattrahni, Matter. I am Pilot and Second in Command–" a small, falsified promotion, but needs must and Sebastian wasn't going to do it "– of this ship – as yet untitled." They rattled off the registration number. "Captained by Sebastian LeaYaPar-Jones. We were on our Assessment for Deep Space Travel and ran into complications." They'd practised this little speech far too many times on the way here. "We request your assistance in healing our harrushetti crew. Our chief Medical Officer, Dimae LeaYaPar-Jones and our Cognitivist, Brruuh TeaYaBin. We were in Clickclick when we ran across some bandits who attacked with a combination of electrical and biological weaponry. Please, we don't have another medical professional aboard and our harrushetti crew have been affected. We are also in dire need of repairs. I don't know who else–" They cut themself off, taking a deep breath. Harrushetti were a proud and prude people. Displays of emotions wouldn't be welcomed, especially not by an ouaeahhn. "Please respond as soon as possible with docking co-ordinates."

Matter ended the message and flopped back in their chair, undoing the top few buttons of their jumpsuit.

All that was left to do was wait for their response.

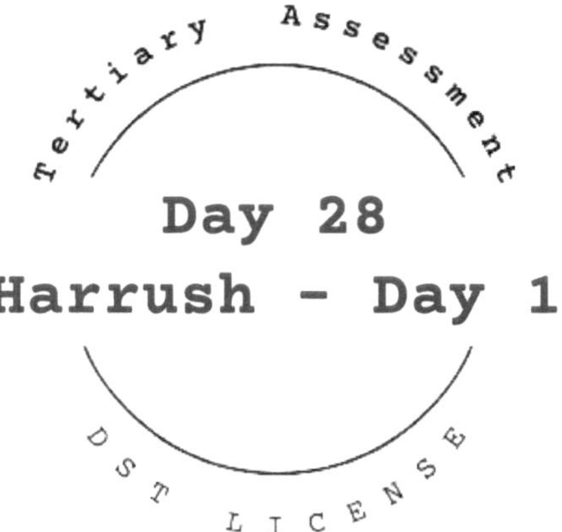

Matter

Matter's wristband beeped with a communication sent to the pilot's console. They shifted out of the aufenthaltsraum and into the pilot's console.

Their heart leapt when the message read as from Harrush but that joy quickly turned to heart-palpitating rage.

"For fucks sake!" They yelled, flinging their music speaker off the control panel, sending it skitter across the glass dome. "Hnanshaatsya! What is the point of me being able to leave a whole message if you're just going to come back with–" They cut themself off, took a deep breath, and re-read the message.

"Greeting from Harrush. Please tell us the nature of your request to land."

Useless tears filled their eyes, spilling down their

cheeks all too easily. They weren't supposed to be the one who had to do this. This was supposed to be Sebastian's job. He was the one with the training not to get too annoyed to act when in receipt of bullshit like this. Basti had endless patience and practise at this. If he'd been the one to send the message in the first place, they probably wouldn't have even asked for this, they probably would have just sent co-ordinates for landing. But Matter was ouaeahhn, and not a captain. And Basti was still at his dying husband's bedside. And Matter couldn't blame him for that.

Their chest hurt. Each breath sending stabbing sensations through their chest. Ripping up their throat like it wasn't just air they were inhaling and exhaling.

They swiped their hands over their face, wiping away what they could of the tears, and pulled up the communications link.

"My name is Ymmattrahni." Their voice shook. "I am pilot of this ship." Once again they rattled off the registration number. "I am requesting a site for landing. We are in dire need of medical assistance. Our two harrushetti crew members have been subjected to some kind of biological weaponry. Dimae LeaYaPar-Jones and Brruuh TeaYaBin."

The automated message responded, "Thank you for this information. Your request has been logged. We will get back to you as quickly as we can."

The tears Matter had been trying to fight back spilled down their cheeks once again. They climbed gently down from the ledge to pick up their speaker.

Surely the harrushetti couldn't refuse to help them. They were all IPA members. Even if just for Dimae, whose family had supposedly accepted Basti as one of their own when they'd got married.

Matter hadn't even been allowed to go. No outsiders at harrushetti weddings. It was a sacred practice and anyone beyond Basti's closest family hadn't been welcome. Half-siblings didn't count apparently. Go figure.

"Matter?" Basti's rough voice asked from somewhere nearby.

Matter swiped their arm over their face, once again hiding any trace of tears, and levered themself back up onto the console ledge. They tried to steady their voice. "Ja?"

"Everything okay?"

They made an affirmative noise but it hitched in the middle. A clear sign of tears. Shit. Basti didn't need to deal with their emotional mess right now. They needed to be strong for him, for Sauraxen, for...

But there Sebastian was, dishevelled and ashen, at the door of the pilot's console.

"I'm sorry," Matter said, trying not to sob. They swiped a hand over their eyes again. "I'm okay, don't worry about it."

Sebastian's arms closed around them and Matter clung tight to him as the emotions they'd been suppressing for days exploded inside them like a firework.

"I'm just so scared. And I'm trying to do everything and I'm not enough. Basti, I can't do it. How do you do it?"

Basti shushed them, rubbing his uninjured hand over their shoulders. "Hey, it's okay. I'm sorry, Matter. I'm supposed to be the captain and that means I have to be in charge even when I don't want to be."

The communications array beeped again. Matter

wrenched themself away from Sebastian, wiping their eyes with one hand and zipping up their blue jumpsuit with the other.

"I am Zyph JaYaPar of the YaPar council." Zyph's voice came through in that same absurdly loud volume as any other comms to the pilot's console. Matter and Basti both winced before Matter pulled up their own video screen.

"Ymmattrahni."

"You claim to have Dimae LeaYaPar-Jones aboard. Where is his husband, also your captain? Why is he not making these requests?"

Sebastian stepped into the screen, messy, dishevelled and all. "I am the only other member of the crew with any medical training, Councillor. Not only that, but, as you can see, I did not escape our attack uninjured and I was loath to leave my husband's side. We both know family is vital to healing harrushetti. But I am here now."

"Good," Zyph snapped. "Your landing co-ordinates are as follows."

As Zyph rattled them off, Matter leapt into the pilot's chair in a most ungainly fashion, inputting the location for the ship to land.

Sebastian

Basti stared down at his husband on the harrushetti medical bed. The healers had taken off the blanket Basti had brought from their bedroom on the ship. Too saturated with the scent of worry, stress, and illness, they'd said. Basti couldn't contest it, no matter how much he wanted to. Human noses weren't able to perceive that.

The medical blanket didn't suit Dimae. It wasn't even the right colour. And he needed something from their nest. The nest they had built together.

It was weird, wrong, bad to see Dimae so ill but with none of the things Basti expected to appear on a sick person. No tubes or wires, no beeping screens. Harrushetti medicine was some of the most advanced in the cluster, in the IPA even. It had to be, since harrushetti were so prone to dying of shock if they became injured. Logically Sebastian knew Dimae was being taken care of. He knew the bed itself was the medical device. He knew how it worked, on a surface level at least. But not being able to see it work made him feel like nothing was being done.

Was this how Dimae had felt when Basti had been suffering oxygen deprivation after that accident with the asteroid on the 2-Eas? When Basti had worked hard to rescue everyone in the compromised bay. Too hard, as it turned out. Was this how Dimae had felt staring down at Sebastian in that hospital bed? IV stabbed into his skin, measuring cables clinging to his chest and fingers, mask strapped to his face?

Helpless? Ineffective?

Or was it different when you had a better understanding of how the medical apparatus worked? Maybe that hadn't helped. Knowing Basti's exact chances of survival.

Basti probably could have understood more if the healers actually told him anything.

Why wouldn't they let him give Dimae a nest blanket? They seemed to resent Basti's very presence. Did they not listen when Basti had said husband? Should he have used pair bond? Bond mate?

Dimae's chest rose and fell in short shallow breaths. Basti rubbed the lets-be-honest-its-a-beard-at-this-point-not-scruff against Dimae's head, ruffling his ears with it. Scenting wasn't something humans could do, but it couldn't hurt to try.

Sauraxen

"Come, lay him among family," the harrushetti healer who hadn't offered a name gestured to the door. Basti wheeled Dimae's bed out of the hospital wing and into a waiting transport to be taken to his family home.

Apparently harrushetti healed batter at home. Which Sauraxen hadn't known – why would she?

With Sebastian and Dimae gone, only Sauraxen and Matter stood over Brruuh's bed in the sterile hospital room, wide windows showing the icy surface of most of the planet. Sauraxen squinted against the light of it, the tiny spots of red where wildlife and plants popped out of the blanket of snow stabbed at her eyes, leaving splotches dancing over her vision.

Matter shifted from foot to foot, yanking Sauraxen's attention away from the way the whole planet reverberated with each movement, clearer than anything she'd experienced before even with the stab-worthy starlight.

She laid a hand on Matter's lower back. "They'll be okay."

"I know." Matter's voice came out soft, barely carrying through the room and setting Sauraxen's hair on end. "And Basti knows the family – they're his family, it's not like I don't trust them with him, with them both. I just..." They shifted again.

Sauraxen stepped toward the healer left behind, legs twitching to run away in a room designed by and filled with such a predatory species. "Is there anything we can do for Brruuh?"

"He has the best medicine we can make for this. Having his family around him, being in his family home, even just his Kitten Blanket would help."

"Kitten Blanket?"

"The first blanket he was wrapped in as a kitten."

"Hatchling," Matter clarified.

Sauraxen peeped. Yes! That was achievable. "Is it on the ship?"

"No," the healer said, hesitant.

Sauraxen peeped again, a little of her annoyance filtering through that one, facing a predator or not. "How do we contact his family, then?"

"You can't." The healer lifted his chart and gestured at Sauraxen with it. As if she could read it. No indentations meant no wave-bounce. "He's a YaBin." As if that answered anything.

Sauraxen chirruped a mixture of anger, distress, and confusion. She wanted to do something. And a healer expecting her to understand a completely alien culture wasn't helping anything!

The healer sighed. "It was years ago now. I was in learning when it happened but the news astounded the whole planet. The Eastern Basin... it was lost."

"Lost?"

"The Basins are a type of homestead here, set into the equator of the planet, inside the huge crevasses that form in the melted ice."

"The scar through the centre of the planet?" Matter asked.

"There," the healer confirmed.

That would explain the resonance.

"Very rarely," the healer continued. "Exceedingly rarely, the Basin's dome cracks." He let out a slow breath. "Normally when that happens, it is repaired before anything can happen. But that year was a heavy snow year and the YaBin didn't notice."

"Snow melts. Basin floods. Harrushetti don't float," Matter filled in, voice filled with horror.

The healer shifted attention to Brruuh. "One did. He was working on some Earth 445 tree. It floated and therefore he floated. Two weeks later he turned up at the Eastern Cave Settlement."

"But the damage is done," Sauraxen said.

"The shift from childhood to adulthood is tough for us. It requires a lot of care and attention from family. He... Brruuh TeaYaBin, the last YaBin spent his adolescence fighting for his life on the planet's face. Alone, and grieving for his loss."

Sauraxen took the time to let the story settle. The room falling quiet as each of them watched Brruuh breathe in their own way. "Right," she muttered. "If he has nei harrushetti family to contact, what can we do?"

"We hope the medicine is enough."

"Has it ever been enough on its own?" Matter asked.

The healer paused. "Not in my experience."

Sauraxen rarely wished to be from a predatory species. She liked surviving on bugs and fruit. The thought of eating animals made her vaguely queasy. She liked that people didn't get aggressive. Even if that sometimes meant they didn't take her all that seriously.

But not being able to show her anger in a way that would matter to this golden tiger-patterned exit-port of a person was making her reconsider her stance. "Then we will be his family," she snapped. "What do families do?"

"It doesn't work like that," the healer said, voice soft and caring like it was a vava to their hatchling.

"Do I look like I care if you think it won't help! Will it hurt him if we try?"

"Well... I don't..."

"We are his Ahthae," Matter agreed. "It is all the family he has."

The healer sighed. "The scent is important. And comfortable things, blankets, pillows. Soft things that smell of... you."

"I will go to the ship and get some smelly things," Sauraxen decreed. She had a better chance than Matter of knowing what would smell. "You stay here and... pet him?"

"Would you bring the whale?" Matter called.

"Your birthday whale?"

Matter nodded, air currents shifting around their free hair. "It's on my pilot's console."

When was the last time Matter had left their hair free, rather than its ubiquitous space buns or a neat plait that hung over their shoulder? They even slept with their hair up in a scarf thing – a wave-dampening material that Sauraxen enjoyed being around for sleep but hated everywhere else thanks to the way it distorted her perception. They took a lot of pride in their appearance for a person who wore a different version of the same basic jumpsuit every day.

Sauraxen loaded Matter's hover trolley with one of the plants from the edge of the botany area – she wasn't about to go inside there, too much a prey species to like hidey spots cultivated by carnivores, even if that carnivore was technically her... paramour? What did harrushetti call it when it wasn't so serious as a bondmate?

She pulled a few cushions off the sofas in the aufenthaltsraum, the whale from Matter's console, Matter's blanket from their bed, one of her own over-worn over-sized t-shirts, some blankets from Brruuh's office. Finally she stood in front of his bedroom door.

Did harrushetti have human-style rules about privacy? Between the way the healer had snubbed them and Brruuh having never invited her into his space, it was probably even more strict. Then again, if a little privacy breach now meant Brruuh could come back enough to be annoyed about it, it would be worth his wrath.

Muttering a quick apology in wrexi, she slipped through the door.

The essence of Brruuh suffused the room, a gentle caress against her scales the way his hands moved down her arms, over her stomach. She wanted to rub herself all over his bed. To curl up here and wait for him to come back to her.

Instead, she grabbed the blanket from the top of the bed and headed back down into the medi-centre.

She hesitated by the door when she heard Matter's voice. If they were talking to the doctor, it would be better to wait. "Then, if you can believe it. The wolf ate Red Riding Hood! I know, it's the most absurd story to be telling young human children. Can you even imagine telling a harrushetti kitten that?" They put on a deep, silly voice, "Beware of going to grandma's house, kits, because she might eat you!"

"Are you..." Sauraxen trailed off, trying to pull herself together enough to ask the question. "Are you actually telling him a very bad version of Little Red Riding Hood?"

"You know the story?"

"Ja, Basti read it to me once."

Matter's face screwed up. "Why?"

"Because he's Sebastian?" Sauraxen offered. Reason enough for her to understand at the time and apparently reason enough for Matter too.

They sighed. "I just wanted him to know I was here, I guess. Like you said, we're the best family he's got."

Sauraxen and Matter set up the bed for Brruuh, layering his blanket under Matter's, putting the whale by his head and Sauraxen's shirt over the rail on the side of the bed. Sauraxen opened the empty coffee jar, wafts of scented air filtering around the room like half-hearted fireworks. Not so overpowering as a new jar but enough to mimic the scent of coffee that had invaded the ship from the amount of mugs brewed there.

"Do you think it will be enough?" Sauraxen asked, voice quiet like she was afraid of causing a rockslide.

"It's better than nothing," Matter whispered back.

Sauraxen handed over a datapad. "So you can read to him, instead of butchering ancient fairy tales – why are they called fairy tales anyway?"

She sank into the chair Matter hadn't been in when she returned as they explained the origins of the term, getting so pulled into their explanation that the tension freezing the air currents around them lessened and the tightness of their voice loosened. If Brruuh was affected by sound waves – even if it was less than Sauraxen – it wouldn't help to make stressed ones.

Matter

Matter swiped the call to close. Sebastian's tear-stained face disappeared from view and Matter sank back down into the uncomfortable harrushetti chair and dropped their head into their hands.

Dimae wasn't getting better. Even surrounded by his family and Sebastian, his state wasn't improving. And Sebastian was starting to lose hope.

And if Dimae couldn't recover in his childhood home, what chance did Brruuh really have?

Matter couldn't move. Couldn't think. Their tiny and precious Ahthae was falling apart – had fallen apart. Again.

They should just stop getting close to people. They should have joined a giant freighter where nobody knew anybody else and nobody made anyone hand knitted space whales. And no best friends turned out to secretly be the love of Matter's life.

It wasn't Matter's first time sat in a hospital room filled with hopelessness.

The last time had been the trigger for Matter to shift their entire medical and personnel profiles to centre on their human side. It was immediately after Matter's last DST license was at its end, in need of renewal.

They had never got it renewed. They hadn't wanted to. Hadn't needed to. Hadn't been able to go back then.

Matter rubbed their wrists, their exposed hands with luminescent skin – impossible to mistake in the right light. They could try passing themself off as human all they liked but it wouldn't work in the long term. At least their wrists hadn't scarred.

Their joined ached from sitting in chairs designed for knees that folded differently from theirs. From the stress. From the still-ignored injuries thanks to the attack. But Matter, unlike the rest of the crew, knew how to work around pain.

Sauraxen had returned to the ship in an attempt to get some sleep. For the first time in her life she needed a locked door between her and everyone else.

Brruuh twitched, as if in pain. His ears flicked back against his skull.

"It wasn't a Space Whale," Matter whispered. "It was a harrushetti, a human, and a uaen. They put out an ad for an ouaeahhn pilot. They claimed they were heading into unchartered space and that only an ouaeahhn pilot would be able to manage the navigation." The words tried to stick in their throat. Even Sebastian didn't know the full extent of what Matter had been through. "There were so many of us, all just out of reach. Aettrae." The Ouaeahhn word slipped out before Matter could think about it. "Many and many," They translated, huffing at the inaccuracy of trying to translate an idiom like aettrae.

They let out a shaky breath. "I was there for – it might as well have been forever. There was no day-night cycle to register. People came and went. Some of the others didn't make it... They didn't bother to move those ones." Bodies piled up in cages, arms still outstretched in the hopes of even brief snatches of life-sustaining contact. Matter had long since given up on such hope. It was the human in them.

"And then the raid happened. It was Basti's old friend, Benoit – he's pah-rushi. He was working on an IPA strike team back then but he changed jobs pretty much straight after this. He recognised me. Because he's come to Terraforming Day celebrations with Jonesy – Basti and my father is called Jonesy. Benoit wrapped me up in his huge wings and the next thing I know I'm waking up in a hospital bed on some random IPA Station with an intensely stressed Sebastian staring down at me like I've cut all the heads off his stuffed animals or something."

They tried to laugh. After all, they claimed not to take anything seriously.

"I felt so guilty. I felt so ashamed. I blamed myself for it, for hurting Basti like that, for gutting Benoit's very promising career. I couldn't even look at another ouaeahhn for a long time. Every time I did, all I could see was that room, those other desperate people. And when I managed to get past that, they... they all give me such looks now. I guess you'd understand that, what with being the only one of your colony left. It's the trouble with being part of a tele-empathically joined culture, I can't even just pretend. I haven't been back to ouaeahhn since."

They let out another shaky breath and touched a hand to Brruuh's. "What I'm trying to say – the point of telling you this is twofold. One: you don't need to feel guilty for this. None of us do. None of us did anything wrong. Nobody is going to be upset with you for waking up whenever you're ready. We'll just be happy you woke up. And two: I trust you, Brruuh. We are Ahthae. Family joined. Family chosen. I haven't trusted anybody else with this but you can have it. You can have that piece of me."

Brruuh

Brruuh leapt for the monster, claws extended. He yanked it into his body, using his sharp teeth and strong back legs to kill it.

Something trilled over his head. A noise of amusement.

Brruuh glared out of one eye.

A white and silver-grey harrushetti looked down at him, ears perked forward with a soft tilt – affectionate attention. Brruuh preened under it.

"I think we should call you Brruuh," the Tea-harrushetti said. "It means playful one. What do you think?"

Brruuh let the monster out of his mouth long enough to nod. He went back to it only to find it was a blanket that had fallen to hang half off a bed.

The Tea-harrushetti petted his head between his ears.

Baba? Was this Brruuh's baba?

But as fast as the thought came, the images were gone. Replaced by fear and anguish and wetness.

Drowning.

Choking.

A hand pulled him from the pit. A sparkling scaled hand of moonlight through ice.

Sauraxen's chin-tilted smile filled his vision. She pulled him into the aufenthaltsraum. The scent of coffee had stained the room, permeating every corner and crevice.

Sebastian and Dimae sat on the comfortable sofas, cuddled up together as they always were.

Matter laughed, the sound coating everything in happiness as thoroughly as the coffee scented the room. They were making eenya in Brruuh's mug. "You can have this," they said.

He turned back to Sauraxen, who pressed her forehead against his cheek. "Come back to me, Brruuh."

The words and tone didn't match the happy surroundings. Brruuh tilted his head in confusion. He was right here.

Harrush
Day 4

Sauraxen

Trying to sleep on an empty ship, alone, and locked in, was always going to be a terrible idea.

Groggy, Sauraxen grabbed a bug-bar and started looking into who had attacked them and the possible reasons.

Research had never exactly been her forte – when you had to wait for audio-versions of articles to get through the text, it always took a thousand times longer than people who could read traditional printed text.

With a huff of annoyance she peeped into her search, "Who had biological weapons that only work on harrushetti?"

"Clickclick is the only known galaxy to develop biological weapons that work primarily against catoids like harrushetti. These were developed as part of the–" But Sauraxen had stopped listening.

Clickclick had been at war with Harrush? Was that why they still hadn't joined the IPA? Unwilling to let go of old grievances?

Had those Clickclick authorities boarded the ship, seen Brruuh and made a snap decision to send them on a suicide mission because of it? They had just been refused a new trade agreement unless they got rid of all their old weaponry. The IPA did not tolerate warmongering. But if they thought it was blocked by Harrush...

What if the whole escapade, the bomb in the briefcase, the illegal weapons, what if it was all in the ultimate aim of taking vengeance against the IPA and Harrush?

Getting ready to head back to Brruuh's hospital room, Sauraxen pulled her hood over her head. It was way too bright in there and, as tired as she was, she wasn't going to put herself through the needless discomfort of a too-bright space.

She peered at the oversized hoodie she had stolen from Matter more years ago than she cared to count and picked it up too. It wasn't that she was cold, but the memory of Brruuh's mumbling about cloak offerings whispered at the edge of her mind.

It was serious, for sure, but this whole experience had told her to stop hedging with Brruuh. There was no need for it. He wasn't another Liz. He was more of a Matter. A forever kind of deal.

And anyway, it didn't have to be as serious as anything since she fully planned on offering it to him while he was asleep.

When she got to his room, Matter was reading him another story; this one was more long winded than the fairytales.

"What is that?" Sauraxen asked, tossing protein bars for Matter down on the chair next to them.

"Love story," Matter answered. "About two people too proud to admit they like each other. There's lots of societal standards and rules, very strict, I thought it might appeal to his enjoyment of romcoms and his harrushetti sensibilities all at once."

"Where are you?"

"About to get to the first proposal. I did warn him already that there's a happy ending so this refusal is only temporary."

Sauraxen laughed and laid her hoodie over Brruuh, whispering in his ear as she did so. "I'll protect you, prey species or not. You have to come back and let me."

She offered Matter a smile and settled into a crouch on the table beside the bed. "Carry on then."

Brruuh

Brruuh's head hurt. Why were the lights so bright in here? Sauraxen would be uncomfortable with enough light to hurt Brruuh's closed eyes. He squinted, trying to see if there was a light switch.

Instead, he found Sauraxen, most of her face hidden in the shadow of a well-built hood, the same one she had been wearing the first day they met. Clever, it shadowed her sensitive eyes from light as well as hiding her face and animate hair from view.

She peeped and leapt to her feet, grabbing hold of Brruuh's hand.

"Where?" he managed, voice rusty.

"Harrush. A hospital on Harrush."

"What...?"

"We were attacked," Matter's voice. Brruuh peered around Sauraxen to spot them slouched in a chair. Their limbs seemed wrong, out of sync with the rest of them. "I still don't know why or by who, but it hit you and Dimae hardest."

Brruuh stretched, fingers tightening on Sauraxen's hand. An unexpected purr escaped his chest at the contact. "Apologies," he rumbled. "I am pleased you're here."

Sauraxen peeped again. "Can I hug you?"

With the briefest glance to ensure they were alone but for Matter, Brruuh agreed.

Sauraxen slithered into the bed, pressing herself against his side. Another unexpected purr escaped him.

Matter chuckled, voice a little hoarse too. "Should I leave you two alone?"

Sauraxen laughed, breath puffing out of her nose where it pressed against Brruuh's cheek.

Neither Matter not Sauraxen asked him any questions about his health or wellbeing. They didn't ask what he had dreamed about. They didn't ask how he felt. Barely caught him up on what had happened since.

Instead, they shared pieces of their past, they told him each of their favourite childhood stories. And throughout it all, Sauraxen lay pressed against his side.

This... This was what Brruuh had been missing all these years.

"Ahthae," he interrupted a story Matter was telling Sauraxen. "This is what it means."

Matter smiled in that oh-so human way and nodded, deep eyes shining just a little of his own silver back at him.

Sebastian

A knock pulled Sebastian out of his thoughts. His back ached from the way he'd been leaning on Dimae's bed. His head pounded with dehydration and lack of food. At least the harrushetti doctors had patched up the rest of his injuries.

"Hey." Matter stood in the doorway. "Can we come in?"

Sebastian lurched to his feet. If Matter was here then Brruuh must be–

A pair of tufty white ears poked over the top of Matter's head, where their space buns normally sat.

Basti crashed back down into the chair. "How...?"

"It's the energy weapons the uaens used and the biological ones Clickclick used in the wars," Sauraxen said. "Those people you reported the weapons to took offence at

Brruuh's existence and set us all up because of it."

"How did you find out about–?"

"I looked up who had weapons like that and tracked it back. I saw quadrupeds invade the ship, so the supposed pirates will have been uaen. And Matter told me they'd found the baited cargo order on your datapad. Which means the Clickclick authorities set us up to die."

Basti sighed, hand automatically wrapping around Dimae's. His heart lurched a little when his squeeze was met with nothing. He licked his lips. "So you know everything?"

"What the fuck, Basti!" Sauraxen exploded.

Brruuh turned to her in shock, but Matter kept their firm attention on Basti – like Sauraxen's personal enforcer, making the point that her anger was more than warranted.

"You can't just do shit like that! You don't get to sign us all up for that kind of–" She peeped a wrexi idiom. "Without consulting us. What, you're happy to pretend to bring us on board for decisions like 'can we take this illegal stuff to the authorities' but not for 'can we take this *baited cargo* and hopefully get *boarded by pirates*'? Do you not see an issue with that? With the crew we have here? Tell me, Sebastian, what security officer did you run this by?"

Sebastian crumpled. He wrapped his arms around himself and wept the tears that hadn't come before.

"Hey," Matter's soft voice filtered through the wails. "Raxen, leave off for now. We can talk about this later. It's not like we're leaving Harrush any time soon."

"Matter–"

"I know. And I get that you're pissed, we all are. We almost lost Brruuh, Dimae is still in trouble. He's made bad choices but laying into him right now isn't fair."

Sauraxen huffed.

A cold hand landed on Sebastian's shoulder and he almost could have believed it was Dimae. Instead, Brruuh's fingers pressed against him, comfort and strength he could barely afford to give.

"How did they do it?" Sebastian managed, gasping breaths breaking up the question. "How did they wake you up?"

Brruuh shook his head. He didn't know or he couldn't say or they couldn't replicate it for Dimae. And Sebastian curled back in on himself again.

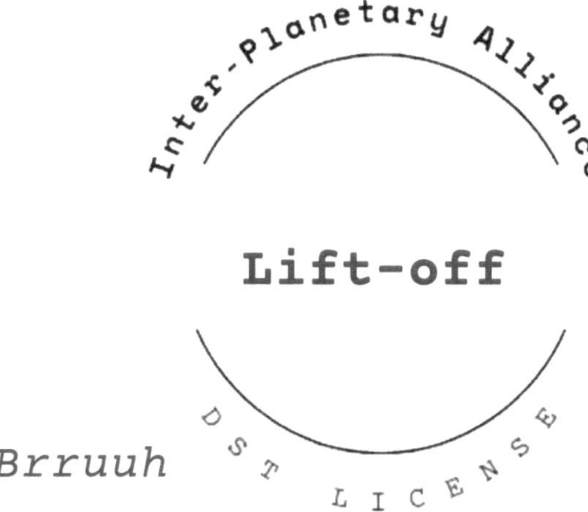

Brruuh

"So," Matter said, leaning on the doorway to Brruuh's office aboard the ship. "Are we going to pass? What with saving your life and all?"

Brruuh's secondary vocal cords rumbled.

Matter's face dropped.

Brruuh pushed up from his chair. "Come, we will all talk in the aufenthaltsraum."

Matter chewed on their bottom lip as she shifted out of his way. "I think you might be surprised about what's in there," they hedged as they trailed him down the corridor.

Surprised?

The aufenthaltsraum was decorated with streams of blue and gold and silver ribbon. They were pinned to the walls, wrapped around chair backs, tied in awkward bows on cupboard doors and around the edges of the botany bays.

A banner hung haphazardly over the sofas, words in messy earth common eurean handwriting read, "Congratulations! You lived!"

Brruuh stumbled, catching himself on the doorway. "What is...?"

"It's a you lived party," Matter clarified.

"But why?"

Sauraxen snorted. "Because you lived, silly. You said yourself that harrushetti celebrate overcoming challenges like illness and injury, you think we wouldn't offer that?"

Brruuh's ears dipped, his heart swelled at the inclusion. And, as seemed to have become a habit, he glanced at Matter: the person who had given him terms for it. Ahni - the feeling of home and family. Ahthae - a family made wherever you were with the people you were with.

"Alright," Sebastian said when Brruuh didn't enter the room. "I can see you want to rip off the plaster."

"Idiom," Matter whispered.

"Get to the point," Basti tried to clarify.

"Idiom."

"Just tell us what's going on!" Basti laughed but there was an undercurrent of tension to it.

Brruuh took a deep breath. He was definitely about to ruin the mood of the party. But at least everyone was already in here, including Dimae, who sat on one of the sofa's wrapped up in what was clearly Basti's cardigan, wide wooden buttons drawing the eye just like Dimae's spotted patterning.

"I will be inputting my report as soon as we get to the IPA Offices."

"Okay..."

Brruuh rubbed the tip of his ears, like a kitten having

been asked if they stole all the ice-sweets. Guilt was the earth common eurean word for it. These people had saved his life, as Matter had said, and he couldn't even promise that it would have been worth it. "The IPA might decide to send a different assessor for a further assessment."

"Why?" Sauraxen asked.

"Because I nearly died. Because I have a request for you all. Because of the whole thing with the illegal cargo."

Matter huffed out a huge breath and leaned over the table. "Well, fuck."

"You're tellin' me," Sebastian drawled.

"What is your request?" Dimae asked.

Brruuh swallowed and stared down at his hands, white and silver-grey fur stark against the dark metal below him. "I would like to remain with you after this assessment is concluded, particularly if you are granted your DeST."

Sauraxen squealed and bounced toward him.

Sebastian cleared his throat, actively wiping the disappointment off his face and offering a slightly strained smile in its place. "All the more reason to celebrate, then."

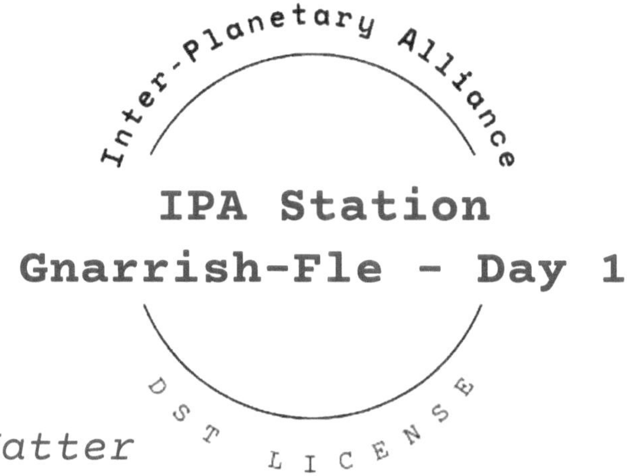

Matter

Matter sat in the uncomfortable chair. Their joints still ached from the aftermath of the attack and everything that had led up to it. Hopefully, with a little time, that pain would ease, but Matter was closer and closer to hover-chair necessity and they weren't mentally ready to accept that yet. Sebastian had actually invested in a hover-chair and Matter kind of hated him for it.

The cognitivist across from Matter said nothing, watching Matter with eyes they couldn't read. Unlike Brruuh, she was dressed in full IPA uniform, her name and pronouns on her sleeve – not that Matter could read it from this angle. She was another bimanual lifeform but had four legs that hooked over the little gaps in the chair back so she could sit on it more like a stool than a chair – at least to Matter's bipedal impression.

Idly, they wondered if that was an unfortunate way to consider the world.

They shifted in the uncomfortable chair. They still

couldn't understand not just having a few different types of chair available. Kil wouldn't be able to sit in these types of chairs at all. Nobody ever seemed to care for the comfort of kil.

"Are you gonna ask me a question, or what?" they blurted.

"I am Dr K'leia."

"Oh," Matter interrupted before she could explain that she was a cognitivist who had been employed to run their assessment, or re-assessment in this particular case. "This is just the tactic. You wait until I break the silence, then introduce yourself as cognitivists as if I didn't know why I was here? That's just the standard?"

"You seem agitated."

"A little. I mean, we're all recovering from the aftermath of the attack so..."

"I'd like you to walk me through exactly what happened."

Matter groaned. They were never getting out of this chair!

"Are you quite well?"

"Nei. These chairs are unexplainably uncomfortable, and I want to know why the IPA are still trading with Clickclick after finding out they still have the biological weaponry they used against Harrush in the wars. I want to know why there isn't an easy access IPA Border Station out there to help people who get into trouble like we did – if we hadn't had an ouaeahhn pilot, we would have *died* out there."

Dr K'leia looked down at the datapad in her hands.

"If you're looking at the fact that I said to Dr TeaYaBin that I would be too dead to worry about being dead the last time I did this assessment, I stand by it."

"I wasn't– you said what?"

"The dangers of Deep Space Travel are always the same: you die, at which point you're too dead to worry about it. You get hurt, which we did but we're all still going so it's not so bad – I probably have a skewed perception of that from the last time I got hurt. Interestingly enough, that was also because of illegal activity."

Dr K'leia hummed. "I was looking to see evidence of your ouaeahhn pilot."

Matter frowned. "*I'm* the ouaeahhn pilot."

"Oh... My apologies. Now, if you wouldn't mind going over the events leading up to the attack."

Matter huffed out a breath but gave Dr K'leia a speedy run down of their experiences surrounding Clickclick. Maybe Brruuh had had an impact on them, they did seem to be taking this assessment more seriously than they had with him.

"And how does that impact your desire to gain your Deep Space Travel License?"

"It doesn't."

"Excuse me?"

"Like I said to Brruuh when I last did this. There are two real risks with Deep Space Travel: death and injury. I am already living with the only one you can live with."

"And how do you feel about returning to the Galactic Whale?"

"What?"

"The ship. It's registered as Galactic Whale."

Laughter bubbled up in Matter's chest. "I feel exceedingly positive about Galactic Whales."

For News About Latest
Releases
Join The Mailing List At:
WillSoulsbyMcCreath.com

ABOUT THE AUTHOR

It's pronounced "Souls-Bee-Muh-Kreth"
As a cosplayer, Table-Top Gaming nerd, and videogamer; fiction has been a staple of Will's life forever. They like to corrupt their friends into joining these pass-times, or at least reading their stories.
Obsessed with every way to tell a story and every possible use for one, Will had few choices other than becoming a writer. A little too nosy for their own good they like to invest their time fixing other people's problems, and when that doesn't work they hand out stories to make you feel better.

The Crew Of The Galactic
Whale Will Fly Back Onto The
Page Soon.
In The Meantime,
Turn The Page For A Preview
From Will's Upcoming Pirate
Novel
NOT THE FIGHTING KIND

The swirl of a ball was a delicate thing. Gowns twirled in a kaleidoscope of colours and details, reflecting light where they shone with gems, trailing fabric across the floor and in swooshes of wrist straps and sleeves. The stiff blocks of gentlemen's clothes breaking the pattern like the lines in a stained glass window.

Nat had been enthralled with the balance of it all for longer than they could remember. Sneaking down from their rooms to investigate to the extent that their father had despaired and begun locking their bedroom door on hosting nights.

That was how Nat usually got into trouble. Caught doing something they shouldn't. Drawn in by something beautiful.

That had to be what had Nat's head pounding with pain. Drawn in by something. Maybe a challenge. Maybe a swirling pretty thing. But no...

A hard floor pressed against their back. A soft swooshing sound filtered into focus. Where in the world were they?

Oh.

Right.

The ship.

Nat held in a groan as they pushed into a sitting position. Everything hurt. And they didn't even have the joy of gossip to tide them over with it either.

But something still wasn't right. A windowless, dark room with the gentle rattle of metal on metal buzzing in the space. A naval bunk this was not.

The twenty-odd other people they had shared the room with were a noisy bunch. Snoring, shuffling, whispering notably absent. And the lantern hung by the door for emergencies that had assaulted Nat's eyes for many a night was absent.

More relevant even, was the lack of bunk, the lack of shitty straw mattress and scratchy threadbare blanket. It wasn't much of a bed. Nevertheless, this was even less of one. Never would Nat have thought they would seek comfort from the naval bunk. Every time it came to mind, Nat wanted to cry. Not that one cried in public, let alone on a naval ship.

Rubbing their eyes as if it might clear the darkness, pain tugged at their attention. Their arms hurt. When did they not these days? But this was different somehow. And Nat would really like to be able to quantify the how and the why but without sight that didn't seem like a possibility.

They shifted in an attempt to better make out the room. If this was some kind of joke by Rodgerson, Nat was going to scream. He was the type to think it was funny to shove Nat into a dark cupboard somewhere and leave them there to get reprimanded by the Rear-Admiral for being late to deck. Again. It wasn't like Nat needed help with that.

Pushing past the indignity of it. If they couldn't see, then nobody else could see them. Nat crawled carefully forward. Their knees called for attention. Another mystery pain to categorise at some point.

The lack of memory concerned them more. A head injury perhaps? Or poison. Unlikely but so was waking up in a pitch dark room one hadn't fallen asleep in.

They ran their hands over the floor: wooden, worn. Where was the edge of the room? Ideally a door Nat could escape through. The blunt edge of an iron bar bit into Nat's probing fingers.

They flinched back and silently cursed themself for it. Returning, more carefully, to the bars, Nat traced them. Flat iron, criss-crossed into squares large enough for Nat to get both hands through but not large enough for any other portion of their body.

At least they had found the source of the rattling metal noise.

Nat sank back on their feet, ignoring the way it would probably leave marks on their trousers. Screw passing inspection at this point. This was a cell.

How had this come to pass?

Blurry, faded images of a rainstorm came to mind. The Rear-Admiral's voice booming, calling everyone to man their positions. Nat's bunkmates had surged to their feet, pulling on some semblance of uniform and grabbing for swords Nat had never before seen them use.

The man who slept below Nat, the one with the nasal whistle that kept Nat up all night, yanked Nat down by a leg. Their knee slamming against the ground with a thunk that carried over both the shouting and the raging storm outside.

At least that explained the knee pain.

"Get dressed," he demanded. "And man your fucking post!" Nobody said naval boys had any manners.

Nat rubbed their face again. What had happened after that? Why had they needed to man posts? And why with swords?

Nat had never used a sword in their life.

There was no point dwelling on the events of the previous night. Maybe Nat would be able to remember the cause of the rest of their pain, maybe they wouldn't. It wouldn't do them any good either way. They were in a cell of some sort, presumably captured by whoever had boarded the ship the previous night.

That could be better. But it left Nat with a potential course of action and that was all they really needed. Find a way out.

Was anyone else here too?

Nat sucked in a deep breath and held it, listening intently for the sound of breath over the quiet whoosh of the sea. Before they could begin to count, a light bloomed in the doorway to their left.

The room itself was long and slim. Nat inhabited the furthest cell from the doorway. A square space with two solid wooden walls and two sets of cell bars. Nat had found their way toward the one with the door, opposite which sat more of that bland wooden walling across a narrow corridor, no wider than the doorway itself.

"Good," the lantern-holder said, voice deep and accented — Kovian if Nat was guessing. "You're awake. Captain will be glad to hear it."

The illumination, still too bright to really make out the pirate beyond broad shoulders, clarified that Nat was not, in fact, completely alone in the row of cells. Three other members of *The Valliant's* crew filled the other three cells in the room. And by what Nat knew of their families, someone on *The Valiant* had sold them out. How else would the pirates have ended up with four prisoners from upper class, well-to-do families?

This was a ransom mission.

ACKNOWLEDGEMENTS

This book, like any other, wouldn't have come to exist without the assistance of several others. Both in helping me create a life that allowed me to write books at all, as well as the actual, functional writing of this particular book itself.
My mum, who taught me to read, helped me find books I could fall in love with, and always encouraged my storytelling. Still does to this day. I owe so much to her.
My in-laws, who still get excited like kids on the way to birthday parties every time I tell them I'm bringing out a new book.
To everyone who bought and read & reviewed any of my previous books. You have no idea how much you make my heart sing, how much you inspire me to keep going. I think I'm pretty terrible at responding to comments and suchlike, but this is how I hope to show my gratitude (the acknowledgement and the continuing to write books).
To my friends, whether we speak every week or once a year, know that I hold you in my heart and you help me build these inter-personal relationships between the people I make up. Thanks again for understanding that I have nothing else I want to talk about so much as my books.
To the writing community online, my mutuals on tumblr, and everyone who shares their writing and publishing journeys for the rest of us to learn from. You make me feel less alone in this endeavour, you make this whole thing seem somewhat sensible.
And,
for the person without whom this and all my other novels wouldn't be possible. My sounding board, the only person I've ever met who can make grammar make some kind of sense. The person who amps me up, reminds me that I have a human body with needs, reminds me to relax but doesn't mind when that inevitably runs back around to new ideas I want to talk through. The absolute love of my life: B. Hope you enjoyed lizard x cat aliens, and yes, Brruuh's botany is based on yours. Obviously.

Thank You So Much For Picking
Up A Copy of
Unlicensed Delivery

For News About My Latest
Releases Sign Up To My
Mailing List At:
WillSoulsbyMcCreath.com

Or come find me on Social
Media, when I'm there I'm
@nopoodles

Enjoy my FREE Short Stories
over on
nopoodles.wordpress.com